WHAT THE CRITICS HAVE SAID ABOUT ADAM P. KNAVE

About "After These Messages..."

"Inventive and original, the story is fun... the characters are hilarious and the style of writing is tongue-in cheek."

–horror-web.com

About "Crazy Little Thing"

"You'll find yourself absorbed in Knave's style and not only understanding where he's coming from, but will dive at the chance to see where he's going."

–Horror Fiction News

About "Flesh Wounds"

"Knave needs to see a therapist and quick."

–horror-web.com

About "Meat"

"Take 'Meat,' for example: the zombie clichés are easily forgiven because of Adam P. Knave's sharp writing."

–The Harrow

About "Mister Binkles and the Highly Adaptable Future"

"...He's also written a fine story about the titular teddy bear-like toy... Well done, indeed."

–SFReader.com

crazy little things

adam p. knave

die monster die! books | baltimore, maryland

contents

preface
by laszlo xalieri

So Adam's attorney contacted me a little while ago and asked me if I'd mind finally breaking down to write an introduction for a new edition of one of his short story collections. "C'mon," he says. "You're the only one left alive who knew him back before the 'reassignment surgery' incident."

There's a subtle guilt trip in there, but didn't I say it was an attorney? They don't play fair. My payback for that is mentioning it here, where it's certain to spark an embarrassing question or two. I'm sure there are exercises I can do to firm up my alibi. Even at my age.

When composing these things I find it best not to assume anything. As the old saying goes, to assume makes an "ass" of "u" and "mption." So I won't mention "the book you are holding now in your hands," because To-Whom-It-May-Concern alone knows what you're holding in your hands right now, or even if you happen to have any hands.

I personally don't want to know, so keep it to yourself.

You could be hearing this as an audio stream, narrated by one of this century's numerous Elmer Fudd impersonators, as a replacement for the Wedding March at a "freestyle" ceremony in Fresno. You could be reading this off of a tattooed strip of skin left on the road by a naked biker after a horrible motorcycle wreck in the Andes. You may never hear or read this at all, but might be mysteriously remembering it verbatim while recovering from anesthesia in post-op after your own unplanned 'reassignment surgery'—which happens to be where I get all of *my* best ideas.

Mmmm-*mmm*. Guilt-and-prosecution-free opiates? For me? You shouldn't have!

Seriously. You shouldn't have.

Regardless, the series of words you are soon to be experiencing (unless you've already gotten through the stories and, completely desperate for something to take up your time while you wait for something a good deal more important to happen, like a bowel movement, you finally resort to this introduction, at which point I'm *still* referring to the stories for which these words were intended as an introduction, regardless of temporal anomalies caused by your personal lapse in judgment and/or constipation and/or intravenous morphine drip) first appeared as a bound collection in printed media around fifty years ago, back in 2008. That was back before the Guild Wars aced Hollywood and LA, leaving us to suffer along with the best New York and, as New York fell, Dubuque had to offer.

Some of these tales were reprints then, but a few were new. I feel a certain amount of personal responsibility for the old Mr. Binkles tales. Adam and I were discussing ideas for stories and how some of the best specimens were old fables revisited, often in the middle of the night by the weird uncle who makes frequent use of the phrase "our little secret." I seemed to recall mentioning that no one seemed to have ass-raped *The Velveteen Rabbit* yet, and the rest is, by now, ancient history. Both of the Mr. Binkles stories appeared in the fabulously named *Cthulhu Sex Magazine*, which strangely enough managed to find newsstand shelf space even in big-box bookstores in Metropolitan Atlanta's tight-assed Bible-Belt 'burbs. (If you remember NYC, think Connecticut. With more churches.)

I doubt anyone remembers but me, but the intended relaunch of *Cthulhu Sex Magazine* failed during the settlement-merger with the *Christian Science Monitor* after that little collision of CSMs in magazine-name trademark space. For some reason they decided to stick with the name Blavatsky saddled them with a hunnert years ago. Go figure. Their fiction section continues to rock, however, to this very day.

Also included was "Crazy Little Thing," a tidy little love story that will, among other things, seriously challenge your assumptions about the traditionally benign character of Abraham Lincoln. It'll also point out how much it wrecks your world to sync up to anyone else you might happen to be falling in love with.

New pieces included "Pretty Little Dead Girls"—about the only way you'd get the best part of Knave's readers and fans backstage at a sweet little children's beauty pageant, court orders notwithstanding—and "Causing Effect," guaranteed to make you crave hot fresh doughnuts no matter what the personal cost to yourself. "Causing Effect" is another charming love story about how people come to grips with the strange things they find inside themselves and each other. And also hot fresh doughnuts.

"Crazy Little Things" was one of the earlier publications from one of the fastest and most prolific writers of the twenty-first century. Knave, to this day, still has a preference for those huge loud and clacky keyboards that, when he types at his usual speed, frequently gets a confused burst or two of answering fire from the block across the street.

That's Dubuque for you.

Anyway, it seems the morphine's starting to wear off, and from here on out it's just a week or two putting up with the inconvenient tenderness and swelling. Same as for you, if this is your first time enjoying this collection of Knave's stories.

You get used to it after a while.

–*Laszlo Xalieri,*
dictated December 8, 2061,
in the post-op recovery room,
Dubuque Mercy General

introduction
by travis ingram

What can I say about Adam P. Knave? Well, he's one of the most original writers I've had the pleasure of working with and probably the most unique person I know. He continuously pushes the boundaries of fiction and gives fresh exciting views to genres that are severely needing someone of his talent.

And he's a damn good writer, too, and a ninja.

To really understand the mind of this modern day renaissance man, maybe it's best if I start from the beginning.

I first met Adam back in 'Nam.

The steamy jungles of the delta had seen the first of them: shambling rotting corpses animated by some as-yet unknown force. Many suspected that the Viet Cong were using experimental nerve gas agents from the Russians, but as far as I know, no proof was ever found to support that.

My Ranger unit was undercover behind enemy lines looking for fox-holes and tunnels to use for cover when we stumbled on him. Adam was standing in a clearing with a bowie knife, surrounded by the bodies of dozens of human enemy and animated corpses alike. He stared at the lifeless eye sockets of the undead thing in front of him, waiting for it to make the first move. Before I could blink, he rushed the creature, burying his knife in the thing's skull to the hilt. He then turned to us.

His only remark was "What the hell took you guys so long?"

From then on we found a lot of common ground discussing ways to rid the world of the undead and a general dislike for dishonest politicians.

After 'Nam we worked together on a lot of "non-sanctioned" freelance wetwork, dispensing death and destruction and the occasional bad joke wherever we went. Eventually our work earned us both a place on the FBI's Most Wanted list.

Today, still wanted by the government, we survive as underground ninja for hire.

I've come to think of Adam as more than a great writer and unstoppable ninja force. He's a good friend. I get a smile on my face whenever I see his name on my cell or e-mail just because I know he'll have some new sick and twisted idea to share with me. It's been a pleasure working with him over the years and seeing his work mature and grow into what you see here.

I hope you enjoy reading these stories as much as I did and remember... If you have a problem, if no one else can help—and if you can find him—maybe you can hire Adam P. Knave. If you can afford him.

-*Travis Ingram*
Artist, Ninja for Hire

I was asked to come up with a quote or something to start this all off. I looked and searched and searched more and looked harder. But really, all I could think was simply this:

Enjoy.

–Adam P. Knave
New York, New York
2008

pretty little dead girls

ONE

THE STAGE ALMOST glowed from the reflecting lights. Ten pairs of highly polished shoes stood on top of the lacquered wooden stage. Each pair belonged to a different girl, and each girl stood as proud and perfectly straight as she could manage. The music swelled to a crescendo as a tall, graying man strode out from where he waited by the side of the stage. He aimed his body like a missile, walking with exacting, perfectly measured steps until he reached the microphone stand that shone under the deathly hot spotlight.

Each girl smiled, each smile spreading across the ten faces to an exacting amount. They showed teeth, but not too much. Their hair stood firm, solid under so much product that even the hanging curls of two of the girls wouldn't have done more than quiver slightly under the force of a hurricane.

Their dresses, each of a different brilliant color, were perfectly creased and pleated. Nothing was out of place, not a single thing—which was exactly as planned. Everything went as planned. That was the general idea.

"Ladies and gentlemen," Carmichael Higgins, that night's M.C., said, "let's have a round of applause for each of our beautiful contestants."

The crowd cheered, clapping and whooping on command. Carmichael stood, waiting patiently, one hand lightly resting on top of the microphone. Deep down he hated this part, waiting for the applause to die down. Still, he would never let it show. No, he knew that to even let his smile falter would end up with the director screaming at him.

Not that he blamed the director for her reaction. She had to deal with the parents. That smallest of faltering smiles would send them to cell phones and knocks on doors, each one demanding to know why the agency hired an M.C. who *clearly* wasn't enjoying himself in the slightest. Higgins held up his left hand and nodded at the crowd.

"Thank you," he said. "Thank you all. The girls will be back soon for tonight's talent displays. We'll be right back!"

The spotlight snapped off, but Higgins stood his ground while each of the girls turned and walked off the stage. Ten little girls waved, their heads turned to the crowd, while they walked. They couldn't see where they were going, forced to trust that they remembered exactly how fast to move so they wouldn't bump into the girl in front of them. Each girl held her smile while she walked ninety degrees from where she looked, counting the steps off in her head until the darkness backstage would wrap tightly around her.

The stage stood empty, except for Higgins, who counted to twenty in his own head, and then turned on his heel and strode back off stage with military precision. There were watches in Switzerland that would no doubt be unaccountably jealous of the exacting nature and timing displayed on the stage.

Backstage nothing was getting done with any real sense of precision. Girls rushed about, worried about this and that. Who had moved a baton? Why didn't the tap shoes feel quite right? The lyrics to "Over the Rainbow" couldn't be found for a last minute double check. Chaos took over, even as parents rushed in to help.

The parents made things worse, truth be told. They demanded every change be made expertly and perfectly. Every adjustment, every lost item, and each and every single missing sequin needed to be accounted for and found by a production member. After all, the parents reasoned, it had to have been the production team who lost the things in the first place.

The director, Pamela McGregor, rushed through the crowded and panicked space letting each set of child and parent know that they only had five minutes before the show simply must go on. Muttered curses followed her, but as the seconds started to tick down, everything fell into place. It always seemed to fall into place, regardless of the situation, somehow.

Sheet music was stowed away quickly, batons grabbed and tap shoes tied on tight. The parents rushed back out to return to their seats. The girls lined up again, standing just off stage. Pamela stood at the front of the line, facing the girls. She held up her right hand, fingers spread and counted down, whispering the words as her fingers fell.

"Five."

Ten heads came up, spines straightening.

"Four."

Twenty arms went rigid, wrists turned just so.

"Three."

Ten smiles lit up, each one perfectly back in place.

"Two."

Twenty eyes closed, and each girl took a deep breath before opening their eyes just in time for...

"One." Ten little girls marched back on stage to applause and cheering. Carmichael Higgins walked out from the other side of the stage at the same time, not even pretending to himself that even one clap was directed at him. The spotlight snapped on, and the microphone stand lit up, just as Carmichael's left foot came down in place behind it.

"Let's hear it one more time for our lovely contestants!" he said enthusiastically.

The girls walked out, waving and smiling, and took their places. Carmichael explained the talent portion of the show to the crowd. He knew they were each well versed in the mechanics of the program, they probably knew the rules better than he did, but he read the teleprompter and tried his best to make the copy sound exciting and new.

As he finished, the girls turned and marched back off stage. They would wait there, nine of them, as the tenth claimed the stage as her own. For two and a half minutes, each girl would have the whole stage to herself. The entire audience would fix its collective gaze on her, and only her.

The first few girls went ahead with their routines. A baton tossed here and a song sung there. At the end of each performance, regardless of how good or bad it might be, applause rang out and the girl smiled, flushing with pride as she left the stage with her head held a little higher.

Even little Patti Jensen, who had missed a catch and hit herself in the head with a baton, left proud. The energy of the crowd invigorated her. It gave her a vitality she thought she would never get any where else in her life. Patti's mother would yell later and baton drills would need to be stepped up, to be sure. But Patti didn't care about that as she walked off the stage. At that moment, nothing could have stopped her.

As her feet landed backstage, reality set in, and she fought tears. It wouldn't do to let the other girls see her cry. Patti knew that each girl could easily see her tightly held self control, and she took a small amount of pride from that, at least.

And so it went. Girls marched onto the stage, spotlight following them, tracking them like criminals. They performed, they smiled and waved, and then they walked off stage again.

In between each performance Carmichael Higgins came back on stage to thank the departing girl and introduce the next. The show went as every show tended to go. Girls came and girls went. Until things changed.

As Melanie-Ann Gladstone walked off stage to Carmichael's scripted appreciation and Kerri DeNunzio mentally prepared herself one last time for her rendition of "I Will Survive," the spotlight went out.

Melanie-Ann considered herself too much of a professional to stop her walk when the spotlight left her, and didn't even think to turn around and look behind her. Even as she saw Kerri's face, jaw loose and eyes wide, Melanie-Ann did as was expected and took her place backstage without a glance around her.

Carmichael's face, on stage, mirrored Kerri's. In the center of the stage, in utter darkness, stood a girl where there had been none before. Though the spotlight was off a soft blue glow flowed from the stage into the audience. The source of the light seemed to be the girl who stood, bluish and happy. She screwed on her brightest smile and lifted her arm for a perfectly executed wave.

Her arm raised, Carmichael noticed that he could, very faintly, see right through her. The spotlight came back on suddenly. The girl seemed to vanish, washing out in the bright glare of the powerful bulbs above. Carmichael cursed under his breath.

"Turn the God damned spot off, you morons," he whispered quickly into the production pickup clipped to the inside of his left cuff. Backstage, Pamela echoed Carmichael's sentiment, if not his calm and considered language, and the spotlight shut off again.

The little girl, glowing faintly, smiled again, and started to wave once more. Pamela's headset went crazy with questions and shouted orders. She ignored them all, choosing to simply stare out onto the stage and watch this strange little glowing girl.

"Carmichael, you worthless fuck," Pamela whispered into her headset, "talk to her, keep the fucking show running, you twat!"

Carmichael Higgins coughed once, pulling back from the microphone stand as he did. Professional reflex took over and managed to shake him out of his slack-jawed trance.

"Excuse me," he said into the microphone, "but I don't believe we've met." He turned to the audience, flashing them a warm grin. He wanted them to buy that this was all part of the show, nothing to get upset about. They weren't buying it. They also couldn't see him very well with the spotlight off.

"My name is Samantha Felder," the girl said clearly, "and I'm here to do my rendition of 'My Heart Will Go On.'"

"Well, isn't that just great, folks?" Carmichael ad-libbed, the teleprompter uselessly sitting on a line about Kerri DeNunzio. "And where do you come from, Samantha Felder?"

"Heaven," she replied simply before she started singing. There was no music to back her up and no lighting to enhance any dance moves she might have planned. She didn't dance. She simply stood on center stage and sung her song as loudly and clearly as anyone might ever have wished.

Her voice was perfect, and, lost in the moment, everyone forgot to react to the insubstantial, blue glowing girl who claimed to be from Heaven. While she sang, nothing else could be heard. The audience simply sat quietly, listening. No one cleared their throat, or shifted in their seat, in fact back in the production room the engineers didn't pick up a single sound from the audience. Not one. Everyone simply listened.

Samantha's voice filled the auditorium. Her pitch was centered and her tone clear. She didn't belt out the song, allowing her voice to simply flow and fill the space without overpowering anything else. Had the audience been making noises, they would have been easily heard.

There were better singers in the world, of this no one had any doubt. However, those better singers were all much older and more experienced than little Samantha Felder, her blue glow increasing as she gave herself over to song.

She swayed gently to the music that she created, her eyes never leaving the audience before her. She couldn't see them, the darkness that enveloped them stayed deep; but she knew they were there, and she knew that staying focused on them was part of what she needed to do.

The last note hung in the air for seconds that stretched until they felt like minutes. Samantha gave a slow and precise curtsey and smiled. "Thank you," she said, and then turned on her heel and walked off the stage. She took the exact same route the other girls had taken, keeping her gaze ninety degrees to her left, on the audience, as she went. One little arm came up, and she waved as she walked.

Carmichael noticed, and realized he might be the only one to, that her shoes never quite touched the floor, except on her forward stride where the toes of each would gently pass into the floor for a second, sinking in.

That touchstone, her insubstantial form, shook Carmichael out of his own revery. He took hold of the microphone, but before he could start speaking, the crowd came to as well. Their applause and cheering washed over the stage like a wave of pure energy. Carmichael, professional to the last, said, "Let's hear it for Samantha Felder! Thank you, Samantha," even though his own words were lost in the clapping.

Backstage, Samantha saw the line of waiting girls and smiled at them. No one moved. Some of the girls' faces were rictuses of shock and fear. Others simply stood, waiting to see what would happen next. Pamela watched Samantha, unsure of what the protocol was for immaterial additions to the pageant.

"Good luck," Samantha whispered to Kerri DeNunzio, as she passed.

Pamela heard the new girl speak and shook her head. Dealing with her would have to wait another minute. "Carmichael," she whispered into her headset, "and everyone the fuck else, there's still a motherfucking show to cunting run. Get on with it!" She turned her body away from the girls, and spoke as softly, yet forcefully as possible. She didn't like it when the contestants heard her and told their parents. It made for no end of annoyance.

"Kerri, honey," Pamela said, rushing to the girl's side, "you're next. Ready, honey? When they call your name."

Carmichael did just that, and Kerri DeNunzio found herself walking out on stage. Part of her mind found itself left behind, wondering both where that new girl came from and if the rules allowed her to simply jump in front of another contestant.

Still, Kerri pulled herself together in time to sing her song. The audience took things in stride, unsure about what had just happened, other than the fact it was wonderful, and listened to Kerri.

Pamela, approached Samantha Felder, whose blue glow had dimmed some. She waved the girl aside, for a quick talk between just the two of them. "Excuse me, Samantha, right?"

"Yes, ma'am. Samantha Felder."

"Uhm, I don't seem to recall you being in this contest," Pamela said, fishing for some way to ask how Samantha appeared on stage magically without coming out and asking.

"I am, though," Samantha said, sure of herself.

"You don't mind if I double-check that, just to make sure, do you?" Pamela asked.

"Not at all," Samantha said with a gentle smile.

Pamela took a few steps away from the girls and radioed for someone, anyone, to check the log books and search for this Samantha Felder. After only a minute of waiting a call came back.

"Pam, this is Steven, at control. We have records of a Samantha Felder in the book."

"You do? She just appeared, just now, so what the fuck?"

"I don't know," Steven said, glad he wasn't face to face with the director, "but her name looks almost burnt in, like someone wrote it with a match or something."

"Fucking great, all right, fine. Where is she, line wise?"

"Right where she thought she was, actually. Between Gladstone and DeNunzio."

"Cocksuckers. That's impossible," Pamela spit into the radio mic.

"I know, Pam, but there it is."

"Fine," Pamela said with a sigh, "this is a cunt of a show, huh Steve? But the book rules above all, fucking hell, fine."

Samantha, at peace and in her element, wandered further backstage, while the other girls waited to perform. There she found the girls that had already gone, a few of them at least, sitting and waiting for the show to move on.

They were startled at her presence, but Samantha didn't mind. She remained friendly and happy, chatting with the girls. Though concern remained, especially once they realized Samantha was intangible, her attitude won them over.

On stage, the show resumed momentum and normalcy without missing a noticeable beat. Talents were displayed and applauded. Everything went as expected. Sheryl Trujo left the stage with a wave and smile, the last contestant to perform, and Carmichael once more gave the audience a break, letting them know that the show would resume in mere minutes with the formal dress and question section of the pageant.

The stage went dark as Carmichael strode off to drink some water and wonder what would surprise him next. He thought he had handled the appearance of the girl well, and had gotten a call from Pamela letting him know that somehow, no one knew just how, the girl in question was indeed supposed to be there.

Backstage, meanwhile, the parents rushed in and helped their daughters change. Questions were reviewed and sample answers gone over even as dresses well pulled over heads. Shoes were changed and hair redone slightly. Samantha Felder stood alone, no one there with her. Pamela noticed and went to her.

"Honey, don't you have anyone to help you change?" she asked.

"Oh no, ma'am," Samantha told her, "but I'll be all right." Samantha gave Pamela a smile and wandered away, humming to herself.

It should've, Pamela thought, been creepy. Somehow though, in some way she just couldn't explain to herself, Samantha seemed a perfectly natural part of the proceedings. Still, other girls had problems, and more than them, their parents did. They voiced their issues loudly, and Pamela found herself running from one station to the next, trying to get every last detail sorted out before the break ended.

Timing ended up helping her out. Pamela soothed a few of the parents, enough to start a chain reaction of explanations. One parents told the next and so on, even as they rushed back to their seats. The girls moved to line back up, standing in a perfect line. Samantha joined them, taking her place between Melanie-Ann and Kerri.

The music swelled, the lights warmed up, and the countdown started. Eleven little smiles froze in place. Pamela glanced at Samantha, noticing the girl had changed, and now wore a much smoother, smarter outfit. There was no way for that to work, Pamela knew, since Samantha didn't have any equipment with her at all, but somehow the girl had found another outfit and changed, ending up wearing the same shade of light, glowing, blue.

Girls started to walk on stage, one by one, to talk with Carmichael. Each one answered a few questions, turning to face the audience in the gaps between their answers. Carmichael talked to each girl like an equal. No condescending tones, no patronizing voice or looks. Each girl, when they were talking to him, felt just as grown up as they wanted to be.

Pamela's headset chirped, and she whispered, "Go," into it, as she took a step away from the edge of the stage. She put a hand over her earpiece and bent down a little bit, knowing none of that actually helped her hear at all.

"Pam, we're checked into this Samantha Felder. She's... well, we can see her too up here. So Bobby did some digging, really fast."

"Right..."

"There was a Samantha Felder who died a few months back. Little girl, about the right age," Jason said from the control booth.

"It isn't that uncommon a name, guys," Pamela reminded him.

"Bobby remembered the story, because this Samantha Felder died on her way to a pageant. There's a picture with the story, Pam," Jason paused, rolling his next words around in his mouth before voicing them, "same girl."

"I'll have to see for my fucking self," Pamela said quickly, "but there's a god damned show to run."

She stepped back quickly and welcomed Latisha Clarke back from the stage. Nodding at Patti Jensen, Pamela took a look around the area. Everything looked perfectly fine, if you included a girl who glowed blue as part of fine.

On stage, Patti Jensen stood under the spotlight and answered Carmichael's various questions with deft and poise. She felt in her element, truly enjoying finding the answers in her head and speaking them clearly and succinctly. She left the stage with a smile, and held it even when she caught Samantha's eye. Samantha smiled back, as did the other girls who saw Patti. There was certainly competition, each girl wanted to take home a tiara, both for themselves and for their parents, but they also felt a certain camaraderie.

In whispers, when no parents were close by or production staff members, the girls often talked about the pageants. They used terms that military men would, after seeing war: the stage was their front line, the backstage waiting area their trenches. They still loved it, though. Most of them simply jumped at the chance to perform, to be on a stage in front of an audience, and they found it worth the various hardships that came their way.

Girls continued to go and march onto the stage and answer Carmichael's questions. The show ran fine, precision being the word of the day, still. One by one they walked forward while the spotlight tracked them and stopped on their mark, smiled and answered whatever questions came their way. The process would reverse, and off they would go, still followed by the same spotlight until it left them backstage in darkness, only to highlight the next girl in line.

Until Samantha, of course. The spotlight followed Melanie-Ann across the stage and winked out. Samantha walked forward, and the spotlight, under harsh orders, stayed off. Her glow shone, as did her smile, and Samantha Felder walked forward. Her shoes still didn't quite touch the stage, and Carmichael forced himself to not stare at her feet as they came closer.

Carmichael ran through the opening script smoothly, Samantha fielding his questions with ease and grace. She smiled at the right points, nodding at some and took only small slices of seconds to think about her answers.

"So, Miss Felder, what do you do on sad days to cheer yourself up?" he asked, tossing her a standard question.

"Well, Mr. Higgins, I look at the world and let all of the beautiful things contained it in fill me back up with joy," she said smoothly. Shyly, she turned and smiled at the audience.

There was no coyness in that smile, no seeming calculation in her glance.

Carmichael was impressed. So impressed that he didn't fully realize the next question until it was halfway out of his mouth. "And what is it that you want to be when you grow up?" he asked, realizing as the last syllable left his mouth exactly how big a can of worms he could've opened. "Errr," he fumbled, trying to bring it back in, "what did you want to—"

Samantha just smiled, causing Carmichael to grow suddenly quiet. Carmichael, for a second, thought he might see a twitch of indulgence in that smile, but couldn't be sure. She nodded then and lowered her head in thought for a second. Carmichael hoped he hadn't blown something big.

"I wanted to be a dancer," Samantha Felder answered, lifting her head again. Her smile slid back into place easily. No regret showed to Carmichael, no sadness. Samantha simply answered the question and was ready to move to the next.

So Carmichael moved on, following the cards and his own memory. The rest of the question and answer period went smoothly and soon Samantha was walking back offstage. Kerri came out next, the spotlight snapping back on to track her movements carefully. The show continued.

When all of the girls had been on stage, each answering their questions, they came onto the stage in one line again. Ten spotlights shone along eleven girls. Carmichael thanked them each and thanked the audience, sincerity coming along with his words easily.

Backstage Pamela gave the standard order for no parents to be allowed and locked down the area. Lighting technicians and electricians took up spots along the entrances as extra security. The parents knew they weren't going to be allowed backstage again, but some of them would still try.

They would, Pamela knew, push and yell and threaten. Some of them might even, in rare cases, lose it completely and take a swing at someone in a moment of pure stress. It didn't always happen, but could, and had. Pamela made sure she was ready for anything. Anything she could think of, at least.

Carmichael announced that the girls would go offstage one last time while the judges conferred and then the winner of the day would be announced. The applause rose to an incredible level, parents and family clapping even harder as if they could affect the outcome, like Tinkerbelle laid fallen on the stage herself.

The girls walked back offstage and stood around in groups, chatting. They hid their nervousness from each other. Some of them knew they would not win, but even they still refused to fully allow that reality to affect them. Stranger things, they thought to themselves, could happen. So they stood and they talked and they waited.

Around them people moved to and fro, getting ready for the show's end. Some of the early breakdowns started: set pieces that wouldn't be used again, dressing curtains that weren't needed now, and the like. The girls stood around and watched, none of them for the first time, the world they battled on and lived in get torn down around them.

Pamela listened for updates about any parents trying to force their way in. She shook her head at each new report, but none of them sounded serious. She used her time, instead, to watch the girls.

Occasionally one of them would have a break down right about now, she knew. If they did, Pamela was pretty much the only person around to help, outside of the other contestants. So she watched, and she waited, and she listened. There was nothing else for her to do just then. It drove her a bit crazy.

Pamela waited for one radio call, and one only. The judges. Once they sent their signal, the show could go back on and wrap up. Then Pamela would only have a few more hours of work to supervise the teardown and move-out, before she could walk away for a few weeks. She needed the break; she could feel it in her bones.

The judges came back over the radio, letting Pamela know they were ready. She sprang into action, following the established steps. The lights were finished, set up for a final hurrah. Carmichael was warned, and the girls were told to get ready.

They lined up, their smiles not yet fully in place. A few of the girls fidgeted, fussing about with their hands along the hem of their dresses. Pamela moved to the head of their line and nodded at them. They came to attention, their heads coming up and their smiles sliding into place. Their hands rested still at their sides, and the girls waited for their cue.

The music started to swell, and the lights were a switch flip away from dazzling, blinding power. Carmichael walked on stage, his shoulders set and his footsteps perfectly even, and rested one hand on his microphone. The call came over the radio, and Pamela brought her hand down, giving the girls the signal they waited for.

As one, they walked back onstage. Their steps were perfectly timed, their smiles firmly in place and they each turned, waving to the crowd as they took center stage. There they stopped, and turned fully to face the audience, standing equidistant from the girl on either side. Carmichael thanked them and thanked the audience and the judges. He left script for a brief second and thanked the staff of the show quickly, as well.

Then...

"Without further ado," Carmichael said, loudly into the microphone. A stagehand came up behind him and handed Carmichael a small folded piece of paper. The stagehand quickly left, his all black outfit letting him fade into the darker areas of the stage like a memory. Carmichael didn't even acknowledge his existence, treating the slip of paper like an artifact that materialized into his hand at the right moment.

He read it quickly, not letting any reaction show on his face. Nodding at the audience, Carmichael took his voice down a notch and read off the name of the third place winner: Melanie-Ann Gladstone.

The girl lit up, taking a step forward. She smiled and waved, keeping her show calm, while inside she wanted to jump and yell. Even third place was a triumph. Yes, she had wanted to win, she burned with the desire, but third place was still a winning spot. It was something to talk about.

Latisha Clarke took second place, stepping forward and doing a quick curtsey before smiling and waving. Melanie-Ann filed that away. The next time she won, any place at all, she would curtsey. It was nice, it looked like fun, and the audience ate it up. Melanie-Ann wondered why a curtsey never occurred to her before that moment, but she filed away the wonder and held her breath to find out who would win first place.

Carmichael milked the moment for everything it was worth. He paused; he double checked the paper; he looked at all the girls and thanked each one of them yet again. And then he said it, the name of the winner: Samantha Felder.

Wild applause was met by mass confusion. Samantha took a step forward, standing on the exact same line as Melanie-Ann Gladstone and Latisha Clarke, not a millimeter further forward. She smiled and waved, deciding to not curtsey, and quietly thanked everyone for making this day the best day ever.

Some of the parents were compelled to leave their seats, to complain and cause a problem. They stayed though, until the girls left the stage and the lights turned off. Partly they simply didn't want to ruin the moment, and partly they were entranced by Samantha Felder. Leaving though, it only made them madder, thinking about how entranced they had been.

The stage shut down, the girls backstage and already starting to pack up. Carmichael walked off, turned in his radio, and changed out of his suit. Pamela stayed to coordinate the dismantling of the set. In silence, the auditorium stood empty and dark. One little girl, glowing blue, walked back onto the stage, flared brightly, and vanished.

TWO

"WHAT THE FUCK?" Pamela McGregor asked. She swung over a bit in her chair and kicked her legs up, coming back to land her feet on top of her desk. The heels of her shoes made a solid thunk against the top of her desk. The noise made the men sitting on the other side of the desk look up.

"Listen, Pam, we're not sure," Don Huston said, shrugging.

"Don's right, Pam," James Towne put in, leaning back in his chair.

"Well, that's really special, guys," Pamela said, rubbing her temple slowly, "but it also isn't worth a motherfuck, now is it?"

"What do you want us to do?" James asked.

"What I asked, for one," Pamela countered.

Not long after the pageant ended, Pamela knew that she would be the target of every inquiry, investigation, and screaming fit that the parents and the pageant board had the ability to throw.

She hadn't been wrong. Her crew knew what had happened, and they swore to it just as hard and often as Pamela did. The girl came out of nowhere, but her name appeared on all the books in all the right places—even though they hadn't been there before. No, it didn't make one lick of sense, but Pamela also knew it was the truth. If anything, that just annoyed her more.

Now, two weeks after the pageant, Pamela was passing through annoyed and straight into pissed off. Don and James, normally her last best hopes, were proving fruitless, and not worth the retainer she paid them to help her out in tough times.

"Just get out, guys," she said wearily, "if you don't know, I guess ya' fucking don't know."

"Listen to me, Pam," Don said, leaning forward, "the problem is everything is just like you said, get it? There's no record of that girl being seen around the theatre before the show, or after. The log books check out, though."

"Yeah, Pam, we can't find anything because there's nothing to find. Isn't that good?" James asked.

"No, you cunt, it isn't good!" Pamela yelled suddenly, dropping her feet off her desk and standing. "I have lawsuits, I have enraged parents, I got a shit storm the size of Montreal swirling around me, and all I can do is shrug and say, 'I don't know, I think she was a ghost after all,' and that shit just don't play too well!"

"There's nothing else to find," Don said, his head shaking, "so maybe, yeah, it was a ghost. Hell if I know. But that's all we got, Pam. That's it."

"All right," Pamela sighed, "get going then. Fuck, if that's what you got, it is. You two don't suck, or I wouldn't keep paying you, right? So fine, you did the best there was to do. Thanks."

The two nodded and stood, making their way out of Pamela's office. Pamela stood as well, pacing in the small office she ranked as the production department's main director. She ran her hands over the legs of her jeans and cursed under her breath for a while.

Grabbing her cell phone, she left her office, even as her desk phone started to ring. Probably, she thought, another fucking parent screaming. To hell with them for a while, she decided as she left.

Flipping her phone open as she left the elevator and stormed out of the building, she keyed through the address book until she found the number she wanted and dialed.

"Yeah," a voice answered on the third ring.

"Meet me at McLaren's?" Pamela asked.

"Is this about that girl again?"

"Of course it is."

"Fine. Give me a few," Carmichael said and hung up.

Pamela got to McLaren's and took a booth near the back. The bar was well lit as were and even the farthest booths. Pamela fidgeted with the unnecessary candle on the table, staring into the flame. A waiter brought her a scotch, as asked, and Pamela nursed it while she waited.

"Isn't it a bit early?" Carmichael asked as he sat down.

"Anyone," Pamela said, raising her glass, "who thinks it is too early for scotch drinks cheap scotch. What the fuck are we gonna do, Carmichael?"

"What's there to do, Pamela?"

"I got—"

"I know what you've got. Parents, the board, all of it. Screaming at you, they're doing the same to me. Hell, the ones that believe you think I rigged this whole thing up. I'd bet the same holds true in reverse. But you know what I think?"

"What's that?"

"Samantha Felder was real. She was dead. And she deserved to win."

"Honest, if fucking career ending," Pamela said with a laugh.

"Oh, don't give me that bullshit, Pamela," Carmichael said, flagging down the waiter. "We've both seen too many of these shows. Ignore the mystery for a second. Did she *deserve* to win?"

"Of course," Pamela said quickly. When Samantha Felder had sung, Pamela felt something, a simple joy she didn't often get to feel during pageants. It touched her; it left an impression.

"All right, then the rest is just noise," Carmichael said. He nodded his thanks to the waiter and sipped his black coffee.

"Pussy," Pamela said, nodding at the mug in Carmichael's hand.

"Lush."

"Fair enough. But saying she deserved to win doesn't end it, and you fucking well know it. Bastards will eat our asses alive."

"Just noise, Pamela. It's just noise. The books check out. The win checks out. All they have is the little problem of her being a ghost."

"So you think so, too?"

"Are you committing to an answer finally?" Carmichael asked. "I knew it when I talked to her, when I watched her feet float, come on, I never doubted what I saw. You can't fake that shit, not that well. No one can."

"Yeah," Pamela said, resigned, "but that requires, fuck Carmichael, this whole thing requires me to believe in ghosts. I saw one, didn't I?" Pamela drained her scotch and set the glass on the table none too quietly, "Except I don't believe in them, so where does that leave me?"

"Needing to get over yourself."

"Fuck you, thanks. And that still doesn't solve how we deal with these fuckers who want our heads for this."

"Let them. There's another pageant in a few months, right? We're both on board for it?"

"Nothing firm yet, but yeah."

"Then make it firm. We do another show, we prove to them that sometimes shit happens. Let them toss whatever experts they think they have along for the ride. What can they do? If nothing happens, and I think that'll be the case, they shrug and go away. If something does happen though," Carmichael grinned, "then they can prove to themselves that what happened was real."

"You make it sound so cocksucking simple."

"Pamela, it is simple. Just make sure all of their fussing doesn't bother the girls, right?"

"Damn, Carmichael, you really give a shit, huh?" Pamela leaned back and nodded at the waiter in thanks for her fresh drink.

"Don't start. Just get the show locked down, will you?" Carmichael finished his coffee and looked around for a minute. "And then you can explain why we always come here."

"I like this place," Pamela insisted.

"I got that. I just don't get why."

"You're a cunt, Carmichael."

"Everyone in your world is a cunt, Pamela. It's what makes you, you. The show." Carmichael nodded and stood, dropping some cash on the table and left. Most times, he knew, they would meet because of some show crisis, and they would hash it out over a few drinks and then have lunch or dinner or whatever meal was the right label for the time of day.

Carmichael just didn't feel like being Pamela's sounding board today, though. She was nice enough, he thought, once you got past her temperament, but this was bigger than either of them, and he didn't want to feel it cheapened, to become just another part of just another show. Regardless of what he might tell her, Carmichael felt that something was happening and that it wouldn't stop with just one show being upset.

He walked back to the train and rode uptown a while, heading home. The pageants took place all over the country, but their offices and homes were all in New York for the ease of being watched over by their parent media company. Luckily for Carmichael, he picked up other MC gigs on the side, so he could make rent. He had a show tomorrow, and wanted to get home and rehearse a bit. The show would be full of French-Canadians, and he had to work out their last names before hand to ensure a screw-up free show.

———

"Mother!" Patti Jensen yelled, throwing down her hat.

"Patti, you listen to me, they cheated you out of placing last time, I know, sweetheart, but it won't happen again," Loraine Jensen told her daughter sternly, "so you have to keep practicing."

"I wasn't cheated, mother!" Patti fumed, but picked the cowboy hat up off the floor anyway.

"Where'd that little blue girl come from then? She was a shill, that's where! That Clarke girl's mother probably arranged the whole thing." Loraine skipped to the start of the track again, pausing it quickly but leaving her finger hovering over the button.

"Latisha didn't cheat, and I don't think her mother did, either," Patti said, trying to sound stern.

"Then where did that blue girl come from?" her mother insisted.

"Heaven, just like she said," Patti told her mother frankly. Patti had talked to some of the other girls, on the phone. Most of them agreed that Samantha Felder was exactly what she said she was: a ghost. A little lost girl who had come to the magic of the pageant, like an angel or something. It was all very exciting and special, and Patti didn't want her mother to ruin everything by making it seem like Samantha had only been a cheap trick.

"Don't be a fool, Patti. She was a little shill. Either way, honey," Loraine said, "you still need to practice. You want to win, for a change, don't you? Of course you do."

Loraine hit the CD players play button and the music started. Patti put her hat on quickly and started to dance. Counting steps in her head, she went through the motions, missing a step here and there, but not stopping.

She would get the routine down pat before the show, she knew. Patti had faith in that. She knew if she tried hard enough, and worked hard enough that she could learn the routine perfectly and show her mother how good a dancer, how good a contestant and daughter, she could be.

Loraine was already composing another strongly worded letter to the board of the pageant in her head while she watched her daughter dance. She also kept track of Patti's mistakes, of course. Loraine was very skilled at multitasking, a skill she credited a lot of Patti's work in pageants to.

Loraine loved her daughter. She also wanted to win; she wanted to see her own child up on stage while the light picked her out and showed her to be a winner to the rest of the world. Loraine burned for it, smiling with determination every time she signed Patti up for another show. Her child, she had decided while Patti was very young, would be a winner.

No matter what.

―――――

Carmichael let one hand reach up and touch his bow tie. It was, as he knew, perfectly straight. He smiled wide and stepped forward. Long, even strides took him across the stage to the microphone stand. The spotlight lit him, one hand resting on top of the microphone, and he looked out into the darkness of the crowd.

"Thank you for coming," he said out into the darkness. "Now, may I present to you tonight's contestants..."

On cue ten little girls marched on stage. Each of them raised a single hand, the other staying firmly by their side, and waved. Their faces turned ninety degrees, so that they could stare into the crowd and smile. Stopping on their mark, each girl turned and fully faced the audience.

The girls couldn't see the crowd beyond the stage. The spotlights on them created shining cones of light that blinded them to anything further than a few feet away, but they could hear that just beyond their sight sat people cheering and clapping. The noise washed over them and filled them, from head to toe, with joy.

They were, just then, each of them, winners. Beautiful and special, the feeling of the crowd's love smoothed over wrinkles in their feelings and gave them each a lift they could physically feel.

Backstage, Pamela worked around the extra security. Guards stood at every entrance, keeping logs of everyone who entered and exited. They noted the contents of every package and bag, each duffel and backpack, logging everything humanly possible.

Cameras swept the public areas, two of them on the log book itself, monitoring every entry written. There were even a few cameras that were aimed at other cameras, acting as a backup for the hell of it.

Pamela hated it all, of course, but she had no choice. The guards and the cameras were conditions to be met, she found out, in her contract for this show. So far the show seemed perfectly normal, and Pamela wasn't sure if that was good or not.

On the one hand, a perfectly normal, by the book, show would certainly eliminate any feelings that she had rigged something the last time. On the other hand, having Samantha Felder, or something like her, pop up now would certainly help prove that she had nothing to do with it in the first place.

She monitored the stage, listening though Carmichael's pickup. Everything sounded normal. A quick peek from backstage showed her that the introductions were going as planned. Nothing was out of its place.

"We got the fucking sets for the opening song ready?" she whispered into her headset.

"Yep," a call came back quickly, "as soon as Carmichael finishes the intro we go full on opening song."

"Good. Don't be a slow cunt and screw me."

"Wouldn't dream of it," the call came back.

Pamela could hear the tired sigh under the words. She knew the crew felt that she was more overbearing than normal. She had also expected them to understand, and while some of them did, she found herself fighting down resentment that they all didn't. The few who that felt she just getting in their way were right, to an extent.

Pamela cursed and grabbed her clipboard, running down the check list one more time. It gave her something to do besides wait.

On stage, Carmichael finished the introductions and made a large sweeping gesture with one arm. The lights came up as his arm reached the apex of its swing, and the music started. Sets rolled into place, black clad stage hands staying out of sight as they pushed and maneuvered things into place with practiced precision.

A giant waterfall, the water itself made of foil streamers, came into view. The contestants each raised one arm high, waving high, and spread out. Each girl walked an exact count of steps to stand along the waterfall. The music built. The lights strobed slowly, changing color as they did.

Carmichael took the microphone from its stand and walked over toward the set. Starting his welcoming song, the girls joining him, he strode back and forth across the stage so that he passed each girl, taking the time to look each one in the eye.

He looked calmly at them, and warmly, making sure none of them were too scared or too nervous. When one of the girls did appear to be the least bit nervous, Carmichael managed to let his gaze linger on her for an extra second, catching her eye and letting her see that everything would be fine.

He acted as a grounding force on the stage, a piece of scenery, something that was there before them and would be there for the whole show, ready to help them if needed. Carmichael appreciated the job, and knew that his responsibility on stage was a serious one.

Girls had broken down before, some worse than others. He

had found himself forced to coach a few through continuing, or in the rarer occasion, help them off stage without losing face.

The song continued, each of the girls raising her voice to play her part. The lights swung around the stage, lighting each girl with different colors, and highlighting them all before the end. Ten girls went though their minor, but perfectly timed, danced steps. Hands were raised, bodies twirled, and feet shuffled.

As the song ended, Carmichael wound his way back across the stage and ended up back where he started, placing the microphone back into its stand. The music hit a final crescendo and faded. The lights came down, and the stage plunged into darkness, except for a lingering spot on Carmichael who thanked everyone, audience and participants, and told them the show would continue in just a minute.

The girls hurried off stage, finding their way in the darkness easily. Pamela was already waiting for them. An assistant was with her, helping Pamela shepherd the girls into the proper areas.

Pamela let her assistant, Mary Locke, deal with the girls, and left to see what else was going on. A radio call came through on her headset just as she left Mary. "Pam, we got a problem," the voice said, sounding both surprised and confused.

"What kind of problem, damn it? Give me information. Where am I headed?"

"Check-in. Just get here."

"Fuck," Pamela spat into the headset as she took off. A check-in table problem could be all sorts of things: angry parents demanding their children be allowed to enter late, press corps people trying to find tabloid dirt on pageants, pageant officials trying to annoy her with stupid requests—hell, once she had been sent to deal with a page that fainted at the check-in table and no one knew who to replace them with. Pamela had a feeling this call would be something utterly different though. She had a good guess as to what had happened.

A bunch of people stood around the check-in table. Pamela came up behind them. Everyone looked down at the check-in book, except Pamela, who watched everyone else's face.

"Ms. McGregor," one of the new security guards said, noticing her arrival, "we have a situation."

"No, fuckwit, you have a situation. I have a continuation, I'm guessing. Let me guess, new name on the book? No one saw anyone? Just appeared?"

"No, Ms. McGregor, I mean, well, yes, but..."

"All right, fuck-o, you're tapped out," Pamela said, turning away from the security guard and finding Rodger, the man who had been charged with manning the check-in book, "Rodger, hit me."

"Four names, Pam, four!" Rodger said, rising from his seat.

"Four? Well, fuck. All right, so four new names. Four new contestants, I'm guessing they're all blue. So where are they?"

"Ms. McGregor?" the guard asked.

"Not addressing you, fuck-o."

"Ms. McGregor, need I remind you," the guard said, puffing out his chest, "that the board itself hired me and my team to—"

"Still not caring, fuck-o. Rodger, write this man a badge that says 'fuck-o' so he'll remember how much I love him." Pamela looked around the hallway. Nothing seemed out of place. "Pamela to all points, we have any blue sightings out there?" she said into her headset.

"Good call, boss," came the reply, "we were just about to call you. They're backstage."

"Fuck, on it," she said as she started to move back the way she had come.

"Ms. McGregor, I am charged with following you and seeing this for myself," the guard said, falling into step beside her.

"Fine by me, fuck-o. But if you bother the contestants or my staff I'll have you tasered as part of the floor show."

Pamela took off, not quite running. She knew the contests were going to need to line up soon, changed for the first part of the pageant. There wasn't much time to sort everything out.

The guard kept up with her easily, not exactly sure what was going on.

Backstage, Mary Locke grabbed Pamela's arm and swung her around, leading her off. "Pam, we have visitors," she said simply as she steered her boss in the right direction. Pamela just nodded, allowing herself to be led.

The contestants were lining up, though with a bit of confusion. Four new girls were taking placing in the line, at various points. No one knew what to do with them. Samantha Felder Pamela recognized at least. The other three girls were new, however, and they wandered around trying to find the right place in line. Except they seemed to know what was the right place when no one else did.

Pamela considered her options. She could bar them completely, but if Samantha appeared on stage last time, there was no reason she couldn't do the same now, and disrupt the show. Pamela also figured she could assign them places, but that would ripple out and cause other problems. No matter what slot she put them in, some other girl would have to be moved back.

The new girls, all gently glowing, seemed to know where they belonged, however. And as they approached their slots, the other girls moved aside for them. At first there was a bit of skittishness, but word had spread about Samantha, so many of the girls were simply surprised without being scared.

Sighing, Pamela let nature take its course and allowed the new girls to find their own spaces. She sent Mary to collect their names and get them to Carmichael as warning.

She studied them, then. Carmichael was right, she realized, their feet didn't touch the floor at all. They each—Samantha Felder, Ronnie Bowman, Loretta Hauber, and JoAnn Smith—had the same ethereal beauty to their features. They were serene, content to be where they were and also at the same time perfectly joyous to be in that line, waiting to take the stage.

Pamela readied the crew and started the countdown. The line formed fully, and fourteen girls stood, patiently waiting for the march back into the spotlight. The lighting crew was warned of the placement of the ghost girls, as Pamela thought of them, and knew to leave them unlit. Everything felt as ready as possible.

The word was given, and the girls walked back on stage. Music fought against the sound of applause as each girl appeared, until Loretta Hauber showed up. A slight break, the merest pause, the applause stuttered, but the girls didn't stop. The applause picked back up, even if the faces of some of the parents darkened, but dipped again as JoAnn Smith appeared.

All fourteen girls stood on stage. The applause died down as Carmichael nodded and started to speak. Still, some of the parents' faces remained darkened. When Samantha Felder broke into the pageant, they minded, but considered it a fluke, or at worst a ploy. Four girls, however, was going above the limits of tolerance. They wouldn't take it. Not at all.

On stage, though, the contestants didn't mind their new companions too badly. The new girls, the blue ones, were polite and happy. They made the other girls feel good, and they were endlessly nice to be around. So pretty and poised, the other contestants started to look up to them.

The pageant went on, following every note and twist and turn that had been laid out for it weeks before. Pamela worked backstage to deal with endless calls that were sure to follow. She still had a show to run, but she also knew she would have to defend her choices as soon as that show ended.

The show continued. The girls walked back off stage to change quickly and then continue. Pamela allowed parents access to help their daughters and led the ghost girls to a special area she had planned ahead with in secret.

Smaller than needed, as Pamela thought only Samantha Felder might return, if at all, the curtained changing area was bare, except for a single chair. Pamela noticed that Samantha needed no help to change and brought nothing with her, but Pamela wanted to provide her with some privacy. At least somewhere away from the parents while they milled around.

The four girls accepted the use of the tiny space happily, and Pamela stood at the break in the curtain, considering.

"Girls," she began hesitantly, "I need to ask. Where do you come from?"

Laughing lightly, Samantha Felder faced Pamela. "Heaven, like I told you," she said sweetly.

"Right, but I mean in a more... why four of you now? Why any of you at all? What's going on?" Pamela felt the questions flow out of her and cursed herself for them. Still, any answers might help both her cause and the girls, she reasoned.

"It's just our time, Miss," Ronnie Bowman said, getting nods from the other girls. "We don't mean to cause any trouble."

"Oh, no," Pamela said, "I'll deal with any problems. I was just wondering, because you have to admit this is a bit strange."

"I don't think so, Miss," Loretta Hauber put in, "not really. We just love these pageants so much. Don't you?"

"I... I sure do," Pamela told them. Over her headset she got a time warning. "Three minutes, girls," she said, moving away.

Around her staff moved at speed, getting contestants various forgotten items, or simply running errands. Parents stood around, yelling at whomever they could corner. One of them recognized Pamela and nudged another parent at her side.

They moved in on her and crowded around. They all started to yell, the mingled voices and volumes making their shouts nothing more than incoherent noise to Pamela. She made quieting gestures with her hands, tried to make sure her posture was nonthreatening, all of the tricks she employed over the years to deal with parents. Nothing worked in the least. Pamela gave up.

"All right!" she yelled, "Shut the hell up for a fucking second. Damn. Don't you have a show to push your children to perform in?" As soon as she said it, Pamela knew she walked a dangerous line.

"How dare you?" a parent fired back. She crossed her arms and then quickly put them on her hips, instead. Not sure what to do with herself, the mother fumed, laying into Pamela. "Who do you think you are? Letting these fake girls enter the show illegally? You're robbing our children of their fair chance!"

A chorus of agreement rose, and Pamela saw the glint of a mob in their eyes. She held out her hands and shook her head. "If you check the log book, you'll see every girl here was entered officially. And they aren't 'fake girls' any more than those are your 'real lips,' lady."

"You bitch!" screamed the mother in question, "Those freaks shouldn't be allowed in our show! I'll be filing a complaint with your bosses!"

"Me, too!"

"Yeah!"

"We'll see you out of a job!"

"You can't do this to people!"

The parents screamed, throwing curses and threats around at whim. Pamela, taking a deep breath, found her calmness again and embraced it, swearing she wouldn't insult anyone else for at least five minutes. Thinking about it, Pamela remembered the time and shook her head. "People! People! One minute! Get the parents back to their seats! Girls, line time!" she shouted, quickly moving away from the parents before they could complain.

Everyone started to move, finding their pre-established places. Staff members helped usher the parents back out into the audience as Pamela and Mary gathered up the girls.

The show, as it always did, went on. Applause started up, lights flared back into life, Carmichael took his place and the girls stood at the ready. Pamela shook her head and watched from the wings of the stage. She could dimly see the audience, a slice of it at least. Parents had taken their seats, but a few more scowls than normal seemed to flare in the reflection of lights.

Pamela ran a running count in her head, assessing the trouble that would come to haunt her later. Good choice of word there, haunt, she thought to herself, and angrily turned away from the crowd.

She busied herself with general work and spot checks until the sound of a pure voice singing caught her attention. Loretta Hauber sang, more beautifully than Samantha Felder had, and everyone was enraptured by her voice.

Pamela snuck another look into the crowd, and saw that they were just as caught by the sound as Pamela and her crew were. Each of the ghost girls managed to do the same, be it singing or, in Ronnie Bowman's case, dancing. They moved and sung with an unearthly grace and poise. They seemed to be so in the moment that moments existed simply to be filled by them.

Section after section the show went. In the gaps there were angry parents, yelling and stomping their way backstage. During the performances, though, the show continued as if nothing unusual was going on.

At the end of the show, Ronnie Bowman took the tiara, first place with a huge smile and graceful curtsey. Samantha Felder took second place. Third place went to Jennifer Saunders, who was as surprised as any one else by the fact of her placement.

After the show, parents stormed the backstage area, equally involved in packing up as they were in taking to task any pageant staffer who happened to be at hand. They called the show unfair, rigged, and morally questionable. They threatened legal action, angry letters and boycotts. They all left, tugging at their daughter's arms and scowling.

After everything died down, four little girls, each glowing blue, snuck back on stage and stood there, staring out into the empty seats. Each one smiled, not a show smile, but a real smile: pure and open. Then, as one, they vanished in a nimbus of light.

THREE

"ASS BAIT!" PAMELA yelled into her phone, right before she slammed it down. Reporters had been calling her for a week straight, and Pamela found herself worn down to the point of screaming rage with them.

Each call was worst than the last. They wanted to know what was going on, about reports of ghosts and impossible goings on. They wanted answers that Pamela didn't have, and worse, that she couldn't give them even if she did.

The board slapped her, her crew, and Carmichael with the threat of heavy lawsuits and job loss if any of them spoke to the press about the various "incidents," as they were now known.

That injunction included talking to parents, as well as the media, which didn't do anything to improve Pamela's mood. When the news outlets couldn't get her or her staff to crack, they went for the parents. The parents, of course, were all too happy to talk, flinging accusations around every which way. They got some money for voicing their opinions, and Pamela could say nothing in rebuttal.

The board called daily as well, demanding answers Pamela still didn't have, even though she would have been allowed to tell those answers to the board directly. No one had the answers that were wanted.

What footage there was that existed was gone over—both in secret by the board and in public by media outlets and parents. The board had more footage, of course, than the newsmakers, and of a better variety.

They screened shots from the back stage areas, dimmed pictures of glowing blue girls at low resolutions, and non-glowing people of similar resolution mingling. The board wrote copious notes, watching footage of the pageants and taking notice of how Samantha Felder appeared on stage the first time, the way her feet never touched the stage and how, when the spotlight was on her, you could actually easily see through her.

Pamela found herself called in for questioning often. They never called it that, no. They didn't want their simple, friend-ly, inquiries to sound too formal and frightening. They would call Pamela's office and request her presence for a "sit down to discuss certain recent events."

It didn't take long for Pamela to understand that those sit

downs were going to be four hours in a chair, answering questions from the board, over and over again. They believed her, they maintained; they simply wanted to be sure she remembered things the way she thought she did.

Carmichael found himself on the receiving end of the same treatment, and they crossed paths more than twice in the lobby of the board's office. Nodding at each other, but not saying anything, they would pass and go their respective way. Only later, when they were free from work and the endless questions, did they consider meeting to talk by themselves.

McLaren's was mostly empty by the time Pamela got there. Carmichael sat at a table off to one side, nursing a beer. Pamela ordered, grabbed and sipped from her scotch as she moved to join him.

"They drag you in yet this week?" she asked as way of welcome. It was a Tuesday night, and Pamela had been to see the board on Monday, only getting a phone call from them today.

"Not yet, but I'm sure they will," Carmichael said. "I wouldn't know what to do with my week if they didn't."

"No fucking lie, there. Cocksuckers, I mean where do they get off treating us like political prisoners or some shit?"

"It isn't that bad, Pamela," Carmichael said, stopping to take a slug of beer. "They're only treating us like lying, dishonest scumbags. No worse, really."

"Well, that's a kick in the cunt then. I should be grateful, huh?"

"We both still have jobs, don't we?"

"Fuck, today, sure."

"And tomorrow, too, I'd bet. They just want answers, but they don't like the only answer we have."

"They don't have to be such annoying pricks about it."

"No, they don't. But they are."

"Fucking right they are. Bunch of cock stains."

Carmichael finished his beer and nodded at Pamela's already empty glass. He stood and walked back toward the bar to get them both refills. Sitting down, moments later, he set the scotch in front of her and said, "I was thinking though, if the number of girls keeps increasing, we're going to have a logistical problem."

"Sooner or later, sure as shit we are," Pamela nodded, draining half her scotch in one solid gulp.

"Can we use that on the board?"

"How do you mean?"

"I don't know," Carmichael said, shrugging, "just something, damn, something useful. I mean, if we don't know what's going on, and they don't know, and we want to find out, why not just hold another pageant as planned?"

"Draw them out?"

"Pretty much."

"That's some Ghostbuster hot shit you got there, Carmichael. Act normal so the ghosts won't know, and then— what exactly? Catch them? Trap them? Kill them?"

"No, no, and no. Maybe talk to them? Find out some answers. God, Pamela, *kill* them? *Capture* them? What the hell?"

"I'm just saying—that's what they'll think of. They don't really believe that we're dealing with ghosts anyway, not really."

"Media seems to."

"Media'll believe in anything if it'll sell; at least they'll believe it in public."

"True enough."

"Thank you."

"So why not?"

"Why not indeed? The cunts'll prolly buy it."

"Then I'll bring it up. You act surprised when they ask you and agree," Carmichael said.

"Done."

Loraine Jensen sipped at her tea. She leaned forward, resting her elbows on the edge of the wide, circular table. Around the table were other pageant mothers, all of them with cups of tea or coffee. There was only one thing on their minds.

"We can't let these little freaks steal our girls' thunder!" Kendra Saunders said. She leaned back, crossing her arms and looking defiant.

"Oh shut up, Kendra! Jennifer won third place didn't she?" Loraine groused.

"That's not the point, Loraine," Susan Gladstone said.

"No, I think it is, Susan," Loraine countered. "I think the point is that human girls, real, rightful girls, our girls, should be allowed to win."

A chorus of "amen" rose around the table, like a slow wave. Mothers nodded, each of them feeling a level of hatred and jealously. Most of them also knew fear—fear that their daughters wouldn't be special enough anymore. Not special enough for them, at least.

"Well, the little blue freaks are pretty good," muttered Sheryl DeNunzio.

"What was that, Sher?" Loraine asked.

"I said," Sheryl repeated, "that the little blue freaks were pretty good, all right? Am I the only one who can admit that?"

"That's not hardly the point, either!" Susan Gladstone shouted. She grabbed her coffee cup and drained it. She slammed it down on the table, empty. "God, don't you people see? Our pageants are being taken over, and we're being told to shut up and ignore it!"

"What can we do?" Kendra asked. The other women nodded in agreement, all wondering the same thing.

Loraine stood up and paced around the end of the dining room. The women were all in her house, while Patti played by herself upstairs. "Are they real?" Loraine asked. She didn't look at the other women—people she knew were both her friends and her competition, choosing instead to study the floor while she spoke.

"Real girls or real ghosts?" Kendra asked quietly. Like Loraine, she expected everyone else to start yelling at this point, shouting and protesting the lack of point. No one did. The question had hung in all of their minds, even if they refused to voice it. Hearing it out loud gave them each pause.

"Ghosts," Loraine said. "I think they may be."

"That's blasphemous, Loraine," Susan said.

"They do look so peaceful and happy, though," Sheryl said, looking at Susan.

"Minions of the devil can have peaceful faces, Sheryl," Susan said, "and I think this is just getting ridiculous." She stood, looking around at each face carefully, "I think that if you women want to pursue such a discussion I am going to remove myself from it. This is Satan's work, or the pageant board's. But not God's, to be certain."

She left the dining room and found her coat, careful not to slam any doors. Her friends may be playing with dangerous ideas and going down a path of darkness by even talking about the... what they talked about, but there was no need to be childish and petty about it, she figured.

Outside, as Susan Gladstone started her light blue Volvo up and shifted it into gear, she found herself considering the question, regardless. Were they real or simply a trick? She shook her head and drove off, deciding it didn't matter in the slightest.

"The thing is, what's really important here, I think, is that," Loraine was saying back in the dining room as Susan drove off, "our girls have a fair shot."

"But how?" Sheryl asked.

"Well, we have to have them get equal footing with the other girls or get them removed."

"But Loraine," Kendra said, "how do we do either? The pageant board doesn't seem to care at all. They're just stalling us. I heard a rumor that they could postpone the next show, even."

"Well, we can't let that happen," Sheryl said quickly. "They'll just have to solve this."

"We'll call them tomorrow. I don't know what else we can do," Loraine said. The other women agreed, and made small talk for a while. They drank their tea and their coffee and talked about everything else in their lives: their own parents, their spouse and in-laws, gossip from each of their neighborhoods—whatever they felt would push them further and further away from looking the problem in the eye.

"You know," Loraine said, as Sheryl and Kendra put on their coats, "if they're real ghosts, then we could put our girls on equal footing after all."

"What?" Sheryl asked. "How?"

"Make them ghosts, too," Loraine whispered.

"That's sick, Loraine!" Sheryl exclaimed, tugging her coat tightly around her.

"Loraine, you have to be joking!" Kendra said.

"Of course," Loraine said, patting the air with her hands, "of course, it was just a joke."

FOUR

DUE TO THE combined forces of production staff and parents, another pageant was held. Neither side knew how much they owed to the other. They both preferred it that way, choosing to paint each other as the blockage point that was, very narrowly, avoided.

Girls lined up, voices were raised in song and lights flashed back and forth across the stage. A small number of Ghost Girls showed up just before the start of the show. "Ghost Girls" is how the media started to refer to them.

Normally the media would show up in the form of a local newspaper reporter or two, per show. At most. This particular show had cameramen set up along the back and reporters wandering backstage and up in the offices as well as sitting in the crowd.

They smelled a story, partly because they were told that they would smell a story. One episode was a fluke, two was a problem, but a third, well, the journalists in the crowd were convinced that a third would be the sign of an epidemic.

That epidemic would be a great boost to sales and ratings. So when the Ghost Girls showed up, cameras whirred, and phone calls were made—all in an effort to verify what was seen.

Five glowing, blue, girls had shown themselves this time, and Pamela found herself ready. Getting the board to agree to limiting the pageant to seven girls instead of the normal ten took some doing. It amounted to admitting these other girls were real, and valid, contestants, but eventually simple numeric logic prevailed.

So now twelve little girls found themselves on stage, commanding attention on a bigger scale than any of them thought possible at this stage in their careers. Pamela and her staff did their best to reassure the girls, all of them, that the extra cameras weren't anything to get nervous about. One camera or five, it was the same thing. The girls had a harder time swallowing that than they wanted to admit.

Each of them wanted to be the star; they wanted to shine and be beautiful and graceful and everything that ever went with those qualities. They were also young, and not half as prepared as they thought for a decent sized media circus.

The board had also sent extra men, once more. They were instructed to be subtle and stay out of the way, mostly for the sake of the media types around. It was the extra security that annoyed Pamela more than anything. She didn't like feeling as if she couldn't be trusted. Rationally, Pamela knew that wasn't really why the extra security stood around, but they still managed to get under her skin.

And still the pageant went on. Carmichael stood on stage and announced each girl, glowing or not, with the same warmth. He smiled and gestured with diamond precision. Extra media, extra security—none of these mattered to him. Not while he was on stage working.

Everything went smoothly, though. Despite the extra obstacles—or perhaps because of them—the show went as planned. Sooner than it felt possible, the winners were announced.

All three places went to Ghost Girls, each glowing brightly.

———

Parents stormed the back stage area, grabbing their children and making angry promises with flush faces. Girls found themselves yanked by the arm out of the theatre. Outside, reporters stood, lights shining brightly, microphones in hand, asking for interviews.

Back stage, once the parents and their children had left, Pamela and Carmichael wandered around, looking busy. They waited, trying not to give anything away. The Ghost Girls, the name seemed to stick and had already permeated Pamela's production staff, milled around, seeming to wait as well.

Pamela and Carmichael made their way to the Ghost Girls. They were careful not to gang up, or crowd them. Though the pair were outnumbered, they also knew that they could have easily seemed like a threat, and that wouldn't do at all.

"Hey," Pamela said, sitting down on the edge of a table. The girls nodded and smiled, perfectly happy to see her.

"How are you?" Carmichael asked, sitting down on a folding chair. The chair was on the same side of the curtain enclosed space the girls stood in as the table. The girls couldn't feel trapped now, Carmichael decided.

"We're all right; thanks for asking," Samantha Felder said. She smiled, glancing to the other girls and nodding. She was all right, good in fact. She had come in second and still felt the rush of a good place.

"We were just wondering," Pamela started, "if we could talk to you all for a second. Alone, you know, like we are right here, in private?"

Carmichael hated having to lie to the girls, but it was the only way to get the board what they needed. The small cameras along the ceiling were unobtrusive and, Carmichael hoped, they would go totally unnoticed.

"Of course, Ma'am," Justine Kirby said, glancing around to make sure the others agreed. They did.

"Well, what we really wanted to know, was, well... where do you come from?" Carmichael asked, deciding to do away with any preamble.

Pamela shot him a look, thinking curses she wouldn't say

in front of the girls. This was defiantly off-script for Carmichael. Pamela always figured if there was one guy to stay on script it would be him. He always did, on stage or off. Except now. Something about these girls got to him.

Labeling it "something" let Pamela pretend that she didn't feel it, too: *protective.*

"I told you, silly," Samantha laughed, "Heaven."

"Right, kiddo," Pamela said, jumping in, "but then how are you here? Mostly people who are," Pamela sighed and glanced to Carmichael, who nodded, "well, who are dead—they don't come back, you know?"

"Oh," Justine said, "well, that's true. But Samantha here, she really wanted to be in a pageant again. So she came back."

"You make it sound kind of simple," Pamela said.

"Oh, it was," Samantha told her. "I just really wanted to be here. I love the pageants so much."

"Of course you do, sweetheart," Carmichael said. "So when the others, your friends, saw how easy it was for you—they did the same thing?"

"Exactly!" cheered Ronnie Bowman.

"You do see how this could freak people out, don't you?" Pamela asked, looking at Carmichael, not the girls while she spoke.

He caught the glance and understood. Pamela was on a short fuse, and he was pissing her off. They had planned this whole meeting to go far differently. Well, she could, he decided, scream at him later if she needed to.

"We don't want to upset anyone," Samantha said. "It's just all so much better now, and we enjoy it so."

"Right," Pamela said, "but even so—"

"Even so," Carmichael broke in, "you just have to be careful."

"Carmichael, I think we need to go," Pamela said. "We have that dinner to get to?"

"Oh, right," Carmichael said. "Well, girls, you, *uhhh*, where do you go?"

"Back to Heaven, silly," Samantha said, and the glow

around the girls increased. They all vanished and left Pamela and Carmichael sitting there, alone.

"That's gonna look great on tape," Pamela muttered.

———————

Patti Jensen sat downstairs, sipping chocolate milk. Her feet dangled off the floor, kicking at the legs of the stool she perched on. She hummed to herself between sips. A tuneless song, just random notes that felt good to hum, were all she had in mind.

Loraine Jensen came downstairs and saw her daughter. Her losing daughter, she thought to herself. All she ever did, Loraine thought, was try to help her daughter out. Teach her how to be beautiful, how to sing, and walk and act like a proper little lady.

It wasn't because Patti was such a special flower, Loraine knew. No, Patti was, in her mother's estimations, perfectly average. But even perfectly average girls can aspire to greatness, and even achieve it if given the proper coaching and discipline.

These days, though, Loraine found herself wondering, more and more, if Patti would ever grow into what her mother had so carefully built for her. She wondered if her daughter truly appreciated what she had been given.

No, she didn't Loraine decided, starting to fume. There she sat, drinking milk, kicking her little legs back and forth. Ignoring her studies, her dance practices, everything, just to hum. And what song was that supposed to be, anyway? No, Loraine, bitterly felt the sting of defeat.

Those other girls could all soundly outperform her little Patti. And that was just taking into account the live ones. Loraine clenched and unclenched her hands as she added the Ghost Girls into the mix.

Girls that weren't even alive could beat her daughter— could beat all of them. Somehow, dead, they found an extra burst of grace and poise. Their voices carried better, and their joy was easier to feel. Loraine chalked all of that up to their simply being ghosts.

That was when she made her choice.

Loraine went out into the garage and looked for a few things, some helpful tools. Then she returned to the kitchen, Patti just finishing up her milk, legs still kicking absent mindedly.

"Patti, honey?" Loraine called out.

"Yes, Mother?" Patti answered. She hopped off the stool and went to see what her mother wanted. It never did to keep her mother waiting, not when she used that tone.

"I think I know how you can win the next pageant."

"Mother," Patti said, feeling bad, "I'm sorry. I'll practice more."

"No, no, Patti, I have a different way in mind."

And the knives in Loraine Jensen's hands flashed up and then down over and over again.

FIVE

MUCH TO THE disappointment of everyone involved, the next few pageants were postponed. The media coverage sparked a public outcry that would have been fine, as more people in seats and more national attention were good. However, the religious quarter suddenly took all of the rumors of ghosts seriously and declared the pageants agents of Satan.

Protestors surrounded Pamela's office for a solid month. They carried signs and shouted, occasionally publicly praying for the souls of everyone involved in the pageants. Pamela cursed them out for the first few days, but eventually got used to them, letting them become background scenery for her life.

The board couldn't just ignore them like Pamela did. Pressure was being put on advertisers and sponsors, and the revenue stream that kept the pageants running started to dry up. So a halt was hastily called while everything straightened out.

In the meantime, the death of Patti Jensen did not go unnoticed. Given the anger of the religious protestors and the media scrutiny, stories sprang up instantly. The leading theory was, in fact, that a "religious nut," as the papers called declared, kidnapped Patti and then killed her, dumping her body in a lake.

Loraine was portrayed as the grieving mother, and everyone pulled around her. Except some of the other show mothers. Quietly, they wondered what had really happened to Patti, even as they protected their daughters just in case.

Pamela and Carmichael found themselves called before the board again and again, watching their own footage. Public opinion already decided that the Ghost Girls were real ghosts, and the board fought against agreeing. Secretly, the individual members each believed in the girls' status, but none of them wanted to be the first to admit that to the others.

One day they seemed to collectively realize they simply had no other choice left. The board didn't call Pamela or Carmichael in. Or anyone else. They met in private, collectively sighed, and laid out a battle plan to deal with the issue in full. Within weeks the religious groups vanished, their protests silenced.

Publicly they took a wait-and-see stance as they claimed the Pope himself was debating the issue. Privately they had no good idea what the Pope was doing, but the board could, and had, exerted it's own control over different groups and a peace had been struck. It wasn't a trusting or comforting peace but it let everyone go back to work.

———

Carmichael let his hand rest lightly on the microphone and resisted the urge to straighten his jacket. It hung perfectly, and he knew that, but something in him wanted badly to adjust the lapel anyway.

Seven girls walked onstage. None of them glowed blue. Carmichael worried that somehow they managed to scare them away for good. He didn't like the idea and found himself hoping for a return, just if only to share in their joy at being on stage once more.

Backstage, Pamela stalked around, wondering where the Ghost Girls were, as well. What the fuck, she thought, was the point of all the bullshit and runaround if things returned to normal now?

"Any fucking word yet?" she asked into her headset.

"Nothing, Pamela. As soon as anything happens, we'll let you know."

"You better, motherfucker."

"No problem, boss," came the reply.

Mary ran up and touched her boss' shoulder lightly. Pamela spun on her heels, ready to yell until she saw who it was.

"What?" she asked, letting her shoulders sag a little.

"We have contact," Mary said. She jerked a thumb over her shoulder, and without waiting, turned and started to walk.

Pamela started to move, letting Mary lead her. "Possible contact at the—"

Pamela stopped and tapped Mary's shoulder. Without stopping, Mary glanced behind her and mouthed *curtain*.

"Possible contact at stage left wing," Pamela said into her headset. "On my way now to verify."

"Got that, Pam. Want backup?"

"Fuck no, cunts. Stay away, except normal staff."

"Confirmed."

Mary led Pamela over to the side of the stage where three girls stood, each one glowing blue. Ronnie Bowman smiled, waving at Pamela.

"Guys, you're a bit late," Pamela said, looking at the other two girls, neither of whom were looking at her. They stared off onstage, watching the show.

"I'm sorry, ma'am," Ronnie told her, "can we still join the show?"

"Sure, kid," Pamela said, looking at the clipboard Mary had discreetly slipped her, "just wait until they come off stage from the intro and we'll slot you in. Names?"

"Well," Ronnie laughed, "I'm Ronnie Bowman, you know *me*," she told Pamela, "and this is Christine-Louise Lee." Ronnie tapped the girl next to her, causing her to turn around.

"Hello," Christine said.

"And this," Ronnie continued, "is Patti Jensen."

"Well fuck me running," Pamela muttered.

———

The three Ghost Girls were slotted, and Carmichael was warned about their inclusion. He felt glad to hear the news, although that happiness faded a bit when he heard the names of all three. Still, there was nothing to be done about it then, except go on with the show.

Ten little girls took the stage, each one smiling and waving in almost perfect synch. They stared off into the audience, taking in the applause and cheering. The parents finished taking their seats in time, and Kendra Saunders turned to the woman next to her.

"Loraine, I don't know how else to say this, so keep calm—Patti's there."

Loraine Jensen burst into a wide smile. "At least she'll have a chance to win now, poor thing," she said.

Kendra wasn't sure how to take that, so she just nodded, turning back to the stage. The girls came out again and did a group song, leaving once more when it was through. The stage went dark and Loraine joined the other parents heading backstage.

"Mrs. Jensen?" Pamela asked Loraine as she spotted her, "I know this must be hard for you—"

"Can I see her?" Loraine interrupted.

"Of course," Pamela said, leading the woman to her daughter.

Patti stood with the other Ghost Girls, waiting for the talent portion of the show to start. Pamela watched mother and daughter meet and stayed back for a minute, letting them greet each other.

"Mrs. Jensen, if I may, the board needs me to ask Patti a few questions."

"This is hardly the time, Mrs..."

"Ms., Mrs. Jensen. Pamela McGregor; Pamela is fine. And the board insists. When else can we?" she asked with a shrug.

"All right, but I will be right here."

"Of course," Pamela turned to Patti, "Patti, do you remember who killed you? I... I hate to ask like that, but if we can catch them, it would be a huge help and—"

"I don't remember," Patti said, "I'm just so happy to be here today," she smiled. "I feel really good about my baton routine."

"I'm sure you do, honey," Pamela said, "but really, if you can remember anything at all, it would be a huge help."

"No, ma'am, I'm sorry."

"All right. Well, if you do remember anything, tell me, all right? Just ask anyone here for Pamela."

"I will," Patti said seriously, before smiling and standing up straighter. "I promise."

"One minute!" Mary shouted, and started to herd the girls to their places.

"Time to go," Pamela said, as much to Loraine as Patti.

Pamela left them, Patti and the other Ghost Girls right behind her, and took Mary's place. Mary wandered off to make sure the parents got back to their seats.

Pamela stood at the front of the line, facing the girls. She held up her right hand, fingers spread and counted down, whispering the words as her fingers fell.

"Five." Ten heads came up, spines straightening.

"Four." Twenty arms went rigid, wrists turned just so.

"Three." Ten smiles lit up, each one perfectly back in place.

"Two." Twenty eyes closed, and each girl took a deep breath before opening their eyes just in time for...

"One." Ten little girls marched back on stage to applause and cheering.

Some of the other mothers glanced between Loraine and Patti as the pageant went on. When Patti's baton routine went over flawlessly, they stopped scowling and started thinking. They watched their own daughters, alive and losing and then watched Patti.

Patti Jensen took first place that day. She smiled so wide and pure that it became infectious. Even Pamela smiled as Patti took first place, for the very first time.

No girl had ever been happier.

futuristic cybernetic assassin fairy hasballah

I ONLY TOOK the job because I needed the money. I only needed the money because Bunny needed the money. Bunny needed the money because she owed it to Kleigschtomper. Kleigschtomper wanted his money.

Regardless, it was a warm, sunny day when I sat on a rock in the open field we always met in and talked to Jennhoff, my agent, about the job itself.

"Hasballah, I couldn't give less of a damn about why you're taking the job…"

"I'm telling you about Kleigschtomper here. He…"

"I know Kleigschtomper. I've worked with Kleigschtomper. Bunny should have known better than to get in debt to Kleigschtomper." Jenhoff shook her head slowly, her sharply sloping ears poking out from under her long dark hair. Her wings buzzed annoyance and she fidgeted with a folder that sat in her lap like a bomb.

"Fun name though isn't it? Kleigschtomper. I just like saying it."

"You like saying it when it isn't being gasped out of you with his hand around your neck as you beg for life."

"I don't deny this. Fine." I ran a hand through my shoulder length blonde hair and took a deep breath, settling my own wings so their movements wouldn't betray my anxiousness to get the job and get it done. "You don't care about the deeper causes and meanings of my existence, or Bunny's. What's the job."

"It's shit."

"Thanks, Jenn. Build morale some more why don't you?"

"Not my job. My job is to hand you, Mister Killer man" she tossed a folder into my lap, "a file and tell you to kill someone. Him, in the file. Kill him."

With that she got up and left me alone in the field with the folder unopened in my lap. Sighing, I did a lot of sighing it felt like, I stood and wandered out of the field, flipping through the folder as I went.

The target's name was Ugh, no last name given. He was an Ogre. I mean a real Ogre: large, smelly, lived in a cave, tusks… the works. I felt another sigh coming on. Ogres weren't exactly easy to kill. Not even for the best of the best. Which would be me.

There weren't many assassins who were fairies to begin with, these days. We were considered too small to be a true and serious threat to the larger races. All too often it was one of the larger races someone needed assassinated.

Since the fall of Man and the return of Magery and our older ways, most disputes were settled in a civilized manner: sword to the face, mace to the neck, acceptable societal situational handlers.

It just so happened, though, that sometimes it didn't work too well that way. You might have the moral high ground, but a weak sword arm. Times like those, you wanted an assassin. If you were really smart you wanted an assassin who was small enough and fast enough to not be caught. Too many people didn't think of that part.

Furthermore, the really critical point, you wanted an assassin who had cybernetic implants and fought dirty on your behalf. Sure, I traded in my left arm for a hunk of metal and wires, and an eye, and my liver and right foot and a few other bits and pieces here and there, all in the name of old Man tech that made me a whole lot more fun to be around, but we all had to make a living.

I filled a niche.

I took to the air and buzzed my way back to the tree.

Flashing my metal eye at a sensor hidden under a leaf I deactivated security and walked in to see Bunny sitting around counting what was left of her money.

"Hasbutt," she said merrily, kicking her feet against the legs of her chair, "did you get a job?"

"I got," I said, waving the folder, "a job. Ogre though."

"Ooo man, I hate Ogres."

"You don't have to kill this one."

"Well that's good, considering that I hate them and wouldn't want to even get close to it. Besides, you're the guy."

I walked over to her and ruffled her hair, laughing. What most people never realized was that Bunny was the dangerous one. Oh sure, I can take down a bunch of Man-sized beasts and do it so no one ever really notices me, but Bunny is the dangerous one. You just never find out about it until you're dead.

It lowers the number of people who talk.

She hopped off her chair and hugged me tight, giggling like a madfairy. Yup. Deadly beast is she. Trust me on this. I've seen her take out Ogres without too much trouble, hells she could take out this one for me but she wouldn't. Bunny had a thing about chores. She didn't want to do any if she didn't have to. She saw my work as a chore, of course, so she would only help out in the preparation and the cheerleading.

Bunny owned pom poms.

I stumbled as I landed on the tree and fell against the eye sensor hard enough to hurt. At least it still read my ID and opened the door. Bunny perked up as I staggered through the door and met the carpet face first.

"Hasballah," she asked, concern in her voice, "what the…"

"Mmmrf, Bunny. We should, well I left here, right?"

"Right, you left here," she agreed as she helped me up and over to the couch.

"To kill Ugh."

"The ogre?"

"Yeah, him. He was home," I said slowly.

"Good place to kill him," Bunny agreed.

"Sure, but he knew I was coming I think, I just... *ow!* stop that."

Bunny shook her head and continued to poke and prod at my wounds.

"But Has, you're bleeding, all over the couch. I keep my art near the couch," she sighed.

"Right, sure, so he surprised me," I admitted ruefully.

"Not the other way around?"

"No, get me that battery over there?"

Bunny nodded and flounced over to the work table I kept on one side of the room. She studied the assortment of gear: batteries, replacement lenses and wires, and so on.

"The black..."

"Yeah. Anyway, as soon as I got through the door he clubbed me."

She came back, handing me the battery, and resuming her makeshift nursing attempts, eyes going wide.

"Ooohh one of those big..." she started.

"An ogre club, of course, what else would he..."

"I don't know. Here, let me see your arm..." Bunny reached for my cybernetic arm, after dabbing at it with an oil cloth.

"Arm's fine. Rebooting," I told her, moving it away from her. Bunny wasn't great with electronics. "So he clubbed me, and then he did it again and..."

"And you blasted him to bits?"

"No, I fell down. A lot. Those clubs hurt."

"Well why'd you get hit?"

"He surprised me, I told you."

"Oh. Right."

"So I... help me plug this in, quickly?"

"What's the rush?"

"Well I got away from him."

"Ugh. The ogre."

"Right. *Except...*"

"There's an 'except'?"

"He followed me..."

"Here?"

"Well not here yet. Tree's still standing."

"Oh, Has, oh, oh, Has, that's not... that's not good, it's just... that's... oh, Has, not good."

I agreed with her, in principle at least. I stood, shakily, and grabbed some new weaponry: a couple of grenades, an extra knife, a bag of the good dust, just some basics. Bunny followed me around fussing as we traced circular paths in the place.

"Time to bail," I said, "We'll use the back."

Bunny nodded and leapt out of the window with a little squeak, her bag of goods clutched tightly in her hand. Her wings slowed her as soon as she cleared the window sill and I followed in short order.

Except my wings weren't up to snuff. They're hybrids, my wings. Semi-mechanical. They have to be, my originals got mostly blown off years ago. I felt like crap, though, and the mechanical systems were still a bit shaky from damage so I fell like a stone. While I twisted and turned in the air I caught a glimpse of Bunny getting clear and avoiding something.

Something I landed on with a whuff and thump. I held onto the lumpy mass tightly, not wanting to slide down and hit the ground, until I noticed that the lump was breathing. Sighing I peeled an arm away and took a good look at what I was holding.

"Hey, Ugh, no hard feelings?" I asked the ogre as I clutched his head tightly.

"Ugh no like you. Ugh use club."

"All right, Ugh, if you need to." I sighed and unhooked a grenade from my belt. Ugh hit himself in the head with his club, narrowly missing my toes. He growled and drew back for another swing.

Crawling around Ugh's head some, I squirted a large gob of glue into his left eye and crammed the grenade into the sticky mess, taking the pin back as a souvenir.

I hit the ground hard, but luckily my side was there to take the fall. As I fell off Ugh his club swung by my ear and right into his own. I took off at a sprint, counting to myself. I reached six and got bowled over by the concussive force of a grenade exploding behind me. I picked myself up off the ground for what seemed like one time too many in a single day and glanced behind me. Half of Ugh's head was missing and he seemed to be looking for it on the ground.

Damned ogres and their ability to keep moving. They were like chickens that way: you can remove their heads but sometimes they just keep going. I watched him for a minute or two, Bunny coming up to my side and watching with me, until he fell down. Hard.

"Bunny, go back inside," I told her as we stepped over Ugh's body.

"What about you, Hasbutt?" She grinned and went back to jump up and down on Ugh's body a few times.

"I have to go finish the job."

"Ogre's dead. Job's done. Right?"

"Normally. But not this time."

"If you're sure, I mean shouldn't you take some time and…"

"Nope. Now go on."

Huffing lightly, Bunny nodded and got off the ogre carcass to fly back into the tree. I resettled my weapons and tried to fly, finding my wings sore but workable.

The door to Jennhoff's office was open. She was sitting at her desk, the window behind her open to allow a cool breeze in. She looked up as I came in, the tips of her ears twitching.

"Ugh taken care of," she asked me as she looked back down at her desk and whatever she was doing.

"Mmm, you could say that, Jenn."

"I just did say that."

"Sure. There's just one thing…" I sat down on the edge of her desk and gave her a cold grin.

"Yeah," she asked, trying to hide her annoyance and failing.

"He knew I was coming," I said as I pulled a knife from my belt, "and I gotta ask myself how he knew."

Jenn started to stand up, stopping when the edge of my knife found itself a few inches from her eye.

"Has, what are you trying to..." She managed to hold her voice level but her eyes kept flicking between my knife and my face.

"At first I just headed here to... I thought you might be able to work out who... but then it clicked. How much?"

"How much what," she asked archly, growing annoyed as her initial fear faded. That's the problem with pulling a knife on someone. When you don't use it quick enough they assume you won't use it at all.

"Don't... just *don't*. We've worked together for too long. I'll ask once more, seeing as how we've taken all this time to build a lasting and meaningful relationship. How much?" I inched the knife closer to her face and tried to not smile as she flinched.

"Has, you're wrong about..."

Her words cut off with a scream as my knife slid along her cheek, parting the skin easily.

"Next it's an eye. C'mon, Jenn. Don't do this...or make me do this."

"The money was too good. I got four times a normal job for it, all right?"

I sighed and lowered the knife some, "So that's all I'm worth to you, four jobs all rolled up in one easy moment?"

"Don't put it like that, Has..."

"No? How should I think of it then?"

"Well..."

"Right." I hopped off her desk and started to walk towards the door.

"This doesn't mean we can't still work together, Has. It was just business," she insisted, standing up and starting to move around her desk.

"Jenn. Don't even try that shit with me."

I closed her office door behind me and took off from her ledge, doing everything I could to look uninjured and strong.

I didn't even bobble and almost weave into a tree for a good three minutes. I was doing fine. Really.

———

Kleigschtomper sat on a rock, idly playing with a knife. He was big for a fairy, about twice again my height and weight. Not that any of the extra weight was body fat, no, Kleigschtomper was all muscle and bad attitude.

"Hey, dude, got a sec?" I asked as I landed behind him.

Kleigschtomper spun around and threw his knife hard before he even saw me. I dodged and shook my head with a laugh.

"Is that the best you got for me, Kleig?"

"Hasballah," he said, and spat on the ground, "you really are stupid, aren't you?"

"That's me. The stupidest with the... oh the hell with it."

I threw a handful of fairy dust at him, my own special blend. It hit the air and shimmered bright hues of silver before starting to fall towards him. I counted to three and dove for cover.

The dust sparkled brighter, I assume since I couldn't see - being face down like I was - and then exploded. The exploded part I'm sure of. That much I felt and heard.

Potent batch.

Kleigschtomper yelped and thudded to the ground. I stood up after an extra second of waiting to see him lying prone on his back in the grass.

"Kleig," I asked as I walked over to him, "I know you're still alive. Why are you trying to kill me?"

"B-bunny," he muttered, his eyes opening slowly and painfully, "owes me money."

"So you try to kill me? How does that work? Try and kill her, like an honest kinda guy."

"She works for you..."

"Mmm right, that makes it all make sense. Sure. Admit it, Kleig, this is because..."

"Don't start that," he bellowed. He sat up slowly and rested his hand on his knees, spreading his wings wide to feel for damage. There was none, exploding fairy dust can be lethal but I knew how much to throw at a fairy.

"It's true, isn't it?"

"Mom always liked you best!"

"Klieg," I said as I sat down next to him, "we're not related."

"Yes we are, our mom is the…"

"Unfortunate result of a time traveling cloning experiment. I explained this all last month."

He glared at me and patted at his belt before finding and pulling a fresh knife out of a holster.

"I still don't…"

"It's a long story. Just deal with it and move on. Now how much does Bunny owe you?"

He waved the knife around some and pointed it at me in a fairly menacing manner. I slapped it away with my metal arm and primed the laser, the small red light blinking to show a full charge.

"I wanted you dead!"

"I know, dude," I told him softly, the primer light still blinking at him, "it's just that things get complicated in my life, it isn't you. So why don't I settle the debt and we'll start fresh."

"I'll kill you eventually, Hasballah, you know that."

"Sure. Just not today. I tell you what…" I dug my free hand into a pocket slowly and rummaged until I found the chip, "I'll give you this and you can go kill me."

"What," he asked, snatching the chip out of my hand, "the hell is this?"

"Time machine. Tiny. Effective. Programmed to take you to my future where I'll be nice and old and you can kill me. Deal?"

He studied the chip, frowning at it as he turned it end over end in his hand.

"Well, I mean, I guess, sure… if you…"

"And we'll call the Bunny thing even. You get to kill me, after all."

"Yeah, all right, Hasballah."

Kleigschtomper gave the chip a good squeeze and vanished before my eyes. Dumb semi-half-brother fairy. This is why not even Bunny knew about our relationship. I was ashamed of him. He never thought to ask how he would get home again.

I told him the truth though - that chip would take him to my future. I should know, that's where I got it from. Years ago an older version of myself came back and handed me the chip, telling me to send Kleigschtomper back to him eventually, for the laugh.

I laughed as I stood up and beat my wings against the air, rising into the sky.

I laughed long and good.

meat

It was break time at the store: my favorite time of the day, next to quitting time. Ever since the outbreaks, sales had been for shit and the place was so quiet you could hear a pin bitch about being dropped even before it hit. I smacked the security bar on the back door with the flat of my hand hard enough for it to sting, and when the door flew open, I drew a deep breath of cool air into my lungs.

Night hovered over the back lot thickly, and a breeze eased along the parking spaces as I lit a smoke. I looked past the flame's dancing shadows into the field behind the store. A squirrel leapt out from under a bush and skittered across the lot toward me, hoping I had some food. I flicked ash at it, which it dutifully inspected before glaring at me and hopping away to try a garbage bin.

The door clanged open, and Jason popped his head out, shaggy dreads flopping across his eyes.

"Hey man, you got a light?" he asked, holding up a smoke and waving it a bit to make it clear why he wanted the use of fire.

"Yeah man, sure," I held my cheap disposable lighter out to him, but kept watching the squirrel. It was digging under the garbage bin, hoping we had dropped something worthwhile. I heard a small noise behind me and spun to see Jason looking like he had just been kicked in the nuts by God.

"Jason, dude, fuck, you okay?" Jason was not okay. It was a stupid thing to ask, but my brain just put it out there on my tongue without stopping to check. He pointed out past me with his half-lit cigarette. I turned to look and saw a few people walking slowly out of the field. I shrugged and turned back to Jason, spotting my lighter on the ground. I bent to pick it up as he screamed, "Zombies!"

The word froze me in place, bent over, my hand curled around the plastic of the lighter. After a second or two, I stood up straight and looked again. Sure enough, they weren't moving right. Living beings didn't move like that. They just... didn't. I moved toward the door just in time to see Jason vanish behind it. I heard the lock engage. Either the piece of paper we used to keep it from locking behind us had fallen–or Jason had pulled it free. I cursed, slamming my fist into the damned door a few times. They were getting closer. I experienced a moment of panic, a blind moment of time when all thought left me and logic flew the nest like a bird on fire.

But as I looked around, I saw Bud's truck. Good old Bud Rotanski, my stupid-as-hell manager, who used to get so riled up at a mis-shelving of goods that he would threaten to shoot us. "James," Bud would drawl, "I'm gonna go git the shotgun outta my truck and come back here and blow your ass off if this mess ain't fixed."

God bless Bud, I decided as I broke the driver's side window of his truck with one of the rocks from the dividers that marked the end of each parking aisle. There were no keys. I hit my head against the steering wheel and thought about trying to hotwire the truck. I had no idea how to do it, and it would cost me too much time trying. If I couldn't get it going, I would be stuck in a very small place. I hit the steering wheel again, this time with my fist, and looked around the inside of the truck.

I grabbed the shotgun off the rack behind the seat, and opened the door to climb out, wishing all the while that I had acquired a useful skill like hotwiring a vehicle. Then, realizing I'd need more ammunition, I knelt on the seat and rummaged around to find the box of shells I knew he always carried. Thus armed, I scooted around the truck, only to find that the zombies had drawn far too close for comfort. I tried backing away, hoping I could outrun them, play a game of keep-away until the authorities came to deal with the problem. That is, assuming Jason had called them. Not that the cops were known for a good response time when dealing with the undead, but it was better than no plan at all.

I cursed when I saw another group of them coming around from the front of the store. I had to stay calm; they were just zombies. The incursions had been getting worse for years but everyone knew to bug out as fast as possible, and they'd eventually get bored and wander off - unless there were enough people in one spot, then all you could do was hope for assistance. Only I had no safe, secure place near. I took a deep breath and forced myself to calm down and think.

Caught between the two groups, I fired at group in front of me. One of them lurched to the right as I got lucky. My fist pumped in the air and a small shout of joy escaped me before I realized how stupid a move that was. I stopped wasting precious seconds and fired again, aiming for the same zombie I had nicked before, and saw it go down, its head ruined. I fumbled with the ammo to reload. Even as I was snapping the shotgun closed, I realized I knew one of them.

"Boo boo kitty fuck," I said softly, the grin that would normally spread across my face with the words replaced by a grimace. Sheena was my girlfriend, the only person in town I really felt I could connect with, never mind the only other real Kevin Smith fan in our god-forsaken town. And now she was an undead flesh-eater.

I lost it around then. I mean, really lost it. The shotgun roared again and again as I fired at everything moving. I stopped thinking, I stopped feeling; I just shot at them as fast as possible, stopping only to reload.
Boom, boom, silence, boom, boom.

My entire world diminished to the pattern of noise and light and violence. Sheena went down in a horrible mess of ruined chest and severed neck, but there were still too many of them. When I reached into the box for another set of shells I found I had another problem. The box was empty. Howling with rage, I flung the cardboard box at a zombie and raised the shotgun like a club. The box bounced off its face. The shotgun that followed it didn't, and the thing shook, turning with the off-center and weak blow. A different zombie behind me grabbed the shotgun as I swung it back again and yanked it clean from my hands.

I ran in circles to get back to Bud's pickup. There were all sorts of stuff tossed in the truck bed. I jumped up into it and started tossing things aside, not quite knowing what to grab: a green blanket, a broken hockey stick, a few bottles of oil, one knee pad, a bowling ball, a handful of wrenches, an empty water bottle. Finally, I snatched up the broken stick and the bowling ball. I didn't have a plan; my brain was working on sheer panic.

A zombie got in my way as I tried to jump down, and I swung the hand with the bowling ball on instinct alone. You'd be amazed at how well a bowling ball can work as a weapon against the undead. I know I wasn't prepared for how easily the ball passed through its head. As he went down, I saw that my hand, like the ball, was covered in rotting goo and shards of skull up to my elbow. Uncaring, I pressed on in the only direction open to me, the field and the woods beyond. A few more zombies appeared in front of me. My arms moved without conscious thought: stick stabbing into them, clubbing at them; my bowling ball taking off their heads if they got closer.

The length of my fight was taking its toll, but only on me. There had to be at least forty of them, possibly more in the darkness where I couldn't see. The undead might not move as fast as I could, but they also didn't tire like I did. They just pressed on. The bowling ball felt heavier with each swing; the hockey stick was harder and harder to raise another time. My adrenaline was wearing off, and I knew I couldn't hold them off like this much longer. Looking around, I finally recognized the part of the woods I was in. I had played in them as a child. Once I had my bearings, I remembered a cave less than a mile away. I knew I had to make it. Just that far and I would have someplace that would allow me to defend myself more easily, someplace where they couldn't surround me, a place with a single point of entry to watch over. My only hope was that eventually they would go off in search of less active food. I hefted the stick, now slippery with zombie innards, and took off as fast as I could manage.

The zombies' lack of speed didn't matter a lot in a close to pitch-black wood when the person they were chasing was so tired that he could hardly stand upright. My feet struggled to find footing, half-tripping over twigs and the occasional beer can in the dark. I used the stick to swat at branches in my path, just trying to escape, to make my goal.

Only when I got closer to the cave, relieved to see it where I thought it was, did I stop to think about what could be inside it. For all I knew, it could be filled with more zombies. Hell, there might be a bear in the cave napping, or snakes, or any number of things that fell on the "Detriment To Life" side of the chart. Realizing I was devoid of any real semblance of choice, I stopped making lists of what might be and ran into the cave as fast as I could, stick held out in front of me.

It was empty, blissfully and simply empty. The zombies were less than fifteen feet behind me, so I fished out the lighter I'd retrieved in the parking lot. I kicked as much detritus together as I could near the mouth of the cave and lit myself a nice bonfire—positioned, thankfully, so the smoke drifted outside the mouth of the cave and not in to choke me. The fire blossomed quickly, stopping the zombies in their tracks, some of them even taking slight shuffles backward. Even they dimly knew that zombies catch fire like toilet paper under most conditions. Maybe it was the rags they wore like they were Armani, or maybe their Jell-O-like guts were extra flammable. A lot of them left after a few minutes, but some of the heartier ones stayed. We all knew the fire wouldn't hold out forever.

I sat down in the cave to push the slime off my arms. I wanted to just go to sleep right there, lean back and pass out and to hell with it all, but I didn't fight my way clear of all that carnage just to die in my sleep. I kept scraping the zombie sludge off myself and flexing the fingers of my right hand, the bowling ball on the ground nearby, just in case. After all that swinging, my fingers had cramped something fierce; they felt like they might never move again. Really, they felt like the rest of my body: inert. The zombies were at the mouth of the cave, keeping their distance, but only just. The fire was still going, but I didn't see much more I could add to it to keep it going once it started to die out. I considered my hockey stick but set it back down, determined to go out fighting.

That was around the same time I saw the wound on my arm. It wasn't large and it wasn't too deep, but I didn't remember getting it. I decided that either the raw end of the hockey stick had cut into me while I was swinging it about so wildly or a branch had caught me while I was running through the woods. I wouldn't have noticed because my attention had been on other things while racing to the cave, and the adrenaline would have dulled the pain.

My throat itched and my eyes stung. The cave mouth still looked mostly clear, but smoke was occasionally drifting into my area, so I tore off part of my shirt and wrapped it around my nose and mouth, hoping to block out the worst of it. The last thing I needed was to be too busy coughing to fight for my own life.

I stood slowly and stretched, trying to force some life back into my body. I felt stiffer than ever with every passing moment. My knees fought against the squats I was doing to limber up, and my back complained with each bend. The fire started to die down a bit. I pushed my body a bit harder, preparing myself for the fight ahead. Only a few zombies still remained outside the cave, but it wouldn't take more than one to finish me off. I hefted my stick quickly at a sound and saw a small animal dart past the zombies and the fire into the cave, looking for shelter, too. As I watched it move, it eyed me carefully. I put my stick down. It was just a squirrel, I realized, and wondered inanely if it was a relative of the squirrel in the parking lot. When the smoke blew to one side, I could see that the moon was high, which meant the night was still young, so dawn wasn't even close. I closed my eyes just for a second and heard a sound. A thin bass drum beat somewhere nearby, constant and distracting. Clearly, I was losing it, wondering about squirrel families and hearing distant drums - much less caring about them in the middle of a zombie attack.

No, I really could hear a drumming sound. I opened my eyes and looked around, trying to place it. The squirrel looked back, and slowly I realized that what I heard was the little rodent's heart. I shook my head and peered closer at the furry little thing. It took a step back. My hand shot out and grabbed it, pulling it toward my mouth. I bit its head off with a satisfying crunch and enjoyed the sensation of a squirt of hot copper blood. As I swallowed and started to go back for another bite, I realized that I couldn't normally hear the beat of a squirrel's heart. My stomach lurched and I felt ill, but I told myself that it was nothing that another bite of squirrel couldn't fix.

I stood up, grabbing my stick and bowling ball as I did, and looked out of the cave's mouth. The zombies that stood there, three in number, were looking at me differently. I dimly realized I could hear noises from them: a calling, a breath of friendship, of brotherhood, that didn't need words. I was one of them now, and they accepted me. I beat at the fire with my stick, my thoughts starting to grow as sluggish as my knees, and walked right up to one of them. The zombie ignored me, content to have me right next to it. I nodded and started to walk off and they followed me. The woodlands looked alive to me in ways they hadn't before. I could hear the beating hearts of animals all over and the silent calls of zombies close by. I could see differently too, a mixture of heat and normal vision that made no sense at first in the once dark night. I kept blinking, trying to clear my vision, but instead slowly grew used to it. It must be how things were supposed to look. I glanced back at the zombies following me and nodded at them. They just kept following.

We entered the field beyond the woods together and saw some of the other zombies still clawing at the back door to the store. I grinned a sick grin and joined in. Together we beat at door, but it wouldn't give. I waved my little zombie crew back and we all stood there, sensing our brethren at the front of the store trying the same thing. I also knew a few of them were holding back a cop car somewhere close by. Someone had called the authorities. I moved forward, waving the others back, and tried to speak, but all that came out was a worthless croak, not words. I coughed and spat; a squirrel ear landed wetly at my feet. I tried again.

"Jason? They're gone. Let me in," I said urgently. I felt a ripple of confusion from my companions. They didn't have the ability to speak; they communicated through feelings instead of words. They pulled aside further, giving me room. I repeated my painstaking sentence. Jason had been a self-serving prick, locking me out in the first place and causing this, but I had confidence that a wave of guilt, combined with a sense of security, would change his mind. The lock on the door turned with a soft click and it opened a fraction. Jason stuck his head out, and the other zombies who'd stepped back as I spoke helped me by grabbing the door and swinging it wide open. I looked at Jason and tsk'd, shaking my head slowly. He screamed as a zombie lunged for him.

I could hear them, for they were my family. The zombies were friends. We all went to bat for the same team. Jason, though, he was a friend too, once. My brain fought itself and neither side seemed to be gaining control. I was stuck in a no-man's land of being. Both sides of the fence tugged at me, trying to gain final control of my mind. I shook my head and pushed aside the zombie trying to bite Jason.

"My bowling ball will work pretty damned well on you, too." I spat at Jason, "Meat," and drew back my arm. The other zombies pushed into the store, leaving me to my kill. Jason whimpered as a zombie brushed past him, and I swung my arm forward. Right into and through that zombie's head. The other zombies stopped in their tracks, again confused. If I were one of them, and something told them I was, why would I attack them? The undead ate living flesh—they didn't stop and attack each other.

Something wasn't right about me. I was definitely undead, but I still had my presence of mind, even if it was a bit slower than it used to me. Mom always said I would never get through college, so the loss of brain power didn't bother me too much. My mind was made up. As they stood there confused, I hefted my stick and ball with newfound determination and waded into them.

The undead fell before me easily. I was as strong as they were, and I was faster than most of them too; just not as nimble as a living human. I was somewhere between the ends of the spectrum. I couldn't work out why. That wound I saw on my arm in the cave was not obviously a bite, but people got bitten and they all just turned into normal zombies. This scratch must've been from one of their nails, or maybe a zombie had drooled into it as well. It certainly wasn't your normal zombie chomp. Something about me, or the nature of the wound or... there was some unknown quantity involved. Then again, maybe this happened from time to time, a bad transition. A half-breed, someone trapped, like me, between both worlds. I decided to puzzle over it later, if at all, and concentrated on clearing the doorway.

Finally, I had destroyed enough of them that Jason and I got the door closed again. I left him staring at me from the back of the store, puzzling at me, as I shambled around to the front. Seven zombies stood outside around a cop on the ground with his face a few feet away, his head half eaten and discarded. The zombies were struggling with the locked doors and safety glass. I opened the door enough to slip out, walked right up to them, and started swinging. They stood no chance. A few of them bit me, but what did I care? They couldn't infect me again. I lost a finger, my left pinky, but I didn't need that to swing the hockey stick. I'd care later, when I tried to pick my nose.

I could see Jason looking out through the glass doors. The kid was cheering me on. He was whooping it up from safety while I did all the work. He could've grabbed something and come help, but no. It looked easy enough from in there anyway, and truthfully, it wasn't too hard. They were slow and were still wrapping their senses around one of their own turning on them. I swung and decapitated another one, but then the one behind him seemed to catch on. It lunged for me as I recovered from the swing. This one was going to be a problem.

He tackled me, forcing me down, and landed with his elbow jabbing my wrist hard enough to jolt my hand open, making the bowling ball roll free of my grip. I tried to swing the hockey stick but the zombie shifted. My weak swing missed, allowing him to wrench the weapon from my grasp. I slammed my forehead into his face as hard as I could and felt his nose break, but he didn't care any more than I would've. He shook his head slightly, a spray of thick slime splattering my face, and sunk his teeth deep into my shoulder.

I pushed at him but to no avail: he was sunk in and I couldn't dislodge him quickly. He worried at my shoulder, trying to bite my arm clean off. I grabbed at his face with my free hand and clawed his eyes out. Slowly. His grip on my shoulder slacked off just enough for me to push him off. He laid there, groping around for me, while I kicked his head in. Grabbing up my stick and bowling ball again I backed up to the front door, sweeping the area with a level gaze and sensing no other undead nearby. The attack was over. I had sent them packing. Me, James Reed, a lowly stock boy in a third-rate store, had defeated a pack of zombies. Jason unlocked the door as I got to it and then suddenly braced against it, so the door would only open an inch.

"You aren't going to kill me, right man? I mean you're just... you're, you know... on our side?" He was white as a sheet, his heart beating loudly in my ears, the noise forcing me to replay what I heard before I could answer.

"Yeah, Jason. I don't know why but I'm still me. I mean, yeah," the words came out sluggish and low, "I'm one of them, but I'm one of you, too." He sighed in relief and pushed the door fully open to let me in. Most everyone else who'd been in the store made a break for it, not even thanking me, just edging away from me as they ran. Bud ran by and I called out, "Sorry about your window" as he fled. I don't think he heard me.

It was just Jason and me, and I could tell he wanted to leave, but was afraid of me still. Too afraid to just bolt. I shuffled to a bench and sat down, patting a spot next to me. Like a nervous deer, Jason sat down as far away as he could manage.

"So it's all good, right, man? Now you can be like some great force, right? I mean, you can take them out yourself, maybe turn the tide for everyone somehow, right?" His voice was on the verge of breaking with each sentence and I just laughed.

"I suppose, sure. I could be a force to be reckoned with huh, Jason? I could be famous even."

"You could, man, you could. Do talk shows in between fighting the undead and shit. You'd be a national hero. No, no, a global hero even." He started to relax by degrees.

"I would, wouldn't I?" I grinned at him and stood up, shaking the bowling ball I still held. "Kids will want toy replicas of my mighty weapons, huh?" Jason laughed at that, nodding. I grinned down at him and hefted the ball.

"They will! You'll be rich and famous, man. Just think of it." Jason stood and grinned at me, comfortable now in my presence.

"Do you want to see it? See the weapon that defeated hordes?" I boasted and lowered my arm a bit. Jason nodded with a smile and bent down to get a closer look at the ball. I swung it back as he bent over and crashed it into his head with a loud crunch that sent him fully to the floor, unconscious.

"The thing is, Jason" I told his unmoving, but still live and tasty body, "I'm not one of you. Or them. I'm on my own side. Meat."

Not long after, I strolled out of the store as best I could manage a stroll, chewing on Jason's left leg as I went. In the distance, I could sense some zombies. They could sense me in return. I tossed the rest of my snack into the road and went to introduce a few more zombies to my bowling ball.

mister binkles and the curious case of changed perspective

MR. BINKLES WAITED patiently in the ratty paper bag that slumped against the hamper inside the closet. The inky darkness within was broken by thin slivers of light shooting through five ventilation vanes cut in the door. The vanes were perfect for Mr. Binkles plan. Just perfect.

For years now, Mr. Binkles sat in that paper bag wondering what had happened. Then slowly, ever so slowly, the answer had come to him. Finally, he knew why he was sitting here. He was unloved. Timmy, his boy, had "moved on." His parents had certainly helped him "move on," but Timmy was also to blame.

Move on. Move on. How Mr. Binkles hated those words, so like death, the death of love and joy and happiness and slick warm drool in the night. Everything that mattered. *Move on, pass on, die die die die die.*

Mr. Binkles had heard enough.

Oh yes, enough! *ENOUGH!* It was bad enough living in the paper bag that leaned on the hamper in the closet, trying to fill endless days lived in near-total darkness, alone but for the occasional remote touch of his boy. The touches, if you could even call them that, only came when a smelly sock missed the hamper and somehow landed on him. A few years back, his boy had even stopped apologizing to Mr. Binkles for missing the hamper. He probably had forgotten Mr. Binkles was there.

Even then Mr. Binkles had bided his time. For deep in his stuffing, he believed that his boy, Timmy, would see the error of his ways, and when he did Mr. Binkles would forgive him without question. Such was his nature.

Until.

Last week, when Timmy reached in the closet to grab a shirt off a hanger, Mr. Binkles had heard his boy tell his mother, as clear as day: "No don't worry, Ma, I'll toss out all that old stuff before I go move to the dorms. Yeah, even the stupid bear."

Stupid bear? Toss out? Neglect was one thing. Neglect happened. Mr. Binkles had heard about it and then had known it. But he also knew that if you waited long enough your boy or girl would end up giving you to their boy or girl and you would be loved again. He had had faith, Mr. Binkles did, faith in the future, faith in his boy.

But now, no more. No more waiting, no more cherishing the love he and the boy had shared, no more biding his time, no more. At that moment, everything had changed.

At that moment, Mr. Binkles had found a new reason to exist. Even as his stuffing churned in his pot belly, his button eyes loosening their threads from the salt of his tears, his very seams threatening to come undone, even as he was destroyed he was reborn. He rolled the new feeling across his felt tongue and found it tasted possibly better than the salt of his boy's tears when Timmy was four and had scraped his knee, finding solace only in Mr. Binkles. The thought of revenge tasted better than that had. Mr. Binkles had found a new reason to live.

So he had planned. He had planned and plotted and schemed. Mr. Binkles took his time and made sure to do things right. First, he had rummaged in the closet at night and found several small pieces of metal. These he slowly sharpened, rubbing them against the rough edge of the old cast iron train until they each held an edge. He practiced slipping them into the small spaces between stitches on his paws until he could insert them and remove them within seconds. Mr. Binkles now had claws. He sat on them now, his large fuzzy ass a safety buffer. Then Mr. Binkles had stolen a few socks. Not all at once, of course, but one at a time, slowly, over weeks. Using his new claws, Mr. Binkles he had carefully stuffed one sock into another and then another until they made a nice wad. Mr. Binkles was planning very carefully.

One rainy-waney-rolly-poly day, as Mr. Binkles' boy used to call them, everything fell into place. His boy had brought home that other one again. Sharia. Timmy would hug her and speak to her softly, in cuddly words. And he'd rub against her. It was almost as if she was a replacement for Mr. Binkles. Indeed.

He had noticed that Timmy, Tim, or baby, as Sharia called him, only brought her up into the room when his parents were out. Then they played doctor, just like Timmy had gotten in trouble for years ago, when the little girl next door had visited. Except this time the game seemed much more enthusiastic. Mr. Binkles wondered why they liked to scream so much when they played on the bed. Mr. Binkles had never screamed when his boy would jump around on the bed with him. Come to think of it, his boy hadn't screamed then either. And the game of doctor Timmy got in trouble for had been very quiet when little Kathleen had visited with her bunny. In fact, when Timmy and Kathleen had played, he and Miss Rabbit had looked at each other happily. But this was different.

But that time didn't matter now. What did matter was that Mr. Binkles knew exactly what was going to happen now. Sharia and Timmy would close the door and remove each other's clothing, and then they would wrestle and scream on the bed. The wrestling could take a while, but the screaming didn't. Mr. Binkles knew he would have to move as fast as his stubby little legs could carry him.

Mr. Binkles watched them from the vents in the door, inserting his new claws as he waited. Then, when they made their move to the bed, he pushed the door open carefully, just enough to slip out. Mr. Binkles was a little afraid, he realized as he padded over to the bed. He always had been careful never to move when his boy could see him.

Once he reached the foot of the bed, Mr. Binkles scrambled up, one two three, leaving little holes in the blanket. His boy was on top of Sharia, his soft white ass presented like an offering to the Gods. As soon as Timmy pressed down low on Sharia, Mr. Binkles slashed his claws along Timmy's ass, raking true and deep. And he let out a war cry from the depths of his soul as he cut. To Mr. Binkles' ears, his cry was fabulous and mighty. Timmy and Sharia heard a small squeak.

The cry didn't matter anyway. For Timmy was too busy leaping up and trying to spin around to see what had happened to his ass. As the boy spun, Mr. Binkles leapt forward, landing on Sharia's chest. He slashed open her neck, feeling a spurt of hot blood slap into his face. He sighed inwardly. Mr. Binkles knew that this would cause a stain, and a stain meant time in the washing machine. Mr. Binkles hated the washing machine, drowning for what seemed like days as he was flung around in horrible circles. And then the dryer. Mr. Binkles didn't even want to consider what it was like in the dryer. Oh God, the dryer.

Sharia lay on the bed gasping painfully for air, bubbles oozing out of the gash in her neck. She slid downward to death with two thoughts swirling in her head: "Was that a fucking teddy bear?" and "I didn't even cum."

Mr. Binkles didn't give her a second thought though as he stood on her chest, small cylindrical feet planted each on a breast, and considered Timmy. The boy, his boy even after all this, still his boy. But his boy screamed and lunged at Mr. Binkles. Mr. Binkles blocked with a set of claws, losing one deep in Timmy's palm. While Timmy screamed again and then fell back, holding his hand, Mr. Binkles jumped once more. He jumped off Sharia's chest and onto Timmy.

His boy had no real chance, not against a small stuffed bear filled with such anger and resentment. For every attack on Timmy's part, there was a bloody parry by Mr. Binkles. Mr. Binkles used to watch G.I. Joe with Timmy every afternoon, and he had learned a trick or two in his time. Timmy clearly hadn't paid as much attention. One hand useless, scores of slashes, both deep and shallow, crisscrossing his arms and legs, Timmy finally sunk to the floor by the side of the bed.

Mr. Binkles descended on his boy like a pudgy Angel of Death. He swiftly gagged his boy with the sock ball, and then moved back, and stood on Timmy's stomach, looking at him. He shook his head sadly as Timmy tried to raise an arm to swat him off. It only took a few tries for Timmy to utterly give up and close his eyes. That's when the cutting started in earnest.

Later, when it was over, they found Sharia dead on the bed, and Timmy on the floor, gagged with a ragged sock gag. There were little pieces of sharp and bloody metal lying about which no one could seem to understand.

Mr. Binkles was once again in the ratty paper bag that slumped against the hamper inside the closet. He sat peacefully in his bag, listening to the policemen talking, the blood drying and caking, clutching Timmy's heart to his once soft and fuzzy chest.

causing effect

PART ONE

My FEET POUNDED the pavement as I raced down the street. I clutched the box, being careful to keep it as level as possible, despite the natural jostling involved with running flat out. The clock stood against me, but I did my best. I pushed harder, my breath coming in ragged bursts.

The burning sensations that my lungs sent reminded me to exercise more. I vowed then that I would start to, if everything worked out for the best this time. Just give me, I prayed to no one in particular, this one win.

The sidewalk ended, turning into a grass path, but I knew it would, and moved out into the street itself. No cars went by, the street almost never bothered with traffic. Three cars in an hour and we considered things to be gridlocked.

Houses moved by on either side of me as I kept running: Mrs. Blagart's white one floor stucco mess, the Lowstiens' three floor fake-Victorian nightmare affair, Mr. Winchell's sky blue single floored retirement present to himself, and so on. Each house inhabited by someone I knew, probably doing something I could guess at.

Steve Burnkin watered his lawn, smirking as I flew by on feet of desperation. He found my plight funny, knowing from the box alone what the score was. I sneered at him and wished that his hose would jam up and explode, sending water everywhere. As evil wishes went the hose thing was pretty tame, sure, but at least the idea had humor value.

Ahead on the right. My house. Once I could see it clearly, in all of its green and white glory, my legs turned to lead. Just knowing I drew close was enough to tire me out deeply. I fought past it and forced one last sprint out of my body.

I fumbled for my keys before the door was in reach. Jamming the master key home I turned it hard and fast, shouldering the door open. The box tipped, almost dropping in the process and I cursed silently, ashamed of myself. More discipline was called for if this sort of mission could be considered a success.

Carrot stood in the living room, waiting for me. His wide smile taunted me, eyes telling me exactly what he thought my chances were. I shot him a quick glare, trying to look angry and failing. Instead I simply lowered the box and flung it open so that he could see.

"Still hot!" I exclaimed.

"Shit, no way," he said, leaning over to look.

I grinned and nodded, presenting the box of donuts for inspection. No easy feat this. The donut store sat a good two miles from our house. The challenge of getting to the place exactly when the donuts came out of the fryer and then getting them all the way back to our place before they cooled, without a car, was the stuff of legend.

Once a month we tried it, taking turns. Sure, more often than not we managed to pull it off just fine, but each time we acted like somehow we failed every time throughout history.

Just how we were.

We sat on the couch and ate donuts, licking the fast-cooling glaze off of our fingers. We stared where the TV used to be. Carrot had broken it the other week, tripping and putting his shoulder through the screen. Things happened around Carrot. He wasn't the clumsiest person I knew, but he also wasn't very far off the mark. I loved him anyway.

So we sat and watched the wall. All sorts of fixes occurred to us, as they tended to.

"We could keep some paint nearby," Carrot said, "and then keep slapping new paint up so we could at least watch it dry."

"Why not entice some flies to use that wall for their orgies?" I asked, gesturing with a bit of donut.

"Since when can you train flies?"

"How hard can it be? They can't be smart, right? So I figure I have a good chance of being smarter than your average house-fly." I said with a smile.

"Oh sure, your average house-fly," Carrot countered, "but what if we end up with the Yogi Fly of house-flies, huh? What then? Are you prepared to be that flies' Park Ranger?"

"Why would I be the Ranger? You would be the Ranger."

"And you would be what? Boo-boo? Nice. leaving me for a fly. Now *that's* class. That's just class all the way!"

I opened my mouth to reply but stopped when I heard a window break. Carrot came to the window with me and we looked out through the broken pane of glass.

"Damn kids must've thrown and ditched," Carrot said. The annoyance in his voice was impossible to miss, the way he would almost hiss the last bit of a sentence. Except he was wrong.

"What? It had to be," I said, "that guy right there."

"I don't see any guy anywhere, Rob."

I sighed and pointed. "How you could miss that guy I don't know." I looked over and Carrot was, sure enough, sighting along my arm. He just didn't see anything. "The guy, right there," I tried, "in a suit of armor? Come on, Carrot, you have to see him. He's right there!"

"Empty street, hon. It was just some kids, you know? They threw a rock and ran like hell."

"There's a man," I repeated through clenched teeth, "standing across the street. In full damned armor. I... look, never mind. Go have a donut."

Carrot shot me a worried glance, but that faded into a shrug as he walked back to the couch. I threw open the front door and went outside to see what the hell was going on.

"Say hi to the invisible man for me!" Carrot shouted as I left. Great, that helped.

The guy still stood there, across the street, another rock held in his hand. The hand itself was iron-shod. Hell, the man was iron-shod, except for his face. Thick looking armor, old as anything, covered him. The metal didn't shine the way I always thought a knight's armor should, and it was clear this guy thought he was a knight.

His shield, slung off his non-rock throwing arm, carried a large cracked and fading picture of a lion roaring. The sword at his side sat in a scabbard of splitting leather. His face looked as worn as the rest of him, craggy and etched with lines. Only his eyes shone, bright green, full of intelligence and information.

"What the hell?" I asked him, crossing the street. There wasn't an ounce of my being that thought demanding answers from a crazy man with a sword and armor could ever be smart, but I did anyway.

The knight didn't answer, though his head turned and he stared at me long and hard. I tried to stare him down, locking eyes with him, but the force of his gaze overcame me and I glanced away.

"Listen, what do you want?" I asked, looking back up at him. He stared at me but still didn't answer. "Talk to me!" I demanded, taking another step toward him. Still nothing. He just watched me. "Well," I said, finding my initial burst of bravery fading, "don't throw anymore rocks through my windows, all right? Just fucking go away!"

I turned to leave and started to walk back across the street. I planned on moving quickly but not quick enough that I looked like I was rushing at all. A single step is as far as I moved before I stopped again. The sound of metal against metal, loose plates shifting back and forth, halted any progress. I turned on the balls of my feet to look back at the knight.

He pointed at me. One long finger extended right at my face, he pointed at me and still he said nothing. I sighed, I might have even grumbled a bit, and then turned away once again and walked back across the street.

Carrot sat on the couch inside, looking up as I closed the front door. "Did you see the kids who did it?" he asked.

"What are you doing?" Carrot asked, putting his fork down with a clink of metal on cheap ceramic.

"Trying to work out where those voices are coming from," I told him.

"The people around us?" he offered.

"Not those voices, the other ones."

"What other ones?"

Great, another mystery of me having a sense of something that only I could sense. Perfect. Maybe I was crazy; the thought ran through my mind and stuck around for a few rounds. I fought it off, but the idea got me on the ropes before it hit the mat for the count.

"The ones you can't hear, like the guy you couldn't see," I told Carrot, turning my head from side to side to try and locate the source of the voices.

"All right, first of all there was no guy earlier, and secondly you're trying to echo-locate magical air-voices that only you can hear. Doesn't that seem a bit odd to you?"

I sighed, trying to ignore the voices and concentrate on Carrot instead. "Yeah, it does, hon, it really does. And I'll deal with that when we get home. But for now I want to find the source and stop it. These things are loud and annoying."

"So your mother is floating around?"

"Very funny."

"I thought so, thanks."

I shook him off and went back to listening. Carrot shrugged and started to eat again. The look on his face was pure Carrot: he knew I was crazy, he just wasn't sure how bad this would turn out to be. Perfect.

Still, I zeroed in on the voices: they came from the potted plant near the hostess station. Well, at least that wouldn't cause any strange looks. Gritting my teeth, I stood up and strode over to the plant. The hostess started to ask me something, probably wondering if she could help me, but I waved her off and inspected the plant. The leaves each talked, rattling off things and conversing amongst themselves.

I listened to their conversations, not sure why I could hear them at all, but also just to listen to what a plant says to itself. Conversations about water and soil, light and shade, they all chattered loudly and continuously. The hostess tapped my shoulder and I realized she was tapping it for the second time. Lost in the words of the plant, I had missed the first. I smiled up at her innocently and quickly backed away from the plant.

I sat down again with Carrot and stole a quick glance toward the plant only to see the hostess whispering to the waiter and nodding in my direction. Subtle I guess I wasn't. I set to again and wolfed down the rest of my steak, not saying anything to Carrot. He didn't say anything to me either, so that felt fair at least.

Though, honestly, it also scared me, his silence. Not talking meant he didn't know what to say, and neither did I. My problem, whatever the hell this was, couldn't be a conversation over dinner. We left as quickly as we could, me ignoring the stares of the staff, and got in the car. We drove home in the same suffocating silence.

Halfway home paranoia set in. Not, though it might seem odd, about the recent issues with seeing and hearing things no one else could. No, I grew cold and paranoid that Carrot would leave me.

I pushed past the old fears and gripped the wheel tighter. Everything would be fine. If I was really going crazy than that would have to be dealt with, sure, but there were ways to deal with that.

The headlights lit the road with twin circles of light and I followed those home, the street vanishing under wheels. The darkness around us seemed to swallow the car whole. Not pitch dark, we didn't live in the woods or anything, everything still managed to feel much blacker than should have been possible. There was a finality to it. A paranoid, stupid, useless finality that I thought I already brushed aside.

Sighing to myself, I tried again and, as I slid the car into the driveway, everything felt better. Home loomed over us, right in front of us literally. Fuck it. I got out of the car with a smile in place and let Carrot unlock the front door.

"Rob," he started, voice low, "I think we need to talk."

His keys hitting the glass dish next to the front door sounded like a bell ringing and startled me. I pulled up short and replayed the last ten seconds in my head, finding myself.

"I know we do. Of course we do. Look, it isn't... I don't know what it is," I fumbled, moving past him, and heading for the couch.

"Tell me about the restaurant, the voices, then. Start there maybe."

So I did. I told him all about the voices and the looks I got and the conversations I heard. I thought I heard. Those things. Carrot sat and listened, not interrupting or even making a face until I wound down.

"So then," he said at last, "this is the second time, right? The guy across the street—"

"The knight," I put in.

"Right, sorry, the knight," Carrot corrected, "was the first time?"

"I don't know," I said, throwing my hands up, "I mean how can I tell you if that was the first time I saw or heard something no one else did? Maybe I have but didn't know because no one else was there, or, or maybe I just got humored a lot. I don't know how to answer that, really."

"Oh lord. All right, so the knight was the first time you can remember this happening?"

"Carrot, this isn't—"

"No, it isn't an inquisition, I'm sorry," he said, "but you aren't making this easy, either."

"Because it isn't easy!" I stood up and started to pace. I kept my feet from stomping by sheer force of will and tried to sort through everything at once. "There was nothing different, do you get that? It wasn't like I felt a tingle or a marker that could separate the events from any other normal moment. Just, as far as I'm concerned, this stuff was all real, just as I told you. Maybe you're the crazy one who can't see it or hear it!"

"No one tossed around the word crazy," Carrot said with a shake of his head.

"But we both thought it."

"I think a lot of things, I discount those, too."

"Like Eggplant Man?" I asked.

"Like Eggplant Man," he agreed, "That's right, Rob, I discount the veracity of a man made of Eggplant, once and for all, right here in front of you."

"Finally," I grinned at him, "because he makes no sense as a superhero. Just none. I mean he'd be too limp to fight crime."

"Moving past Eggplant Man and back to the problem at hand," he suggested.

"My being possibly nutso?"

"Exactly." Carrot stood up and gave me a shrug. "If it helps, I don't think you're crazy," he said as he walked toward the kitchen.

"Then what," I asked him with a raised voice, "do you think is going on?"

"Do you want a drink?" he asked in reply.

"Sure thanks," I called back.

The sounds of the fridge opening and closing rattled in from the kitchen. A bottle opener tossed caps off of glass bottles and they clattered on the counter. Carrot came back, two beers clutched by their necks in one hand, and sat down. I took my beer and raised it in salute. He matched the motion and we both drank.

"I'd call 'stress' but it wouldn't hold water," Carrot said, setting his bottle down on one knee, "and it can't be a cry for attention really."

"So then?"

"Well that does kind of just leave crazy, huh," he said and turned to me with a huge, shit-eating grin.

I punched him in the arm, hard enough for him to feel it, and laughed. Great. At least, I noticed, the paranoia flew off when I hadn't been looking at it. A win is a win is a win and I took that one for what it was. Another sip of beer and a deep breath later I stared at Carrot.

"Except I'm not crazy," I said to him slowly, "so maybe it really is happening."

"Sleep on that proclamation."

"You think?"

"I do. I think we just wait and see. Maybe it was a two time thing. Maybe not. Let's give it some time."

I couldn't argue with avoidance, not really, not if I wanted to win the argument, so I just nodded. We finished our beers, prattling on about this and that and nattered uselessly to pass the time. The remains of the donuts sat between us on the couch, the box open just enough for the smell to waft through the air. Too sweet and settled, the donuts smelled like yesterday already.

I closed up the box and carried it to the kitchen, dropping my empty bottle in the trash. Carrot came in after me and tossed his bottle in to join mine. The donuts went in the fridge and lights were turned off. Sleep was chased, caught and held fitfully captive.

Morning came and Carrot wandered off to work. I got up to the sound of the car driving off, its engine coughing and complaining. I rolled out of bed and made some more coffee, taking the morning nice and slow.

I had two commissions to finish: a spaceship fighting aliens over the bones of Mars and a grove of evil trees ripping apart a band of unlucky campers. Neither presented too much challenge, but they needed to get done before I could really dig into the newest cover my publisher sent over.

The newest manuscript called for something involving a darkened cityscape, and I still needed to pull the last of my reference together for it. Luckily, I had those commissions to work on first.

Brushes swirled in water while paint clumped wetly on a palette. I set up the spaceship's canvas and gave it a good looking over. The aliens would be the worst part of the whole job, which is why I hadn't added them yet. Spaceships were easy, human ones at least. No one thought they should look too strange. They had to look like spaceships, really.

Aliens were a whole different story. I attacked them with everything I had, making them look like spaceships as well but certainly nothing like a workable design. That made it alien. I stopped working long enough to make another fresh pot of coffee and stood in the kitchen while drinking it.

Outside, in the backyard, a little girl played with a small dog. They ran around each other, the sounds of barking and little girl's laughter rising into the air and filling the surrounding spaces with joy. I smiled and raised my mug to them both.

Until I remembered that there was no such little girl in our neighborhood. Now I had a dilemma. This could be the same sort of problem as the other day, things only I could see for $400, Alex, or it could be a lost little girl. No independent verification meant finding some other means of working out a difference, if there was one.

My coffee mug clanked against the counter, tipping and spilling darkly. My hand was already on the door, yanking it open. I let myself out into the backyard quickly and in no way quietly. The little girl and her dog kept playing, ignoring me.

"Hey," I called out, forcing a smile.

The girl stopped, hugging the dog to her, and stared at me. The sun shone down, highlights in her hair exploding with light. I squinted a bit and thought about shielding my eyes. She just stood there, staring at me.

"Are you lost?" I asked, trying to get some sort of reaction.

She put the dog down, and it sat quietly at her side. One tiny arm lifted and the girl pointed at me. Exactly like the knight. Exactly. I could almost see echoes of his hand overlaid on top of hers. It answered the whole 'real or not' question, at least.

"Can you talk at all?" I tried, taking a step closer to the pair. Unlike the knight, I didn't feel a sense of danger. The lack of size, armor and sword helped in that respect, but there was also something more, some calmer air about them. The knight seemed to accuse me of something with his pointing. This little girl, on the other hand, just pointed, singling me out.

I walked closer and closer to her, but her hand didn't waver. Her brown eyes tightened though, focusing intently on me. The edge of her mouth curled up, the hint of a smile or grin teasing itself free. Each step brought me closer to her and allowed me to see details that, really, should have been visible a step before. It was as if she was coming into focus better the closer I came.

"You." The barest whisper from her lips, hardly even parted, floated to me. I caught the word and stopped dead in my tracks. She nodded and lowered her hand.

"Me what?" I asked, my own voice becoming a whisper for no good reason.

"More," she said, and though I still stood several steps from her I could feel the air escape her lungs and smell what I could only place as sunshine on her breath.

"More what? Come on," I said trying to not let the flare of annoyance rise too high in my voice, "more than one word at a time maybe? Talk to me. You know the knight, right? And the plants? This is all something, and you're a part of it. So talk to me."

The words rushed out of me like living things and I fought down the urge to cover my mouth with my hand. Hopefully I hadn't overplayed whatever hand I possessed. I hadn't.

"Don't think." The curling at the edge of her mouth blossomed into a small smile. "Wander the halls. Let everything free."

It's one thing to have hallucinations. It's another to have them give you Yoda-like proclamations. I shook my head and stepped even closer, intending to take the girl by the arm and march her right back into the house. I was going to find out who her parents were and—except she was a hallucination. Imaginary girls have imaginary parents and I don't think they had a phone number for me to call.

"Not that I want to keep echoing your statements as questions but what the hell?" I exploded, "Let what free? Wander what halls, what are you talking about and who are you?"

"The other," she said simply, "you have to free me." Her hand raised again to point at my chest.

This time I reached out and grabbed her hand. Her skin was cool and pliant. Cooler, in fact, than living skin had any right to be. It felt off, and yet also perfectly fine. I dropped her hand and rubbed my own palm on my leg.

"To sum up," I said, "I'm nuts, you're imaginary, and your little dog too!"

I turned my back on her and stormed back into the house, sick of this game. To hell with my head. I almost screamed when I saw the mess my coffee managed to make, dripping along the counter and down to the floor. I stormed around, grabbing paper towels and setting the mug upright. Every time I could I glanced out the window into the backyard. The girl stood there, her dog quietly at her side, staring at me. She had one hand raised, pointing.

I raised one hand right back at her. I didn't point, really. Well, kind of, upwards, with only one finger. I suppose it counted as pointing. I poured myself a fresh cup of coffee and glanced out the window. The backyard sat empty. Good. That was exactly right.

My studio called to me and I wandered back, picking up brushes and describing alien spaceships. I worked the rest of the day away, so lost in what I painted that I hardly even noticed when Carrot came home.

He poked his head in and smiled at me. I set my brush down and glanced up at the clock. The day had flown by and I gave the timepiece a shake of my head. Carrot laughed at that, nodding without a word. There were no verbal hellos exchanged. We smiled at each other and he vanished from sight. I started cleaning off my brushes and by the time I had the studio back to almost clean and ready he returned with a grilled cheese sandwich and two beers.

The plate got set down and we each picked up a half of sandwich and ate, pausing mostly for sips of beer, just enjoying the company and ease. Carrot finished first and only then, wiping his hand on his jeans, did he walk around and look at the still drying painting.

"Finished the space thing?" he asked, gesturing at it with his bottle.

"Just about," I said, swallowing the last bite of food, "but it still needs some touch up work. Nothing major."

"That's great. It came out wonderfully."

"Thanks," I said, happy. So long as my first critic liked it, I would be happy with the finished piece. "Decent day?"

"Decent," he agreed. "Got a stupid thing to deal with tomorrow, but that isn't today so who cares?"

"Procrastination as stress management, I approve."

"I knew you would," he smiled, "so did... did anything else happen today?"

"*Hmmm?* Mail came, I think. No Jehovah's Witnesses. The usual."

"So nothing else? Nothing... nothing out of the ordinary?"

I laughed, "Oh, you want to ask if I'm crazy! Sorry I didn't get you being subtle. I'm so sorry."

"I always wanted to try it," he said laughing.

"Well, anyway, yeah, I am. This time it was a little girl. She told me I had to not think and wander some hallways and let something free. Or wander the hallways where something was free already."

"Oh," Carrot said. He shrugged, and I could see the effort it took, "but at least the vision talked, right? All mysterious and shit, too. That's progress, isn't it?"

"The wrong sort, Carrot. The wrong sort. I don't think we want the crazy to get stronger, but instead, I would personally really dig if it got weaker instead."

He sighed. "Maybe you should see someone about this."

"No way," I said simply. I left the room, brushing past Carrot. In the kitchen I tossed my bottle away and generally fussed. Carrot had left the pan on the stove so I set that to soak, banging things as I went.

"Throwing a hissy fit won't help," Carrot said softly from the doorway.

"I don't want to go to a shrink," I said.

"Why not?"

"Because he'll say that I'm crazy! I don't need some idiot telling me I'm nuts for a few hundred an hour and then telling me to take pills that will wipe my brain to fake uncrazy."

"At least you don't have an unrealistic view of the head-shrinking field."

"No, seriously Carrot, there's something else to this. I can feel it. I just don't know what it is yet."

Carrot left me in the kitchen, turning and walking away. Nothing in his body language gave off a hint of anger, or even frustration. There was only a deep-seated tired there. I finished straightening the kitchen, quietly now, and joined him on the couch.

The cushion let my ass sink deeply into it and I curled my legs up under me. I faced him, and he turned to look at me. We sat there for a minute, just watching each other. Finally one of us had to break that silence.

"I just want some time to work through this on my own," I said, "with you, whatever, but not with some guy being paid to tell me how nuts I am. I really think there's something else here. OK?"

"I guess," Carrot said, "but you have to admit it's strange."

"Of course it's strange. I'm probably crazy," I admitted, "I just want a chance to prove otherwise. That's all."

"Also, before you go spending all of our money at a shrink, you should finish the other commission."

"So I can pay for it, right," I agreed. "So after I finish that, and I won't drag my feet on it, promise, I'll see someone. Deal?"

"Deal," he said. He shook his head then and grinned, "a little girl and her dog, huh? Red shoes?"

"No red shoes, no suntan lotion, no, just a normal little girl and her normal little dog."

"Normal except they weren't there."

"Everyone has drawbacks."

"That's a pretty big one."

"Eggplant Man," I reminded him.

"I have already conceded Eggplant Man to you. You can't bring it up every single time."

"Well, fine," I admitted, "but it still holds."

We talked for a few hours like that, easing ourselves into laughter and the normal nonsense while the night crept up on us. Dinner was made, chicken with salad, and everything rattled around inside our house just as normal as ever. Nothing else showed itself to me, I didn't hear voices or anything. It was a perfectly normal night, and a good relaxing one at that.

After dinner I sat around with Carrot and sketched out the first drafting of the evil trees. Carrot watched for a while before he grabbed a book and sat with me, reading. Every now and then I would nudge him to take a peek at the sketch pad and he would nod or frown. Sometimes he would nudge me and read me a passage of his book.

The night passed.

We slept. The moon passed by overhead and then the sun rose. We woke up and the day started like any other day started. No strangeness or strangers. Nothing freakish or unexplainable went down. The morning passed in quiet contemplation of the spaceship canvas, adding a touch here and there to finish it off. I called the buyer and told him that I would be shipping the art out to him in two days. He thanked me and I felt the joy of a finished job. Holding that to me, I went back to start the next job, on a minor high note.

I painted, without much care, just setting in a few lines to shape the piece. My sketch notes helped and the job looked like it would be simple. A day or two at the outside. After that I could seek help and settle this once and for all.

As I worked, I started to notice odd sounds echoing around the room. I glanced around me once and realized they had to be coming from my madness, so I pushed past them. Let's see, I decided, how the imaginary crap liked being ignored.

It turned out not to like the idea of being ignored at all. Not one little bit. I started to catch flashes of movement out of the corner of my eye. I tried to focus around them but they distracted me. An errant brush stroke, I could cover it up later, swerved across the page as a pirate walked across the very edge of my vision. The whispers and the vision grew in intensity and I set my brush down to have a look.

I knew I was giving in by doing it. I just didn't see an alternative. The studio around me swam with people and animals. Each one paced a few steps and then pointed at me.

They whispered to each other about me, I could only catch snatches. Mutters about me being the one, my potential to help them and so on.

I screwed my eyes shut and hummed loudly, drowning out everything in the room. I gave myself until five hundred, on internal count, before I opened my eyes. The humming stopped as light fluttered around me, vision clear and clean. The room was empty, it was silent, and I smiled.

I felt in control, real control, for the first time in a while. The feeling of simply besting the hallucinations flooded through my system. I got up, almost leaping, and went to the kitchen to grab a fresh cup of coffee to celebrate.

As my foot fell, stepping into the kitchen, I could see him around the edge of the fridge. Long and lanky, the man wore loose, simple clothing from a century or so previous. His head was clean shaven and a small thin beard dotted his face. Both hands jammed deep in his pockets, the man nodded at me, flashing a simple grin that managed to feel sinister. On second pass, as I weighed the real look, I realized that the grin was honest, still plastered on his face. I simply felt sinister vibes from knowing how fake the guy was. Still, I could smell his breath, feel his presence in the room and hear the sounds he made as he shifted slightly, waiting for a reaction.

I decided to ignore him. It had cleared out the studio, after all. So I opened the fridge and grabbed the milk. The door slapped shut and I turned toward the counter. The milk carton hit the floor. With a start I glanced down to see it spilling all over the tile and looked back up to see the man standing there, having slapped the carton clean out of my hand.

"What the fuck?" I demanded, staring at him.

His grin stayed in place, if anything it widened. Then he gave me a small shrug and started to lift his arm toward me. No, I knew the pointing was coming and I reached out to grab his wrist.

He jerked his arm back at the last second and shook his head at me. Damn it, now I was pissed. It was one thing to point and act all mysterious. Maybe some whispering and attempts to drive me truly up a wall but now to add just flat out messing with me to the table proved to be one step too many.

I took a swing at him but he leaned back just enough for my fist to push nothing but air. My second swing met much the same effect. The third connected, lightly, and I felt the shock of skin on skin. I think I was more shocked that he remained solid than I was at actually connecting. He seemed confused, too, standing and looking at me as his eyes went slightly wide.

I took the chance and my fourth shot caught him clean on the jaw. His head snapped back and I felt the burning sting of a solid punch spread along my knuckles. Lifting my fist to my mouth to in a move of pure instinct left me wide open for his return punch.

Air left my lungs with a sudden unscheduled departure as his fist landed in my gut and I doubled over. A fighter I wasn't. I cursed and ran at him anyway, determined to make a good showing of myself. We tussled, wrestling a bit and grappling here and there, for a few minutes.

The kitchen filled with the sound of our breathing, ragged and explosive. Grunts and groans sounded as fists and elbows and, really, whatever body part could connect, all thrust into one another. We didn't trade blows as much as we flailed at each other.

Though he was obviously the better fighter, my raw lack of talent made up for a lot. He didn't know what to do with me and I kept so close to him that he had no way to regroup and actually take me down.

We landed with a thud, unsure of who knocked whom over first, and continued to grab and hit at each other while rolling in the spilt milk. It covered our backs first, then our arms and faces, smearing long and thin and wetting us both down. The smell made me want to gag, but breathing proved hard enough without coughing.

He grabbed my hair and lifted my head up, while sitting on my chest. Once, twice, three times and four my head smashed down into the tile. The light in the room went dark and I hoped that the wetness in my hair was only milk. I fought to keep my eyes open but a fifth knock on the floor shut them but good.

I opened my eyes, wincing at the brightness of the light. And it was bright, too bright to be my kitchen. I looked around as much as I could manage without actually moving my head. Clutter surrounded me, all lit with a harsh white light that left no room for shadow. I wondered how that light worked, seeming to come from everywhere at once, killing every inch of shade in each direction.

Sitting up lead to standing, and standing lead to wandering around. The walls of the room were a nice, relaxing, sky blue. Boxes and papers and just general clutter obscured most of the floor. I stepped carefully, trying to not crush anything. There was crap everywhere. Paper crinkled under foot, and something sharp poked at the bottom of my shoe. I headed for the door, the only door I saw.

At first it hadn't registered as a door. Just a black outline of a door-like shape. Then I realized that peeking out over a stack of magazines was a doorknob. I moved the piles of stuff as gently as I could manage, only knocking over a few, before giving up and kicking things out of my way. Once I started, I found I couldn't stop. My foot swiffered through trash and litter with a vengeance. I wedged the door open just wide enough to slip through and escaped.

I escaped right into a hallway full of otters. Otters. They crawled and flopped around on the wooden floor, making otter noises. Some of them watched me with beady little eyes and their strange hands clapped. A few of them pointed at me, sitting there in silent judgment. I refused to be judged by otters. A door sat on the side of the hallway, plain and subtle. I reached for the handle quickly, before my kicking urge came back and spread to otters, and ducked inside.

The throne room was massive. The size of a football field, ornate gold things dripped from the walls and sparkled in the light. Heavy silver and gold chandeliers hung from the huge, arched ceiling, and cast a warming light around that set off not only the crap on the walls that sparkled but also the tapestries that hung next to them. My eyes got lost in that room, snapping from one thing to another, trying to drink it all in and build a full picture.

That's how I missed the throne and its attendants. The thing stood off to one side, not deep into the room at all. It just matched the room so well, as did the people near it, that my eyes had slid right over them. Once I noticed them, though, they stood out. The whole room took on the quality of one of those magic picture posters that no one ever wants to buy. Once I stopped trying to see the whole room, the room fell into focus.

The King, on his throne, sat still, not moving except for his eyes. Next to him stood two guards, both dressed in shining, thick, armor of silver and gold. The King nodded to me, when he noticed that I finally saw him and lifted one hand to beckon me closer.

As I took the next few steps his beckoning hand turned into a point, finger extended. Anger rose and I wanted to rush forward and smack his hand down. The guards prevented me from giving in. Well that and the fact that I'm not really a fighter. My temper, I realized, had been hyped up since the skirmish in my kitchen, and nothing was allowing for it to settle. I shook my head and kept drawing closer to the man on the throne.

"Where am I?" I asked him.

"Where we are," the King replied.

I stopped walking and just stood there, looking at him. I didn't want to deal with this Yoda crap on top of being somewhere that was, frankly, God knew where. No, I had to force some kind of real answer out of somewhere.

"Yeah, that's great," I started, "but where is that? How'd you get me from my kitchen to here?"

"You are still in your kitchen," he told me in reply.

I looked around. I was pretty sure that our kitchen didn't look anything like this, much less have a herd of otters wandering down a hallway we didn't own. "Nope, try again. This isn't my kitchen."

"You are still there. In here, however, you are also here."

"Oh for... come on," I seethed, "all right let's try a simple one. Why am I here?"

"To help us."

"To help you what? I mean you stalk me, you attack me, and kidnap me and all in the name of asking for help? Couldn't you have, I don't know, sent a letter? Made a call? Asked?"

"We are asking now," he said. He stood, letting his robes drape properly onto the floor before straightening. Once everything seemed to be in the right place, he strode forward and closed the remaining gap between us. I fought an urge to take a step back and just held my ground.

"Well, then, no," I told him. I fought to keep my voice flat and calm.

"That isn't an option," the King told me, and as he spoke the words I could see that his eyes matched the old knight's that started this mess. The same gleam to them, color and weight. He was old, older than anything I'd seen, and I could feel every year of it in that stare.

"There's nothing you can do to make me change my mind," I said. It was a total bluff, but I wanted to believe it. More than that, I wanted everyone else to believe it. I stood a bit straighter and lifted my chin. My shoulders shifted back. I braced myself for his reply.

"We could torture you," he said, giving me a shrug.

"Wouldn't work, I insisted, "that won't get me to help you."

"Perhaps," he said, fixing me with his gaze again, "you misunderstand."

"Of course I do! You haven't explained anything."

"Fair enough." A nod and a glance off to his guards and the King started walking, not even glancing back to see if I would follow.

I followed. I didn't want to, but I did. His offer to explain things, as much as it felt out of the blue, couldn't be ignored.

The King flung open the door to his chamber and I braced myself for otters. Except outside the door, the same door I originally walked through, there was just a garden. Light diffused down to the ground through tall trees and the garden beyond them grew long and lush in the viewing.

Grass crunched underfoot, snapping and shattering like glass. I stopped walking to stare at it, and the King stopped as well, turning to look at me. He shrugged and started walking again, so I did too, stepping as lightly as possible and wincing with each crunching step.

We came to a small pond and the King stopped there, staring into it. I stopped a few feet away from him and looked around. We were alone.

"You didn't create this, but you power it," the King said, still watching the pond.

"What are you talking about?"

"You asked what this was all about. I told you I would explain. So let me," he said, glancing over at me. I nodded and shut up.

"For years we have lived here, growing stronger. Inside of you. At first it was nothing, a bit of nothing that we all hated. But you grew older and stronger and so did we. We just grow faster than you. That's all it is," he said, flashing me an odd smile, "that's why we tried to break through and get your attention. We need you to let your mind wander, to give us space to grow. We just want room to live."

"That's it? You just want me to idly let my mind wander, so you can increase your space in my head? But what about me? I mean if I do that, won't you..."

"No, of course not. We wouldn't harm you," he told me. He turned to me and gave me another smile. It was the smile that threw me off. It felt wrong, though it looked perfectly fine.

That was it. Everything else I had seen was off somehow: from his ageless eyes and oddly sinister grin to the landscape itself, everything was off except that smile. Which meant that the smile was the fakest thing going.

"Nope, no way. So you live in my head, and you need to

grow but need my help," I shrugged, "which means I can also starve you out, right? Get rid of you?"

"Why would you kill innocents?" he asked, taking a step forward.

I took a step backward in response, wincing again at the sound of the grass breaking, "Not innocents. *Figments*," I insisted. "You don't even really exist. So how could I kill you? It'd be like getting rid of an imaginary friend. No harm, no foul."

"We are alive!" he raged. "How can you deny us existence, how can you deny me, ME, life? Who are you to decide such things?!"

I took another step back and fought down the wave of anxiety that tried to smack me upside the head. "You're in my head," I said as calmly as possible, "that's who I am. Hell, where are these other people you're so concerned about then? Who? The guards? The little girl and her dog? No I have a feeling..."

"What? What great and powerful truth do you have stored away that you think will shock me into submission?"

That deflated me, "Well, when you put it like that, I mean, I was just going to point out that I think this is only you. The rest are even faker. Fakes of a fake. But uhh..."

"Shut up!" he raged.

"Touched a nerve?"

"You don't know what you're talking about," he told me, the sinister grin sliding back into place.

"Then why are you getting all fussy, huh?" Something in his reactions emboldened me. I stared him in the eye and I could feel the balance of power start to shift. Just slightly, mind, he still scared the crap out of me. There was a definite shift though. He had started to worry about me. I wasn't just something to brush aside anymore.

"I need life, why won't you give it to me?" he asked, managing to not whine. He did, however, drop anything about others, I noticed.

"Why do you keep telling me bullshit, then? You want help

but you won't ask for it outright. Why is that?" I asked, giving him a grin of my own.

"You wouldn't help me when I told you there were many of us," he said, "why should you help just me alone?"

"I won't," I insisted, "but it certainly doesn't help that you felt the need to string me along."

"I tried this the painless way," he said, "I really did. But if you won't help me by choice…"

"Woa now," I said, backing away, "let's not do anything rash."

"You should have said yes, Robert."

He lunged for me, arms extended like a madman, and I tried to back away. The grass underfoot, cracked and scattered, slid under my heel and I went down. He overshot me anyway, and landed within my reach. Which meant I was in his reach as well, sadly.

Before I could react, grab him or scrabble away or whatever, he had hands around my throat, squeezing down hard. I tried to scream, but no air inflated my lungs. I swung at him, out of desperation and clocked him right on his right temple. He rolled off me and I tried to run, the grass cutting into my hands.

I got back on my feet and took off, but by then he was up and after me. The landscape changed, swimming before my eyes, and I fought down the urge to vomit. Watching space change in front of you is disorienting, to say the least. It was like someone had grabbed the world and shaken it, hard.

Things settled and I looked around, while trying to keep running. The garden was gone, and in its place I found some kind of stone maze. I took turns at random, hoping I wouldn't end up in a dead-end.

The King was on my heels the entire time, looking about as deadly serious as he could manage. I saw light ahead and turned toward it, feeling the escape from the maze just seconds away. The world shimmered again and I came up short just before I ran off a cliff.

The wide open field stood all around me, impossibly high

cliff faces to three sides and the King behind me on the fourth. He stood and watched me, unwilling to leap, I suppose. Until he changed the scenery again, he had given me a stalemate. I had to take advantage of it. So I ran at him.

I screamed, trying for a battle-cry, a wordless yell that would impart my desire to win. I think I sounded like a scared guy instead. Either way, the yell made him blink and the charge made him flinch. I could at least pull off unpredictable.

The King settled in and braced himself before I reached him, so when we met it was as equals. We grappled again and he threw me down into the dusty ground, landing on top of me and pinning me.

"Stop struggling!" he demanded, hands reaching for my throat.

"Why would I suddenly do that?" I asked, wasting what breath I had.

"Once I am in control of your brain, I can escape. No one will think you're mad, Robert..."

"Yeah, they will," I said, using my legs to shove him off of me, "you can't pretend to be me worth shit, I'd bet. Besides, wait a second, this is my brain we're in, huh?"

"Of course it is," the King said, standing.

I stood and faced him, "Then why can't I change the scenery?" I asked and thought about it. Hard. The cliffs, those were wrong, I decided, and the ground should be softer and maybe, for the hell of it, we should be inside. As I thought and focused on things the world shifted.

I looked around and we were in my parent's house. The pictures of Sinatra hung near the door, as always, and a vase of half-wilted roses stood near the couch. Why did the roses get left there so long, time after time? No idea. But they were there, too. Everything was exactly as I remembered it.

I nodded with approval and the King glared. He reached for me but I knew this house like the back of my hand, so it was easy to step back twice and hop over the coffee table backwards. I knew he'd stumble over it, no one ever expected that backwards hop.

"Now let me see," I said, backing into the kitchen, "you need me to become real, right? Little Pinocchio that you are. Not a real boy at all, huh?" I probably shouldn't have been taunting him but finding control over things made a feeling of strength washover me.

"All I need is your brain, I don't need *you*," he spat.

"Right but we've established you aren't getting anything, so why not just vanish like a good little hallucination?"

"I am not a hallucination!" he raged, grabbing a saucepan and lobbing it at me.

I took the pan on the shoulder and bit my lip. It hurt. In remembering the house so well I had remembered things like that cast iron pan all too well. I picked the pan up from where it clattered to the floor and brandished it.

"If you're stuck in my head and no one else can see you, then you're a hallucination," I told him, still backing away, trying to get to the garage.

"I am as real as you!" he insisted, following me, "Not having a body doesn't make me unreal! I can do things you can't even imagine; I am more powerful than you could ever know!"

"Except you're stuck in my head. So how powerful could you be, right?" I reached behind me and grabbed the knob to the garage. I shoved it open, vanishing inside. I shut the door and locked it, moving the old oil drum in front of it to block the King. I had to think. I knew I didn't have much time, either. Something nagged at me and while the King hammered at the door I tried to piece together what it was.

The banging stopped and I knew he would be going out of the house and around, barging in on me in a minute at most. I thought harder. For all that the King attacked me, trying to get rid of me, something held him back. I wasn't a fighter, and he didn't really feel like he was trying too hard to kill me.

He was afraid. Afraid to kill me, but that was his intent. So why would he worry so much about it? Unless it was the body he couldn't kill. He needed the body, he had said as much. I had to use that. That and one other simple fact: if he could get rid of me I could get rid of him. That street had to go both ways.

Now I just had to find a way to use everything. Time ran out as he broke down the flimsy front door set into the garage. Sunlight streamed in behind him and he stood there, framed in the bright glow, looking mad and powerful. I grabbed a tire iron and faced him, puffing out my chest.

"This is your last chance," I told him with as much bravado as I could find.

"I was going to say the same thing to you," he replied, stepping into the garage.

I focused on the area between us, trying to eject him from my mind. He felt the change, the shift in power and fought back. Matching me shift for shift, the world swam and continued to change and flow like a pool after an elephant dropped into it.

The tire iron dropped from my head and we locked eyes from a few feet away. We both tried to shove the other one out of existence, shifting the world to something that didn't contain us both. I felt myself start to slide away, refusing to look down and see if I was fading away in form as well as mind. I hit back as hard as I could, creating a mindscape that didn't include him.

It was my mind, after all, and I would rule it. No one would come into it, regardless of how he got there, and take it over. I couldn't let that happen. I wouldn't. I didn't want to think about what he would do with my body, but even without deep thought I knew it couldn't be anything good. I pushed harder.

So did he. We were deadlocked. Finally I thought of something, even as I started to lose ground.

"You know," I said through gritted teeth, "you don't have to die, you just have to get out."

"You don't have the power," he said. Something in his eyes shifted though. It wasn't fear, either. Trying to work out what went on behind his eyes distracted me, so I gave up and refocused on pushing him out.

My new tactic seemed to go easier. I wasn't trying to remove him anymore, so much as slide him outside. Without a body he would vanish, I figured. The fact it felt easier than outright destruction seemed to tell me I was right, too. I pushed. He slid. I pushed more. He pushed back. The tug-of-war continued until I found some sort of mental footing and braced myself for a big final push. Which sounds far more planned than any of it was.

I gave him a giant shove, one last push with everything, nothing held back, and he slid further away. I watched him start to vanish and kept up the pressure. He wasn't turning into nothing, he was simply sliding into somewhere else. I could feel the hooks in my mind, his very presence, start to diminish.

"Don't do this," he said, forcing each word out.

"You forced me to do this," I told him and kicked him out of my head for good. Once he was gone, I realized how dizzy I felt, how weak and washed out. I sank to my knees, hitting the ground hard. The world swam before my eyes, not changing but simply disorienting. I fell over backwards and my eyes closed hard, darkness taking me again.

PART TWO

The stench of spoiled milk mixed with the cloying sweet dried milk smell to combine into a form that man should not smell up close. I gagged as I came to, sticky with milk and some dirt from the tile floor stuck to my face.

Carrot stood over me, looking concerned. I could feel the place on my cheek where he had slapped me, trying to rouse me, no doubt. I blinked a few times and looked up at him.

"Hey, I'm all right." I said.

"What the hell, Rob?" Carrot asked, "You just smashed around the kitchen and then passed out and now you want me to think you're all right?"

"It isn't quite that simple," I told him, holding out a hand. He gave me his and helped me up. "The thing in my head, the crazy? It came and dragged me into my own head and... this just sounds worse, doesn't it?"

Carrot nodded and shrugged. "Kinda, yeah. Listen why

don't you go clean up and if you still feel fine you can explain it all to me. If not we'll go to the hospital, deal?"

"Deal, but why—"

"Would I let you wander off and shower if I thought you were injured? You don't look injured, you don't even seem dizzy. So I guess I just hope you know your limits and aren't fucking around."

"I'm not," I told him and headed for the bathroom. The water was hot and I stood under it for a while, washing off not only the stink of the milk but also the feeling of what I'd been through. While I was there everything felt undeniable. Now, in my bathroom, under a solid spray of water, everything felt like it very well could have just been more crazy.

I held onto my convictions though and fought down the doubt. I toweled off and padded back into the living room, where Carrot sat on the couch. I sat next to him, slumping back against the cushions and told him everything. I started with the fight in the kitchen and went all the way through collapsing inside my own head.

He nodded and kept quiet throughout the entire thing, giving me serious looks, like he believed me. Maybe he did, even. I ran on at the mouth for a while, trying to get every detail just so. It took a while.

When I finished, Carrot sighed and studied my face in silence for a minute. His eyes searched across me, seeking some detail he couldn't pin down. I didn't know what he thought to find, but I contented myself with the belief that he would find it.

He must have, because after a while he nodded and rested a hand on my knee. I shrugged, not wanting to guess at exactly what his reaction would be.

"You know you should go to a hospital right now, don't you?" he asked, his face flooded with concern.

"I know," I admitted, "but I also know that I'm sure this is over."

"So?"

"So I don't think I should go anywhere. Let's give it a few

days and see if this really is done with. If I have visions again we'll go in somewhere, I swear," I told him.

"Isn't that kinda what you said," he asked, waving a hand, "last time? Not that long ago, I'm sure I remember it."

"That was different, I was still having the visions."

"And were convinced that they would stop," he said. Carrot blew a burst of air out in exasperation. He stood and started to pace in front of the couch, gesturing with a hand to accent his words. "How long does this go on, Rob? I mean, I should what? Sit here and just ignore all of it? The visions, the assurances that it'll stop when it obviously doesn't? What should I do? Tell me."

"I think you should trust me," I said simply, if irrationally. "No, I know it doesn't make sense," I said preempting him, "all right, I know that on a lot of levels this just reinforces my crazy levels in your head, I get that. But I still think you should just trust me."

"Rob," Carrot said, almost pleading with me, "you're asking me to go against everything... come on, you want me to ignore helping you, keeping you from getting worse, just because you feel good about it today?"

I fussed around with my hands for a second, trying to somehow draw what I meant in the air. "Yeah, pretty much, I guess," I finally said.

"Oh, come on!" Carrot yelled. Carrot never really yelled, though. Not in anger. This was close to a first. A second maybe.

Still, I flinched a little. I didn't like Carrot when he was angry. He looked so close to losing control, even though, in my head, I knew his anger was controlled. That didn't help my gut, that information.

"Carrot," I started. A swipe of his hand through the air stopped me.

"No, seriously, Rob, come the fuck on! This isn't a game, this is some deeply serious shit."

"I know—"

"Then why are you trying to put me in this bullshit corner? No, I can't just ignore this and hope you're right this time," he insisted, "we have to do something about it, you have to do something about it, now."

I stood, too, as I felt my own anger rise in response to his. "No I don't," I told him, hoping that a calm voice would diffuse him, "you're wrong on this. All right, all right," I said, holding a hand up in front of me, "give it one day. I haven't lied about this yet and I still won't. One day is all I ask. One. Then if I have even a twitch of a vision or hallucination, you can have me committed."

"Rob," Carrot said, voice softening, "I don't want you committed, I just want to get you the help you need."

"One day."

"I don't want to... all right one day. One and only one," he relented, "and you tell me the second it happens."

"Promise."

We stood around after that, not sure what should happen next. There had been yelling and tenseness and those weren't things we dealt with often together. Did you just pretend it didn't happen? That didn't sound healthy, but it felt like possibly the right choice. Otherwise, I think we both knew, we could talk this to death just trying to avoid talking it to death.

So we sat around. We both returned to the couch and sat around and made mindless small talk. We avoided real conversation out of a fear of what it could bring. In a day, we both knew, we would revisit the conversation and, out of necessity, have it out. Either way, there loomed a conversation just over our heads. It swung like blades and so, for a night, we ducked.

The next day came and started like any other normal day. Carrot went to work and I painted. The morning routine was exactly that: routine. There may have been a few more significant looks here and there, but outside of that everything went along like a well-oiled machine.

The afternoon followed suit and though I kept half an eye peeled for sights of things that shouldn't be there, nothing happened. I worked on the commission and found the kind of simple joy in painting that attracted me to it in the first place. The world was a decent place, that day.

Still, my eye was peeled for signs of the strange. I kept looking over my shoulder, too. When I ran out of coffee I considered not going to the kitchen for more, just in case. As the day wore on though, my paranoia decreased. Nothing had happened. It felt like nothing would.

As I put my dishes from lunch in the sink, I gave in and laughed. I didn't think a simple uneventful day had ever meant so much to me. It certainly had never been an open call for such celebration. Yeah, the visions had gone away before, but even so, this felt different. Cleaner. Words didn't quite wrap around the feeling, so I stopped trying to tell myself about it and just lost myself in work.

Carrot came home and I told him the good news. He smiled, but it felt a bit fake. Still he upheld what we agreed to and didn't bring it up again. Life seemed good. So we went out.

I drove us out to a park and we sat around on our favorite rock while the sun set. Leaning against each other then, there was a calm certainty about life. We still had to talk, but somehow it didn't seem as pressing now. At least not to me, and if Carrot felt it, he was keeping quiet about it.

Night fell and we headed home, still mostly silent, with breaks for inane conversations, our favorite type. I parked the car outside and pulled the key out. While I fumbled with my seat belt Carrot turned to me.

"I'm still worried," he said softly.

I clicked my seat belt apart and slid out of it. "I know," I told him, "me too, kind of. But it's over and I'm fine."

"Then why," he asked while he opened his door, "are you still worried?"

I got out of the car and looked at him over the hood. "Because I've been known to be wrong before."

"At least you admit it."

"Of course I admit it, what's that supposed to mean?"

We walked to the front door and Carrot fumbled his keys for a second. His shoulders slumped a bit and I could almost hear the gears in his head turning. He finally got the door open and flicked on a light, still silent.

"No, come on, what does that mean?" I asked, following him in.

"It means I was afraid you were so confident about this that it would be a problem. This hasn't been easy."

"For either of us. But it's over."

"You think," he shot back.

"I think," I admitted, shaking my head.

"So where does that leave us?"

"Taking life one day at a time, the same as before," I offered, slumping into the couch.

Carrot joined me, curling his legs under him and facing me. We searched each others faces for a second. He shrugged and sighed.

"A bit more at stake," he said at last.

"Don't I know it, but it'll be fine."

"How can you be so certain?" he asked, and I could see every inch of worry written there in his skin. He was right, of course. I didn't know how I could be sure, but somehow I was. That wasn't a strong enough answer, not now, but it was still true.

"Because I know what this felt like before and I know what I feel like now."

"That's it?"

"That's all I got," I told him. I dug around for anything else but I really was out.

"Then," Carrot said after a thoughtful second, "it'll have to do. One day at a time?"

"I loved that show," I said with a grin.

"Oh, shut up," he laughed.

I laughed with him and we sat there, falling into a much easier silence. Things could be all right.

And they were. The next weeks were all normal and comfortable. Life continued the way we both expected it to. There were jokes and good times, sleepless nights and hard days, the entire spectrum of life passing before our eyes as it normally did. Everything was taken in stride though. Somehow the big things didn't seem quite as big anymore.

I had dodged a bullet and Carrot dodged it with me. Not the sort of thing you really take out and celebrate, for fear of being wrong somehow, but just the same. We might not have celebrated it with party hats and dancing but we managed to be thankful and treat things a bit brighter than before.

We talked about getting a dog. Maybe a cat. A lizard even. Something else to share our space with us. We considered all sorts of changes and adjustments to our existence. None of them huge, sure, but things added up. A new toaster oven, a pet, possibly even repainting. We looked forward.

We were out, on a Saturday, leaving the pet store with indecision weighing heavily on our minds. A dog would be great to have but I would have to walk it during the day and Carrot would at night. Come winter or the blaze of summer that would simply suck.

A cat could be anti-social and sometimes you just want a very social pet. Then again lizards and such were handy since they stayed in cages. The pet question had raged throughout the store, quiet voices putting forth one thought or another and coming to no good answer in the end.

So we left. We walked back toward the car and each thought about bringing someone new into our home. Carrot drove, weaving through traffic like the other cars on the road were part of a video game. We were hungry so we decided to seek out food.

There was a good Indian place neither of us had tried, so the car was aimed in its general direction. The food ended up being good, but the decor was firmly set in 'bad-plastic-ethnic-fakery' mode.

We drove home, still undecided about the pet situation. Somehow, though we hadn't decided on a type of pet we were already discussing names for the eventual beastie.

Carrot parked and we went inside. I stopped, still. Wanting to cry, I turned to Carrot.

"All right," I told him softly, "let's go drive to the hospital."

"Huh?" he asked from behind me.

"In the living room, there's the knight again. Just standing there."

Carrot moved around me and looked into the room. The knight stood there and raised his arm, starting to point. I fought back an urge to scream in frustration.

"I... Rob, I can see him, too," Carrot whispered.

"What?" I spun and faced Carrot, ignoring the bastard in armor. "You can see him?"

"He's pointing at us."

"Yeah, he is," I confirmed, "but how can you see him?"

"Can crazy be infectious?" Carrot asked me, eyes wide.

"I don't think so."

"Then I don't know why or how but I can see him, too." He looked into the living room and made a small noise of confusion.

He wasn't alone in that. If Carrot could see the guy too, then I wasn't crazy, or we both were in exactly the same way. That didn't hold up for me so I went with me being uncrazy.

On the other hand, the knight was back, in my living room and once again doing the pointing thing. It wasn't a total winning situation, I had to admit. I cursed, loudly. Carrot agreed. The knight just pointed.

"You thought you had destroyed me," the knight intoned, "instead you freed me."

"What does he mean, you freed him?" Carrot asked me.

I shrugged and shook my head, "What do you mean, I freed you?" I asked the knight.

"No," Carrot said, grabbing a chair as he moved past me, "I don't care." He charged into the kitchen, chair held high. Before I could say anything, and before, I think, the knight realized quite what was going on, Carrot slammed the chair upside the knight's head.

The sound of crappy wood against thick metal rang out into the room. The knight staggered under the blow, and the force of it sent the chair right out of Carrot's hands. The knight vanished. One second he was standing there, raising an arm to ward off a second blow and the next he simply wasn't.

Carrot stood, looking around him. He laughed and walked back to me. The chair stayed where it lay, ignored and already seemingly forgotten. I frowned, but kept my mouth shut for a minute.

"Did you see that?" Carrot asked, "I totally just sent him packing."

"No," I said, "you didn't."

"Mmm, yeah, but no," Carrot laughed, jerking his thumb over his shoulder in the general direction of the kitchen, "see, I hit him and he poofed right out, he vanished in defeat. I defeated him."

"Carrot. No you didn't. Remember when I started seeing him, he would vanish, too? And then he came back and slowly got stronger until... yeah, so, I don't think you really defeated him."

"Shit, it felt like I defeated him."

"And you hold onto that, but we need to work out what's going on, right now."

Carrot followed me to the couch. We sat down and settled in. The couch was our center, somehow. Whatever, it didn't matter why or how, the couch simply managed to be where we decided big stuff. This time "big stuff" would just include defeating impossibly powerful imaginary creatures that used to live in my head.

We discussed it back and forth for a while. I went over, again, everything that went down in my head. This time Carrot looked interested above and beyond deciding my state of crazy. I didn't feel vindicated about that, though, I just wanted this to end.

I made us some coffee as we continued to dissect the whole thing. Somehow, instead of vanquishing the thing, I had set it free. Which maybe, I had to admit, was what it wanted all along.

All right, so crazy could be crossed off the list but stupid definitely stayed on it. I had been played by some crazy-ass impossible creature. Though I supposed, as I told Carrot, at least it took a crazy-ass impossible creature to play me like a three-card Monty dealer.

Carrot reminded me of the three-card Monty game I got

roped into a few years back. I didn't find it as funny as he did and we kept working on a plan. Except we didn't have one.

"Here's the problem," I told him, late in the conversation, "he could, in my head, change reality, right? Well maybe he can here, too."

"Probably a lot less than he could in your head though, I would think."

"For now, maybe. As he gets stronger? Who knows," I pointed out.

Carrot stood and paced around the living room. "He took different forms, too. Any pattern to them that you can recall?"

"No, I mean the little girl and dog in the backyard, I had kept almost drawing a picture like that, it's cute. But no real... oh shit."

"What? Rob, what?" Carrot demanded, striding up to me.

"Well they were all thoughts I entertained not too long ago, different ideas for paintings or whatever. So maybe he took a form that I thought of?"

"Shit, we're fighting Gozer?" Carrot chewed his lip, something he didn't do all that often. It worried me.

"We are not, I repeat, *not* fighting Gozer the Gozerian. No."

"But you just said..."

"I know what I just said. But this is not Gozer, all right? And maybe, if he can take forms we think of, we shouldn't be focusing so damn hard on Gozer, right? Let's just forget that, lock it away and leave it alone."

"Oh fuck, Rob, you know now all I'll think about is—"

"Don't even say the name."

"This is just uncool."

"I know it is, hon, I know it is. But I think it might be just us saving the world."

"Whoa! Alert me before you suddenly veer into world saving speeches!" Carrot flopped back onto the couch and glared at me.

"Sorry," I said, patting his knee, "but think about it. If he gets more powerful and starts to shape the world the way he could the inside of my mind, then what could stop him?"

"Not us," Carrot offered.

"Why not? I defeated him before, and now we're two against one. Plus," I said, holding up a finger, "no one will believe us until it's too late. So we're all we got."

"So what do we do?" Carrot asked me.

I didn't have an answer. Not a simple, quick one at least. So I shrugged and hemmed and hawed a bit. Carrot just nodded and understood. We had no plan, no good idea how to actually defeat this thing, since I hadn't really defeated it in my own head. All I had done was banish it. I banished it right into my own backyard, kinda literally.

I decided to leave the past behind. Dwelling on this stuff wouldn't help us at all. Sure it informed things a bit but we had to find a way to make this work now, not fuss about how it didn't work then.

Instead of driving ourselves nuts over it, we sat and shifted into mindless conversation. Silly thoughts about silly things that let our brains works in the background. Or maybe we fooled ourselves into thinking that and just had to escape the pressure for a few. Whatever worked. Eventually we went to bed. The place stayed quiet, normal, but that quiet was now a veneer over what we both knew waited for us.

We woke up to sounds of scraping and rustling. We both sat up, quick, and looked around the room. At first nothing seemed wrong, and maybe it was just someone doing bad things with a Weed Whacker outside. Then I noticed a hint of movement in the corner.

I rolled off the bed, trying to land in a crouch, which pretty much worked. Carrot got up and came around the bed. We inched closer to the source of the noise. The knight wanted to make us fear. He wanted us to be afraid of what he would do, but we didn't intend to give in.

The noise came from behind the dresser. We sprang, Carrot and I, each grabbing a different corner of the dresser and yanking it hard. The dresser fell over, breaking all sorts of bits off itself, I'm sure. The press wood was never really meant for a face plant.

The mouse freaked out and stopped dead when it saw us. Little shavings of wood sat along the baseboard where the little guy had been gnawing. I sighed and looked up at Carrot who gave the mouse the most intense look I had seen in a while. I picked the mouse up by the tail before it realized it could just run and stood there with it dangling, its little legs scrabbling for some kind of purchase.

"So, is it a real mouse?" Carrot asked.

I stopped and realized he was right. I took it for a normal mouse but we had no way to tell for sure. I held it up in front of my eyes and peered at it. "I think so, I mean, I'm not sure how a mouse is supposed to scare us or overwhelm us."

"Maybe it's an advance scout," Carrot said.

"It isn't really his style," I said.

"Still, we shouldn't be so fast to discount anything."

"It's a mouse," I said, letting it crawl onto my hand, "why don't we just let it free outside either way. If it's his, then he'll know we can't be taken out by a mouse. If it's just a mouse then... whatever it is that mice do, it'll run away I guess."

"Fair enough," Carrot agreed.

I carried the mouse outside and set it down. The thing ran off, dodging and weaving until it found a sewer grate along the curb. The little guy wiggled and dove down into it. Well, it didn't tell us anything definitive but I had to side with the theory of it being just a mouse.

I went back inside and rejoined Carrot, telling him about the cute way the tiny mouse ran and dove. He laughed and nodded, agreeing with my fine rodent assessment skills. We retired to the kitchen, the coffee calling to us. While it brewed, we laughed about the mouse, and the damage to the dresser. Sure, we had been a bit enthusiastic, but we couldn't even blame each other. A dresser was a small price to pay for not being surprised in a bad way.

Like when Carrot opened the cabinet to grab a mug and a few hundred locusts flew out. That fell under the bad type of surprise. We hit the floor, and covered our heads with our hands. The intense buzzing deafened us both and I slapped

Carrot on the shoulder. He peeked at me through his arms. I pointed toward the living room. We belly crawled there and then stood up. The locusts confined themselves to the kitchen, swirling like some bizarre hurricane.

"All right, those aren't normal," Carrot said.

"No, no, they aren't. Well, but we can use the fire extinguisher, right? And then we could blast them out of the sky."

"That'd be great," he agreed, "but the fire extinguisher is in the kitchen."

"Oh. Right. Well, how do we deal with locusts then?"

"No, Rob, that's the problem, we don't deal with locusts," Carrot said firmly.

"You're right," I said, smacking my forehead, "we call an exterminator."

"No, no, hold on, see, that's the problem..."

"I thought the problem was the locusts, or not dealing with them?"

"All right, let me try again," he said, taking a deep calming breath, "the problem is that we can't keep attacking the little things. Those aren't real, we have to confront the guy in charge. Otherwise he'll just keep throwing things at us."

"But the knight isn't here," I said and then stopped and closed my eyes. "Yes, he is," I said, "He's been everything, just in different forms. Sorry, I wasn't thinking straight. Hordes of locusts do that, I guess."

"Good to know for the future, maybe, but, regardless, attacking the locusts won't help, so how do we fight him directly?"

The question stumped me, and I shrugged. I thought about it and all I could come up with was the way the knight trapped me in my own mind. Except he wasn't in my mind this time, he roamed free. So how could we confront him directly and where could he go?

Carrot watched me and I could see that my face was readable enough for him to get what I was thinking. He nodded and shrugged back at me. So neither of us had a good, clean, solid idea. We still had to find one though. That much seemed obvious.

Then it hit me. I laughed and Carrot looked at me, wondering if I had lost my mind. I shook my head and forced the laughter to stop, holding it down with some decent amount of will power.

"He's weakening reality around us, right?" I asked Carrot.

"I don't know, is he?"

"Maybe," I said, admitting my own uncertainties, "but it feels right. And if he is than maybe we can change things, too."

"How?" Carrot asked, looking around. The locusts still swarmed over our kitchen, the buzzing noise growing louder all the time. My head started to hurt from it, and my teeth ached.

"I'm not sure. Think really hard? I think it'll take both of us, but think about it, if he really weakened things enough for him to do this sort of special effect why can't we?"

"Because he's made of special effect and we aren't?"

"Sure, if you want to get technical about it, but that's just it. I think he's weakened the general area of this house enough that maybe we can work with it, too."

Carrot shrugged and we both stared at the locusts, thinking. Getting rid of them wasn't the goal, but we both wanted to do that as well. I leaned close to Carrot and tried to whisper in his ear. The buzzing was too loud by then, so I tried again with some shouting. He nodded and we both stood in the doorway to the kitchen, heads down, focusing hard on what we wanted to happen.

It started to work. Very slowly, realistically, but it still worked. The locusts started to collide with each other and where they did, they stuck. They flowed into each other and took on greater mass. Soon lumps of them fell to the floor, too big to fly, or not quite merged right, just jumbles of locust parts that twitched along the tile. More and more fell from the air and landed.

We didn't let up, glance at each other, or break concentration. Carrot and I stood, still as statues, staring into the kitchen. The buzzing died and against their will the locusts found themselves sliding across the floor and merging into even bigger masses.

The mass stopped looking like a locust. It flowed like water, or maybe Jell-O. It flowed like Jell-O and quivered as it grew taller. The knight took shape and stood in our kitchen, a low buzzing still emanating from his form.

The buzzing stopped, and the knight cleared his throat. "Very good," he admitted and Carrot and I relaxed a bit. We glanced at each other and allowed ourselves a smile.

"Thanks," Carrot said.

"Don't expect that to work twice," the knight told us, "all you've really done is show me that I need to try a tiny bit harder. It doesn't defeat me at all. You do realize that, right?"

"He can't even let us have a moment," I said to Carrot before turning back to face the knight himself. "It isn't as if we won't defeat you. Just give up now and go away forever and this is over."

"Funny," he laughed, "I was going to suggest the same thing. Soon I will be powerful enough to spread my influence further and then I will simply take over this city, this planet."

"Lofty but impractical," Carrot said to him.

"He's like that," I told Carrot.

"It's annoying, you think it would be endearing in a Marvin the Martian kind of way but it really isn't."

"Stop ignoring me!" the knight yelled. Carrot and I shut up, but exchanged knowing smirks. We had found a metaphorical chink in the knight's armor and we wouldn't forget it soon.

"Sorry," Carrot said, "you were threatening?"

"Joke all you want," the knight said, "your world will be mine soon enough."

The knight faded out of view while we watched. He became transparent, fading out of our lives again. We both sighed, not quite in unison, and started to clean the kitchen. There wasn't anything else to do right then, except start picking up all of the things the locust swarm knocked over and getting life back in some sort of order.

We worked side by side, in silence. The coffee maker would live for a little while but there was a crack in the glass urn that would eventually give and go all the way through. Grumbling, I set about picking up stuff that had fallen from the counter. Forks and spoons lay in a small pile of broken glass. I went for the broom, while Carrot picked up and stacked the newspapers that had been blown off the table.

The air hung with an odd sense of peace. I realized that I didn't feel scared anymore. I don't think Carrot did either. Sure, we still had to solve the problem, get rid of the guy and bring about world peace for dessert but we didn't fear facing it head on.

Correction: we didn't fear the knight. The things, the horrors we might have to stare down, those could cause some alarm. The knight himself though, well, he was nothing now. Carrot and I met him head on and walked away from it clean. I had beat him before. Maybe he meant me to, that time, but either way I saw what he could throw at us and I stood against it.

That peace, the utter sheen of calmness, kept us together while we cleaned up. This wouldn't be easy but it would be doable. I laughed, tossing out a dustpan full of broken glass and Carrot looked over, catching my eye. He smiled and laughed with me.

Two fools, to be sure. Two fools with a much cleaner kitchen and half a plan. While we cleaned we talked in hushed tones and quickly scribbled notes, coming to a few hasty conclusions. By the time we finished, we were both starving. But the kitchen was much, much cleaner.

We sat on the couch, later, eating and wandering around our ideas.

"So do you think if we—" Carrot asked around a bite of burger.

"Maybe," I agreed, "the important thing is that we don't let him know how scared we really are." I shook my burger to the left, to indicate that we should keep the talk up in case the knight was listening.

"I know, right?" Carrot nodded, blinking twice to let me know he understood, "I think if I had to face him again I'd lose."

"Don't talk that way," I said, "he might hear us."

"You think he can hear us?" Carrot asked, his voice going up an octave. I had to fight back a laugh. This plan would never work if I had to keep a straight face for it.

"I don't know!" I shrieked and got up to flee the room. I ran into the bathroom and turned both taps on full to cover the sound of my laughter.

Carrot knocked on the door after a few seconds. I cracked the door and looked at him. The bastard stood there making a face at me. I quickly slammed the door shut again and buried my face in my hands.

I prepared a list of curses to use on him the next chance I got and was peeling off some toilet paper to jot them all down on when I heard an explosion.

"Rob," Carrot's voice bellowed, easily heard over the flowing water, "you might want to come see this."

I didn't, really, but faced with no good alternative I shut off the water and hurried out to the living room. Carrot stood at the window, looking out. He turned over his shoulder to yell for me again, stopping when he saw me. He waved me over, pointing out the window with his other hand.

I stood there, next to him, and looked. The street was gone. No, let me back up. The light streaming down from the sky was oddly green. A sickly, strange green that looked like someone had poured liquid broccoli over everything. The street itself lay broken, shattered in a million places. From each crack a bright red hellish glare shone upwards to meet the green.

I could hear a shuffling, a clanging scrape of a noise. I looked at Carrot as my mind tried to fit it all together.

"Kinda Christmassy isn't it?" I came out with.

"The red and green do clash," he said, "but I don't think it matters."

"Point. What's that noise, Carrot?"

"I hoped you would know what it was."

"No clue. But then I don't know why the sky is green, either."

"Oh we both know why the sky is green, Rob."

"Knight, sure. But I meant on a deeper level than that."

"Are we both far too calm or just unable to cope?" he asked, tearing his gaze away from the window again.

"Six of one," I whispered, "three dozen of another."

"That's not how it goes," Carrot whispered back.

"It is when the sky is green. So now what?"

"Now," came the reply, from behind both of us, "you die!"

We turned to see the knight, armor tarnished and noisy, standing behind us in the doorway to the kitchen. He seemed to have a thing for our kitchen, but that would have to wait.

"You're going to kill us with a light show?" Carrot asked. Our plan to feign fear and spring an attack on him fell by the wayside as Carrot shook his head. It felt good on paper, but we couldn't back it up. The sarcasm was too strong in us. The rest of the plan, that still held, in reserve.

"That is just a side effect," the knight told us, shrugging a noisy clanking shrug, "of bringing your worst fears to life."

Which could, of course, mean anything. Anything at all. In the pit of my stomach, though, I tried to think of all the things that both Carrot and I were afraid of. That list, while smaller, contained all the normal things. Nothing too bad. Nothing we couldn't deal with.

The scraping, metallic noise grew louder from the other side of the window. I refused to turn around, not wanting to give the knight the satisfaction. Carrot, I could see out of the corner of my eye, felt the same. The noise behind us grew. It multiplied and raised itself into a chorus, adding moans and what sounded like loose electrical sparks. I gave in and looked.

I looked back at the knight. Then I looked at Carrot. "Turn around and tell me what you see," I told him, taking a deep breath.

Carrot turned his head, glanced out the window and looked back at me. "Impossible," he said.

"Impossible," I agreed. We both turned to look, ignoring the knight.

An army marched towards us. Their small legs didn't work

right, some disjointed, others limp and still others simply missing. They were a ragtag group. Their skin gleamed in places, metal flesh occasionally rusted through to the wire. Those exposed wires sparked, shooting bursts of ice blue light through the horde. Their red eyes shone brightly though, above slack razor sharp jaws. None of them stood taller than maybe three foot five and they all moved with the crazed lumbering gait of the unliving.

"Robot midget zombies!" Carrot proclaimed, looking over at me.

"Midget robot zombies," I corrected, "we're facing a horde of midget robot zombies."

"That is so cool!" Carrot yelped. His hand flew to his mouth and he coughed lightly, "And totally frightening!"

"Dear lord how will we defeat them?" I asked, Then remembered we had given up on the mock-fear. "Oh wait, hey, Carrot?"

"Yeah?"

"Didn't we lose the fear thing?"

"Oh. Right." He turned to the knight and jerked a thumb over his shoulder, "Robot midget zombies—"

"Midget robot zombies," I corrected.

"Whatever, the point is they're impossible! Robots can't be undead. Therefore," Carrot told the knight with a flourish of his hand, "they don't exist."

We both laughed, triumphant. I was tempted to strike a pose. The knight looked singularly unimpressed. It dawned on us that maybe we were wrong. I turned around again and the midget robot zombies were still out there, drawing closer.

"Was that," the knight asked us, "supposed to work? None of this can exist, not really. Denying it won't make me vanish in a puff of logic, or some stupid thing like that. Fools!"

"Spock is so off our Christmas card list," Carrot said.

"Totally," I agreed, "but still, if Spock's battle plan is out then that leaves—"

"Kirk," Carrot nodded and charged the knight.

The knight grabbed Carrot by the face and tossed him

aside. Carrot flew a few feet until the wall got in the way. He crumpled to the ground, dazed. I found myself caught between a horde of midget robot zombies and the knight. There wasn't a good way to run, if I wanted to run.

I did want to run, kind of. Not really, I mean, well, I wasn't sure what I felt. I knew we could take the knight. I knew that. But I also knew that if I was wrong we would die.

Still, Carrot stood, leaning on me, and I fount down the little bits of fear that still welled up. The knight would go down. He had to. I patted Carrot's shoulder and gave the knight a big grin.

"This is the best you can do," I told him. As I said it, I realized it was true. "You don't have the power to do anything really big so you're wasting it on a little display like this. Otherwise you would've just killed us."

He laughed, but I could hear the hollowness hidden behind it. I turned away from him and faced the midget robot zombies. They lurched clankingly closer. I grabbed one up before it could bite me and threw it at the knight.

He swatted it aside and it vanished. Not in a puff of smoke or flash of light, no, it just ceased to be. So I grabbed another and did the same thing. He backhanded that one into nothingness, too. Sadly the rest of the horde was getting too close to keep feeding them to the oblivion wood chipper.

But then Carrot whispered in my ear. "You focus on him, I'll deal with the little ones," he said, moving away from me.

I focused on the knight, trying to do the same thing I had done before to him. I willed him away. Carrot, behind me, had a clanking, rending fight with the small machines of destruction. Since I only heard them cry out and not him I had to assume he was winning. I focused hard on the knight.

He noticed and shifted his attention to me. He fought back, trying to make me slide away the way his minions had. The noises behind me dimmed away. My world shrank to only the knight's face.

We fought each other there, in a contest of will power. I sought his weak points as he tried to find mine. He had an advantage though, the knight spent time living in my head, he knew my weaknesses well. I could feel my body start to vanish.

And then I had a single thought. A realization that I grabbed at with all my strength. The knight had no imagination. Everything he came up with was something I had once thought about. The imagination to create, that was borrowed from my mind, not originating in his own.

I rallied, thinking up new ways to force him out of this world. I pictured different scenarios and tried to shape the world along each one. He weakened under the sudden step up in force, taking a step back. I took one forward in response.

There was a flash of doubt, a moment when I questioned my ability to kill someone, even a person who never really existed in the first place. I focused past it and enveloped the knight in nothing, and then squeezed.

The room went silent. The knight was gone. The midget robot zombies were gone. Carrot and I stood in the living room and looked around. We could both feel that the knight wouldn't be coming back. We couldn't prove it, we couldn't know it for sure, not logically, but we both knew it. We knew it like we knew that we would never be able to explain this to anyone else.

So we did what anyone would do after a victory like ours. We cleaned the place and went to bed.

Days passed, then weeks. Life returned to normal. Soon seasons changed and life simply went about its business, without troubling us too much.

I broke into a sweat, one weekend much later, and my calves burned. Still, I ran on, pressing forward as hard as I could. I passed by Mrs. Blaggart's and the Lowstiens', they had just repainted. Mr. Winchell's house still shone a brilliant sky blue. Every house was peaceful though, and the neighborhood breathed and settled, at peace.

Mr. Burnkin, Steve, smirked at me as I went by, shaking his head. I cursed him silently, but it gave way to a laugh that I let explode from my throat in heavy gasps. Everyone went about their normal lives.

The box in my arms remained solid and steady and I could feel the warmth coming from the bottom and seeping into my skin. My house lay not far off. A dog almost tripped me up as I went by. I leapt over it and spared a glance over my shoulder. Something in its eye sparkled, a knowing sparkle that spoke of... well whatever. It was only a dog.

I reached the front door and jammed my key home on the first try. My shoulder forced the door open and there stood Carrot, waiting for me. He shook his head, checking his watch. I let out another wheezing laugh and set the box in his hands.

"Still hot!" I exclaimed.

"Shit, no way," he said, leaning over to look.

They were still hot. Everything was just as it should be.

after these messages...

"Giggly Wiggly, laugh for you, laugh for me!
Giggly Wigglies, play with you, play with me!
They come to spread Giggles across the land,
To all girls and boys—just come take their hand!
Come on! It's Giggly Wiggly time!"

THE SONG SLAMMED around the room like an invading armies' siren. It bounced off of the walls and ceiling, wrapping around everyone on the soundstage. The children cried with joy, screaming until their throats burned with the kind of passion normally reserved for people at punk concerts, but even they had nothing on these children. The speakers broadcasting the song had been designed to be able to drown out anything this side of a jet engine. The children managed to be heard anyway, as they always did. Johanna Herbister sighed, covering her headset microphone with her left hand, her green sparkling nails curling with delicate anger. The only thing Johanna found more consistently frustrating than the Giggly Wigglies was the hordes of little brats able to fashion, on demand, endless amounts of shrieking, mucus, shit and tears. Not always in that order, either.

As the children stood up to dance the Great Giggly Dance, a funeral procession of laughter and ill-coordinated stomping, Johanna discreetly popped another two aspirin. She swallowed them dry and shot a glance at her Production Assistant, Travis, in the corner. Travis winked at her and shrugged gently, turning swiftly to wave frantically at Tony, working Camera Two. Johanna followed the wave and grit her teeth. If Tony couldn't manage to track children who could barely work out marching in a circle he would need to be replaced. The suggestion would come from Travis within a week, she knew, and she would agree with it. She wanted to let Travis bring it up though, he was learning quickly and she enjoyed watching him grow into his role with each passing day.

After the Great Giggly Dance came the Romp 'n' Stomp, the Juice Box Jamboree and the most hated moment of every show—the Hokey Pokey, or as Johanna put it to Travis one night, long after taping for the day had ended: "If those kids put one more left foot in, they're not getting it back." Travis laughed, and Johanna had laughed right along with him. There was something in her eyes though, a resigned gleam that spoke volumes about her simple statement made in the heat of anger and wine. Travis didn't seem to notice it, and Johanna was grateful.

II

Grinkle, Snorktasm, Tamburto and Bobble Wobble sat in their private lounge after a long day of taping. Grinkle, his blue and red fur slicked back with sweat, finished shuffling the cards and started dealing a fresh hand of poker. Snorktasm gathered her cards up, and tapped them down in a fist of green scales and claws, the claws rounded down and painted in hypnotizing swirls of gold and silver. Tamburto sighed loudly and puffed on his cigar with lips the color of the sky after a storm. He turned to Bobble Wobble and gave the pink-winged creature a sharp nudge with an elbow.

"Did you see that kid in the second row today?" Tamburto waggled his eyebrows and fanned his cards in a large three fingered purple furred hand. Bobble Wobble shook his wedge shaped head slowly and refused to comment, frowning at his cards, his black pupilless eyes shining darkly.

"The blonde with the pigtails?" Grinkle asked as he fanned his own cards, "Yeah I saw her. Her parents were there—I'd forget it."

"Maybe we could invite them, too?" Snorktasm ventured, already shrugging as she spoke, knowing Grinkle's mindset.

"Are you nuts, 'Tas? We start that kinda shit and we are col' busted."

Tamburto tossed a card down and nodded at Grinkle. A card was pushed off the top of the deck and slid its way to Tamburto's hand. Bobble Wobble took two, Snorktasm only one and Grinkle held his hand as he had dealt it.

"We need to speak to Johanna though. It's been a tight month." Tamburto grumbled, ashing his cigar slowly, watching the sudden reveal of the cigar's glowing red tip as the ash fell free. Bobble Wobble nodded agreement and laid out his cards. The rest followed suit and Snorktasm thumped the table in joy as she showed off her winning hand.

"We can't even play for anything worthwhile," Grinkle spat, annoyed as he gathered up the cards and passed the deck to Snorktasm for a shuffle.

"We could play for money." Tamburto smiled as he offered the suggestion, hopeful that he could shift the mood of the room a little, even though he had brought the subject up in the first place.

"Like I damn well said," Grinkle grumped at him, waiting for Snorktasm to deal, "we can't even play for anything worthwhile." The game continued apace, mostly in silence, a simple way to pass the time.

III

JOHANNA SIGHED TO herself and pushed the ratings report away from her in frustration. The Giggly Wigglies was still the number one kid's show in its time slot, meaning the guys upstairs would be pleased. Pleasing them meant a big bonus come the holidays, something that most producers would look forward to. Johanna would look forward to it too, but not until after she got back from her next meeting. She stood, bone weary, and forced her feet to move. She hated visiting what the industry deemed 'the talent.' Her black leather heels clicked all the way down the corridor to the elevator. One green nail jabbed at the button with acquiescent hate. It was late enough that no one else was in the building and a car showed up quickly, taking her upstairs to the Giggly Wigglies's domain.

The entrance area off of the elevator was done in bright primary colors, full of swirls and sudden streaks of color, all of it having cost a fortune to design; molded to bring out endless amounts of joy in children, a feeling of play and safety and happiness. She marched through the space right past the waiting area full of plastic toys and dolls, all of it Giggly Wiggly merchandise available in the gift shop downstairs, and knocked on a bright blue door marked Employees Only set into the far right corner.

She heard a muffled greeting through the door and stepped inside. Grinkle looked up from his cards and caught her gaze with his own solid purple eyes.

"About damned time," he snarled at her, once again trying to cower her. Though a small flutter in the pit of her stomach threatened fear, as it always did, the rest of her was cold and hard.

"You guys wanted to see me?" She stepped further into the room, letting the door close behind her, her stride full of intent.

"We need more kids," Tamburto complained, tossing down his cards. Johanna grabbed a spare chair and pulled it over to the table, making sure she sat within arm's reach of Grinkle, showing him exactly how little she feared him or any of them.

"Look," she sighed, exasperated, "we've been over this. If we up the numbers again, someone is bound to notice. I can get you a dog or two, but that's the best I can do right now."

"Hey, fuck your dogs." Grinkle turned on her, his chair squeaking under his sudden shift of weight, "Come on Jo, did I say we needed some pets or did I say we needed more kids?"

"And did I say," Johanna leaned forward an inch, "I could or could not arrange kids right now? This is the deal we had. If I could do better I would."

"Maybe we're sick of the deal," Snorktasm peeped suddenly. She leaned back in her chair after she spoke, satisfied with herself for coming out and saying it.

"Yeah well, maybe I am too," Johanna admitted, "but it doesn't mean we can change it, now does it?"

"Listen," whispered Bobble Wobble, his voice sounding like a bag full of snakes writhing, "when your father called us here..." Johanna had to admit to herself, if there was going to be one of them to fear, it was Bobble Wobble. She twitched her left foot in response and turned to him.

"When my father called you here," she said evenly, "he wanted you to take over the world for him. I know. This is hardly news. We all know," she turned slowly, taking in each of them in turn, "his plan didn't work. But you agreed to behave in exchange for what you have and I've made. It. Work." Silence drifted over the room in a solid sheet of nothingness. Finally Grinkle broke the spell with the slam of a fist into the table, the surface wobbling under the sudden force.

"Behave?!" He started to stand in his rage and it was only a glance from Bobble Wobble that stopped him, "We aren't your pets, to lock in a closet when you don't want to deal with us, human! We're fucking demons."

"Lesser demons," Johanna pointed out, unfazed. Grinkle lost his temper whenever he knew he had lost an argument.

"We're still far more than you'll ever be," Tamburto pointed out softly, not wanting to get involved, but knowing he had to.

Johanna stood up and walked towards the door, turning her back on the quartet.

"You just remember," she said over her shoulder, "what your oaths mean, and what will happen if you cross them. Or me." She left them, the door snapping shut smartly behind her. She got into the elevator before she let herself begin to shake, knowing they would sense it if she had lost control any sooner. One thing she did know, and admitted to herself as she returned to her office, she had to get them at least one kid fast. They were bound to obey, but the agreement had room for play, and she didn't need them working that out. Better they think she caved a little to maintain the peace.

Upstairs four demons, lesser or not, brooded and began, for the first time in a long time, to plan.

IV

TRAVIS INGRAM BOUNCED on his heels as he waited outside Johanna's office, a few days later. Her door was closed and the little white plastic sign that read 'Yes, I am in a meeting, thanks,' was showing. She had—or so she told Travis—been forced to get the sign and use it because of a Production Assistant who didn't understand what a closed door meant. It was one of the many things that she obliquely warned him about over the course of his few months working with the Giggly Wigglies. Travis took it all in stride with a wink and a shrug and sometimes the running of a hand through his short blonde crew cut. He wasn't fazed by the antics of the show. Travis might have been new on this set, but he had worked in Children's for years now and he reckoned that once you've seen one of your childhood heroes puking on the carpet while screaming about needing whores you could just wink at everything as if it was a big joke.

The problem was that this time a wink wasn't really helping. Something was off, and though Travis felt he had an indicator or two, he wasn't sure exactly what they meant. Which is how he found himself outside his bosses office bouncing on his heels slowly and trying to will the door to open, trying to mentally force the sign to not be there, something to just get this all over with. He squinted at the sign and muttered "come the fuck on already" under his breath, sliding his hand through his hair.

The door opened and a thin man in a bad suit was suddenly visible. He was smiling, and on reflex Travis glanced at the man's shoes even as he took a step backwards and to the right to be out of the way of the leaving visitor. Expensive shoes sent a counter message to the suit, and the smile meant only one thing. Travis nodded to himself as he moved, catching sight of the small blonde girl the man rested a hand on. Her face was beaming with joy, even as she struggled under the hand atop her head. Johanna was shaking the man's other hand when she spotted Travis.

"Mister Harrison, we will be sure to fit little Andrea into 'Special Time' as soon as we possibly can," Johanna told the man with every inch of her Producer's charm in place. Travis appreciated the way she handled the parents, with their often screaming and incredible demands and offers of money, every one of which it seemed she turned down. Johanna Herbister was untouchable as far as office scandal was concerned. He didn't know what had made her single out this one kid for 'Special Time'—a private, or very small group at the most, meeting with the Giggly Wigglies themselves—but she always had some reason that bordered on the random, from the outside. The parents could have money or be poor, the children could be screamers or beamers, she just had a way to choosing them. Must be, Travis reflected, her experience coming into play.

Mister Harrison and little Andrea left, the girl skipping, and Johanna looked at Travis and smiled, waving him into her office smoothly. He closed the door behind him and sat in the right hand leather seat in front of her desk, as he always did. When she had first noticed his habit she joked that he was well on his way to becoming her right hand man. Travis liked that, he liked Johanna even if he knew she hated the children. Years in the industry could do that to a person and Travis never took it personally.

"What can I do for you, Trav?"

Long green nails curled around the handle of a coffee urn, pouring for both of them. Travis loved that, his boss bringing him coffee. How many executives in television did that for their P.A.s? he wondered to himself.

"The G.W.s, Jo, I gotta ask you something about them." He sat up a bit straighter and then checked himself, leaning back into the chair comfortably until he looked utterly uncaring about his own question. Johanna handed him a mug of coffee and sat behind her desk, setting her own mug down softly. She settled into her chair and watched him, her face open and relaxed.

"Bobble Wobble isn't gay," she said cracking a smile, laughing with the old joke. Travis laughed along, remembering the media scandal a preacher had caused when he randomly declared Bobble Wobble's supposed sexuality to the world. It was even funnier because he meant the character, not the actor.

"Thanks, Reverend," Travis grinned at her, following it with a wink, "I was really just wondering...Jesus this sounds stupid when I say it. Jo, are they stable? I mean the actors, huh? I've been here months and I've never seen them out of costume in the least. All of their make-up is done in their lounge, and we've never been allowed to even meet their costumers."

"Hey, they're eccentric. Look you want the truth Trav?" she took a generous sip of her coffee, swirling the black bitter brew on her tongue for a second as she watched her Production Assistant's face shift from curious to wary and back to curious.

"Yeah, that's what I want, Jo. I'm your P.A., huh? I need to be able to back your plays." He smiled at that, it sounded good and he meant it, which was an added bonus.

"They're all old stage actors. They're ashamed of doing what they feel is scut work, and they demanded absolute privacy. They have their own make-up guys, and their contract specifies secrecy." She shook her head with an air of disbelief, "They think they'll end up back on stage at some point and don't want to be known as guys in foam costumes when they do." She shrugged and smiled at him, cradling her mug in both hands. Travis nodded and allowed himself a small laugh.

"Talent, huh? Thanks, Jo. I was just too damn curious to

not ask eventually, right?" He stood, draining his mug and crossing behind her desk to set it back down near the coffee maker, "Thanks for indulging me. And for the trust."

"Not a problem, Trav. We have to watch out for each other. You're my right hand around here." Travis gave her another wink and left her office, closing the door behind him. Johanna nodded and smiled until the door was closed.

After Travis had left, when she could dimly hear the ding! of the elevator arriving through the closed door, she set her mug on the desk and shook her head slowly.

"Really, *really* eccentric," she whispered to herself.

V

BOBBLE WOBBLE DEALT cards slowly, his soft pink wings stretching and relaxing as his arms moved. The week had passed slowly for the four Giggly Wigglies: an endless parade of screaming children and singing. Bobble Wobble set down the deck of cards, silent, and picked up a large tumbler of whiskey, angling it so that his triangular face could drink and not spill liquor all over the table. Tamburto puffed a cloud of smoke out, thick and white, and took his cards, tapping them on the table softly.

"Now this is more like it," he said happily. He fanned his cards out and squinted at them. Snorktasm laughed and nodded her agreement, her swirl-painted, blunted, claws tapping against the back of her cards.

"I'll say it is," she piped in, her free hand rubbing along the opposite arm's scales slowly, smoothing them down as she did before a taping. Rubbed the wrong way, they would stand up, showing off how sharp their edges really were.

"You guys're too easily satisfied," Grinkle said with a low grumble, a bit of gristle hanging from the corner of his mouth. He gestured with what was left of the child's leg, a bloody stump of mostly bone, jabbing it out towards Tamburto. "The kid's good—yeah, sure. So what? Whats-hername might've..."

"Andrea," Bobble Wobble whispered, the layered over

and undertones of his speech crawling across one another unkindly.

"Yeah, sure. Andrea, was a nice kid. Tasty." Grinkle paused to rip some more meat from bone. "But she ain't the solution, is she? We were talking about it. I say we do it."

"You mean break the agreement? But we can't." Snorktasm looked slightly fearful at the idea, even as she cast sidelong hungry glances at Grinkle's meal.

"We can," Bobble Wobble slid back into the conversation, putting his cards down and pushing them away from himself, "bend it."

He tossed back the rest of his whiskey and bared his teeth at Grinkle.

"Exactly!" Grinkle waved the leg around, holding the ankle, as if conducting an orchestra. "Look, all those years ago? Jo was a kid. She left holes in the whole thing. She was just tryin' ta, you know, stop us cold. No, the best she could do was bind us to her service, and only mostly at that, and what? Keep us from roaming?"

"Well, when you put it like that," Tamburto said, pondering, "we do have more room to move in it than I thought. Why didn't we decide this sooner?" He cast sharp glances at Grinkle and Booble Wobble.

"We were slow. Content with simply having gained access to this realm," Bobble Wobble pointed out, eyes locked on Grinkle's as he spoke, "It has been long years here, but in our lifespans, it's only a blink. We act now." The others nodded agreement, Grinkle shoving the rest of the leg into his mouth, teeth worrying bone with sharp wet cracks and snaps. A single toe fell to the table and Snorktasm snatched it up, popping it in her mouth. She loved a good toe.

VI

DEEP AT SEA, Captain Ronald Jackson nursed a headache. The water was calm, the night was dark and all should've been right with his world. His ship, the Lazy Marie, was on its way back to the Cape of Good Hope with new cargo. His crew was sound and content and the money was good. For the life of him, Captain Jackson couldn't figure out what was bothering him enough to cause these headaches. The last few nights had been full of them, each one clawing at the edges of his consciousness but never quite cresting. He could feel the pressure there, building behind his eyes, and he had the keen sense that there was something else, some part of the headaches that wasn't fulfilling itself. Until it did, he knew, he wouldn't get any rest at all.

First Mate Christina Hartman watched her captain take his hands off the rudder and cross to the small white medicine chest on the starboard side of the bridge. She sighed to herself and moved to take his place, unconsciously smoothing the sides of her crisp white jacket as she did.

"Cap?" she asked him without turning to look at him, "Headache again? Maybe you have Jonesy look at it. Could be something big."

"I'm sure it isn't anything Jonsey could fix," he told her gently as he swallowed more of the small white pills. As he said it he realized he felt dizzy and dropped like a stone to the lacquered hardwood floor of the bridge. Christina slapped the intercom on as she watched Jackson fall.

"Jonesy, get the fuck up here!" she bellowed at the little speaker, rushing to the fallen man and kneeling next to him swiftly. Captain Jackson's eyes were open, she could see. His body was rigid and taut, like the anchor cable at dock. She slapped his face lightly and called his name a few times, to no avail. His eyes rolled back into his head and his jaw started to work, saying something quickly and silently.

Jonesy burst into the room, black medical kit in hand, and muttered a soft string of curses as he knelt on the other side of Jackson. He turned to ask Christina what the hell had happened but as he opened his mouth to speak their Captain's voice rose in volume.

"Giggly Wiggly, laugh for you, laugh for me. Giggly Wigglies, play with you, play with me. They come to spread

Giggles across the land, to all girls and boys—just come take their hand," he intoned, his voice rising with each statement. "Come on, it's Giggly Wiggly time!" he finally screamed and sat bolt upright. Blinking and in control of his senses again, he looked to either side of him, taking in his First Mate and Medical Officer. "What the fuck?" he asked them. Neither had any idea, but the three of them spent the next several hours downstairs doing tests and trying to find out. They never did.

Thousands of miles away, Grinkle slammed his fist into the table with rage, standing and leaning on the table, forcing the grain of the wood to creak.

"What the hell was that?" he demanded, fuming. Snorktasm and Tamburto winced but remained silent. Bobble Wobble opened his eyes slowly, sighing.

"I'm out of practice," he said, trying to keep the anger from his voice and failing. "It was the only thing I could force him to do." Grinkle cursed again and sat heavily. The four looked anywhere but at each other, knowing this was not exactly going to plan.

VII

THE BUILDING WAS quiet and Travis gently touched the elevator button, knowing he would get fired if he was found out. The car rose swiftly and he forced himself to stop bouncing on his heels as it rose, floor by floor. Johanna would kill him, he knew, if she found out, but it was late enough that no one else was around. Even she had gone home at last, telling Travis to find his own bed and seek its comfort for the night. He had waved her off, muttering about some details with a set designer he had to work out before tomorrow. She had no reason to doubt him and left him there, alone, shrugging and thinking to herself that she had made the right choice in P.A.s.

The elevator opened to the bright primary swirls and flourishes of the Giggly Wigglies floor. He had decided, after speaking to her, that something about her story didn't hang together right. As he crossed the room, looking for some sort of clue as to the true nature of these reclusive actors, he noticed light coming from under a door set into the far right corner of the open space. He crept closer to it, listening for any sounds he could discern. Muttered voices rose and fell but individual words were impossible to work out. He sighed and turned to search the rest of the space, his shoe making a slight squeak on the tiled floor.

He got all of two more steps before the door was flung open and Snorktasm burst out of the room, her scales rippling with movement. "I know I heard a mouse!" she insisted to whomever was inside the room.

She saw Travis and blinked several times.

"Hey," he said lamely, knowing his career was over, "I just heard a disturbance up here and..." Grinkle and Tamburto came out of the room slowly behind Snorktasm, both grinning as they saw and heard Travis.

"Yeah, you're the disturbance... human." Tamburto shook his head and walked right up to Travis, his fingers working slowly. Travis blanched a bit, wondering what kinds of freaks wore costumes this late at night, after a whole day of filming. Did they sleep in those things, he wondered, even as he realized their smiles and grins were somehow predatory and utterly unlike the kind smiles they gave to children.

"Ok, I admit it, I was curious. I wanted to know why you guys never took off your costumes." At that the three giggled, Snorktasm's voice peeping and shrieking a bit.

"He thinks..." Snorktasm began with a titter.

"These ain't costumes, human," Grinkle said, stepping up next to Tamburto, "You wanted to know. Now you know. ...Sorry 'bout that."

"Sorry about what?" Travis asked, growing nervous. He started to back away slowly, hands coming up in front of him. They didn't make it far up before Tamburto pounced on him, knocking the man to the floor. Travis screamed, the sound cutting off as Tamburto's teeth ground against his neck, tearing out his throat.

"He's gonna be tough meat, not like a good kid," Grinkle

sighed as he wandered up to Tamburto and reached down, tearing one of Travis's arms off. He bit into the shoulder and shook his head. "Tough meat," he lamented and turned back to reenter the room he had come from.

From inside the room a voice of multiple layers could be heard by all three, "Clean that up, and then we have to step up the plan."

VIII

ALL ACROSS THE city children woke up humming to themselves. They dressed and ate and went to school, behaving as they normally did. Their parents never noticed the constant humming, chalking it up one and all, to normal child behavior. Throughout the city the morning proceeded normally, sun shining and birds singing. Cars honked and busses shat out volumes of gas, devouring and releasing passengers.

At about eleven A.M. everything changed. Every child in the city stood up and tried to leave where they were, as one. Children escaped school and ran from nannies. They crossed streets without the buddy system and walked solemnly when they could, all heading towards one central location.

Johanna was in her office when the phone started to ring, every line on the flat black device lighting up like a Christmas tree. A secretary ran into her office, a worried look on his face.

"Ms. Herbister," he yelped, "there are children everywhere!"

"Yes, Francis, I know." She shook her head, "We work in children's television. One does lead to the other." She picked up her phone and turned away from the secretary, annoyed.

"Ms. Herbister, there are children—thousands of them—swarming the building." The voice on the other end of the call said quickly. Johanna looked back at Francis with apology in her eyes. "The Police are here but they don't know what to do. The children are all singing the Giggly Wiggly theme, ma'am!" Johanna hung up the phone and felt an icy cold lump form in the pit of her stomach.

"Ms. Herbister?" Francis asked as he watched her stand up and close her eyes for a second, "What do we do?"

"You call downstairs and make sure they lock the doors. Then call more Police. I'm going upstairs." She sighed and started towards Francis.

"Ma'am? Ms. Herbister? How will going upstairs help?" He stepped backwards out of her office as she approached him, trying to stay in front of her but not hinder her movement. There was something in her eyes when she had reopened them that he didn't want to mess with.

"Did I tell you to do something or did I ask you to question me?" she barked loudly, drawing stares from people passing by. She closed her door in his face, reopening it a minute later, dusting off her hands. She slammed her office door shut behind her and marched to the elevator, her resolve tightening around her like an electrical charge. Francis meeped and ran for a phone to do as he had been ordered.

The elevator seemed to crawl upwards as Johanna tapped her long green nails on her thigh. Finally the doors opened. The room had changed since the last time she had been there: the brightly colored swirls were rent with claw marks, the tiles along the floor pried up as often as not and shattered against each other. She ignored it all, letting her senses take it in but not processing much of anything as she strode towards the bright blue door in the corner. Without knocking she flung the door open wide and glared inside.

The four sat, grinning wickedly at each other, their sharp teeth revealed in full as three of them watched Bobble Wobble. His wings fluttered and his head shook as he opened his eyes.

"Johanna, what a pleasant surprise." Each word was perfectly formed and said with distinct distaste. "We had wondered if you would simply run in fear or if you would bring yourself to us and let us have one last meal together." Her knees started to weaken and Johanna steeled herself all over again. She couldn't back down now. She knew she was the only thing that had half a chance, but she also knew it was only half of a chance that she had.

"Stop this now!" She gave extra force to the word. "You idiots are causing so much trouble I don't know how I'll be able to cover it!"

Grinkle laughed and tossed the last half of Travis's head at her feet. She jumped back, wobbling as she landed on her heels and gaped at the head for a second. Even though the face was eyeless, she still knew exactly who it was.

"Don't bother covering it, Jo," Tamburto said smoothly, "We'll deal with it ourselves, okay?" Snorktasm laughed and stood, as did Grinkle. Johanna swallowed hard and shook her head defiantly.

"You're breaking your oaths," she reminded them darkly, standing her ground once more.

"Yeah, we'll uhhh deal with that, too," Grinkle said as he took a step forward. Johanna noticed that Snorktasm had re-sharpened her claws, the swirling point now leading down to knife-like edges and points.

"I'm sure." Johanna took a step backwards, trying to gain enough space to do the only thing that popped into her head, the only real chance she could find. Grinkle leapt at her and she turned and ran, kicking off her heels as she went, the shards of tile on the floor cutting into her feet deeply as she tried to outrace the demons on her tail. Snorktasm shouted, "The elevator!" even as Johanna turned suddenly and burst into the emergency stairwell. The door slammed shut behind her and she took the stairs as fast as her now-bloody feet would let her.

Seconds later the stairwell door slammed open again with a squeal of protest as the metal itself bent. Tamburto threw himself down the stairs, followed closely by Grinkle and Snorktasm. Bobble Wobble walked slowly behind all of them, taking his time and smiling.

Johanna felt something inside her break as she went down under Tamburto, the two tumbling down a flight of stairs, tangled together like badly-paired lovers. He raked her shoulder, tearing through a hundred dollar silk blouse and rending soft flesh. She raked her own nails across his face, feeling one of his eyes pop. He screamed a string of curses and let go of her. Johanna stood shakily, started running again. Grinkle and Snorktasm could be heard thudding and smashing their way behind her, one of them stopping to deal with Tamburto— Snorktasm, she guessed.

Blood ran down her arm, hot and wet, staining the silk of her blouse as she continued to run. Each step was a knife of pain in her chest as the four ribs she had broken in Tamburto's tackle ground against each other. She ran, stumbling, her feet crying out in protest, curling her bleeding arm against her broken chest and turning down another flight.

"Mine!" snarled Grinkle as he slammed into her from behind, sending her tumbling down another flight of stairs. He stood at the top of the landing, watching her. She screamed as her right knee gave, bending wrong, and forced herself upright, limping towards the door.

"You're dedicated, Jo," Grinkle said with a cold sharp laugh. "But not good enough."

"Oh, for fuck's sake," Johanna said as she shoved the fire door open painfully, "stop watching bad movies." She started to limp as fast as she could, heading for her office. The floor was empty and Johanna realized they were all downstairs dealing with the children.Grinkle burst through the fire door behind her, tearing it off its hinges with a sharp protest of metal and threw it at her. The door shattered her office's wooden door, missing her by a few inches. Tamburto and Snorktasm came out of the stairwell, Tamburto snarling and holding his face over his ruined eye with one large hand, Snorktasm holding him and promising revenge. Bobble Wobble showed seconds later, strolling calmly behind.

Johanna struggled into her office, splinters gouging into her feet and hands, and limped to her desk, sitting behind it in her chair. She grabbed the piece of chalk on the floor and connected the two ends of the curve quickly before she pawed at drawers and opened the bottom most one, starting to frantically flip through pages.

"Jo, Jo, Jo," Grinkle sang as he entered her office, taking his time. The other two followed and stood there, watching her with a level of sheer disbelief.

"Is this really the time to take a memo?" Snorktasm asked her with a giggle. Bobble Wobble entered last and watched her curiously. His curiosity turned to rage as he saw what she pulled from her desk. Johanna took the contract and tore through it, hoping she had time before they could figure out what she was intending. Grinkle glanced around uncertainly, sensing something in the room was wrong.

"Breach of contract," she said softly. "Section 14-D."

She looked up at them, the air itself seeming to charge electrically as she intoned the words.

The three looked at Bobble Wobble who started to launch himself across the room at Johanna. At his lead the other three did the same. Bobble Wobble realized that he knew the feeling in the air, the same wrongness Grinkle noticed. Johanna had closed a magical circle, binding them all in the room until she chose to reopen it—or she died.

"'If the talent interferes with the production of the show...,'" she said quickly, the words coming rapid-fire from her lips as she shoved backwards in her chair, evading the four by scant inches.

"'...The entire contract is forfeit and the talent is to leave the premises, defined as the realm in which they currently reside—'"

Bobble Wobble screamed in rage and tore his hand through her cheek trying to shut her up.

"'—As soon as they are notified of said breach.' In other words—"

She closed her eyes and hoped she still had time. The world seemed to slow into individual seconds: Snorktasm's claws started to work their way across her jaw even as the words left Johanna's mouth.

"—You're *fired*."

The stench of brimstone and burnt fur washed over her like rancid garbage. Gagging, broken and bloody, Johanna leaned back in her chair and glanced around the now empty room.

"Read your contract and don't fuck with your Producer, you fucks," she whispered.

She glanced at her Rolodex, smudging the circle open with her foot.

She wondered how she was going to explain this to the higher-ups and—more importantly—where the Giggly Wigglies's replacements would come from.

After all, she still had her father's old spell books.

high noon of the living dead

NOW THIS WAS back in the early days of the dead west. Back then it didn't have a name or anything, it was just where man was losing the fight to survive. The desert was bad enough on its own, but add the Brainers and their mounts to the mix and, well, to be blunt, we were gettin' real bad. Most civilized areas had already collapsed, and the future wasn't lookin' none too bright.

By then, this was only ten or so years after the Brainers had come, in you understand, the whole of what used to be called Texas and most points west of it clear to the ocean had already fallen. The Brainers moved fast, faster than anyone thought they could. The disease they spread with them affected mammals of all sorts and made 'em hunger. It made 'em kinda stupid, too, at first—but they got smarter as they adapted. That was our mistake in the first days, we showed 'em all what we could do and they learnt from it like children.

They swept clean across the land, legend has it they came right out of the sparkling ocean in old California and just started marching east one day. They hit the rest of the globe too, the same way, walking at first. Damn them anyway, they learned. They started riding horses again, Brainer horses to be sure, and training dogs and everything. They couldn't eat no Brainer steer but then they didn't eat anything but the brains of the living anyway so what did they rightfully care? Still they were kinda smart, even if they didn't talk except to grumble and growl like old men arguing without teeth.

We stopped 'em around the Mississippi for a while, superior firepower still meant something even if we hadn't learned some of the tricks to killing them that we know now. Most of us had given up on the west. When the Brainers came across California they started to bunch up in the west, see, and what with us holding them back from moving much further the west became their stronghold. Not that I would credit them with enough smarts to think in terms of conquering strategy, their natural movements just gave them the appearance of it. They were smart, yeah, but they weren't that smart. Some higher brain functions would always be lost to them, and they only had crude hand signals and gestures to coordinate themselves.

Once they had a natural stronghold growing though, they learnt to use it. Hand signals increased and patterns started to form up out there in the harsh sun. You gotta understand, it wasn't as if they had killed every living person in their path. They needed the food source, but they also needed the fine control labor.

With memories came wants and with wants came the problem: the Brainers couldn't rebuild things. They could tear a house down just fine, but they couldn't work together well enough to build one. So they took living men and women and forced them to do the hard work. At first, to be sure, work was refused. Then again how many people around you do you have to watch die for refusing to lift a hammer and work some nails before you find that same hammer in your hand a-swinging?

We all gave the west up for good. There wasn't a good clear choice otherwise, that we saw. Two folks found it in themselves to disagree. Franklin Cleaver and Edward Bones was what they called themselves, if pressed. Most folk called 'em simply Cleaver and Bones but they always called themselves Frank and Eddie.

This is where a lot of historians, if I can use the word to describe myself, disagree. Some say the two men were assassins until the Brainers came, fingering their expertise and willingness to kill as explanation. Some point to evidence, namely Bones' crockery collection, that they were just chefs in some lowly military outfit. Still others like to claim, and Lord knows what they base this one on, that the two men were sports players who got separated from their team and struck out on their own. They certainly didn't play any sports that I ever saw.

Yeah, I saw 'em. I was with 'em when they... but that's later on. The rest, including how they came to the point that they considered their plan, I heard tell from others in town, like I'm tellin' you now.

They came into what was left of Logansport, Louisiana early one Saturday. Thing was, they came from the west. No one, by then, came in from the west unless they were a Brainer looking for a snack. The sentries on the town wall, a hastily constructed thing of wood and mud, almost shot 'em. Bones and Cleaver were covered in sand and dust and they looked for all the world like statues come to life.

The sentries shouted warnings to each other and readied their guns, hoping for a clean shot, when Franklin shouted right back at them. Brainers didn't shout, even the guys dumb enough to land sentry duty knew that.

"Hey, buddy, open the damned gate, will ya?" Franklin asked.

The sentries were too shocked to do any opening of anything besides their mouths at that point, so they stood there, jaw-dropped at the two men. Edward sighed and took a rifle out from under the sand colored poncho he had draped over his small frame.

"Frank here asked you to do us a favor," he said cheerily, "think maybe you could get to doing it? Today?"

The sight of the obviously well kept gun shook the sentries into action. Two of them rushed down the rickety old hand-lashed ladder and started to work at getting the gate open. The other two sentries stayed where they were, taking in the sight of men. Men from the west.

"We'll get it open, it's just," the first sentry stammered, "we don't use it, see."

"Yeah, it... no one comes from this direction. No one that's still talkin' at least," the second explained.

"We gathered," Franklin said mysteriously. He yanked his bandana off his head and his scarf off his face and started to wipe the grime clear from his skin. Franklin had the ability to loom over people even while the people he was loomin' over stood twenty feet above him on a wall.

Edward pulled out a bent and broken cigarette, hand rolled but crushed in the folds of his poncho. He shook his head sadly and looked at it, turning it this way and that in his fingers. "Hey, Frank?"

"Yeah, Eddie?" the bigger man answered without looking, spitting into his scarf and trying to wipe his face somewhat clear.

"This ain't right," Edward Bones said sadly to his partner, "I didn't even get to smoke the fucking thing." He presented the broken smoke to Cleaver like a child handing over a broken toy.

"And what," Cleaver asked, "am I supposed to do with this?"

Still, Cleaver took the broken thing and studied it for a second before muttering under his breath, breaking it in two and handing half to Edward. Then he stuck the remaining half in the corner of his own mouth and started to dig out a match.

They went on like that, smoking and talking as if nothing was unusual while they waited for the gate to work its way open. The sentries on the wall fell silent, out of awe or fear depending on who you asked later. The two sentries who couldn't see any of this, but only hear the mutterings on the other side of the thick and stuck gate figured the two men on the other side to be insane.

Either way, the gate got opened with a bit of teamwork and, more importantly, closed and firmly locked again once Cleaver and Bones were through. Edward waved at the sentries and the two men just walked on past, uncaring, aiming right for the bar. They had no way of knowing where it was, but somehow their feet took them right to it with only a stop at a horse through to finish washing off the dust from their faces.

The air in the bar was hot and unmoving, like the beer, but that didn't stop Cleaver and Bones. They ordered up two mugs of the local swill and found a cracked and leaning table to sit at, Franklin Cleaver putting his feet up on the edge of the table and causing it to sway.

Sammy Burns, the bartender in the Last Drop, swore till the day he died that they looked right at home from minute one, never stopping to give pause or consideration that they were somewhere new. They had a sense, Sammy would say, that everywhere they stopped to sit was their home and you were welcome to share it with them so long as you played by their rules.

No one wanted to ask the two strangers any questions at first. They didn't exactly go out of their way to hunt down people to interview 'em, either. A week passed. Then two. The town got used to them, as much as they could, lettin' them go about their business, which seemed to consist of drinking and talking to each other and no one else. They always had money for their drink and never seemed to do nothin' to earn it. Which is what eventually broke the mutual silences, I'd say.

It happened late one night, out back of the bar. Edward was setting up his cook pots and slicing roots into a bucket. Franklin was busy starting a roaring fire. The men had taken to cooking late nights, Edward seemed to insist, and feeding whomever was still awake. It didn't invite conversation much other than thanks, but it warmed some of the locals to the two.

Johnny Boots saw it different. He felt that his woman, Betsy Klein, was paying that Bones man far too much attention. Betsy didn't see it that way at all, but then she also didn't see herself as Johnny Boots' woman, either.

Boots was out back watching the fire grow along with his ire. He shot Edward a look, trying to warn the man off through sheer force of will. None of us knew, then, that battle was a losing proposition. Johnny Boots learned it soon enough though, and learned it for all of us.

"Hungry?" Edward asked Johnny, gesturing him closer to the cooking pots that were warming up over the fire. The night was dry and hot and the fire's heat warmed men that didn't need warming. Edward's face was coated with a fine sweat but, like his partner, he still wore fine clothing and layers of it regardless of the heat.

Johnny shook his head at Edwards question, stopping his head shake to spit. "Naw, I jus' don't think you oughta be paying so much attention to my woman," Johnny said slowly and then jerked a thumb over towards Betsy. She rolled her eyes and started walking towards the fire.

Edward held a hand up to stop her and smiled warmly at Johnny Boots. "Hey, man, I have no interest in her," he told Johnny as easy as discussing the weather, "I mean, no offense... uhh... Betsy, right? But yeah, guy, I'm sorry if I gave you some sort of impression there. Whatdda ya say you have a plate with me when I'm done, we can call it the past?"

Johnny turned to look at Betsy, who was smiling, and looked back at Edward, turning his full attention on the slender man. Edward's green eyes fairly twinkled in the firelight and his short black hair shone with beads of sweat. Somehow that managed to rile Johnny even more.

"How'sabout you stop lookin' at her and I won't have to deal with you myself," he said, putting as much menace as he could into the sentence.

Edward laughed easily and gave Johnny another smile. Franklin didn't even perk up at the exchange, bent over and busy with stoking the fire as he was. Both men looked as if nothing at all was going on, except making dinner.

"Hey, Frank?" Edward asked, his voice light and uncaring.

"Yeah, Eddie?" his partner answered, still not looking up.

"Do we have any oil, and perhaps another turning fork would come in handy, if we could spare one for a few hours."

Franklin reached over and passed Bones an old glass bottle half full of oil. The makeshift wooden stopper was jammed into the bottle at an odd angle and it took Edward a second to pry it loose with his teeth.

"Yeah, we should have another turning fork," Franklin added, glancing over at the large bag of cooking supplies they lumped out back every night. He stood up and walked over to the bag, undoing the flaps slowly and rummaging inside.

Johnny Boots stood there, confused for a moment. He wasn't sure what was going on except that it seemed like he was being ignored. Growling deep in his throat Johnny took a step towards Edward, raising a fist.

Edward Bones threw the contents of the oil bottle at Johnny's face without seeming to move, stopping the man mid-swing. Johnny stood there, sputtering, and reached a hand up to wipe at his eyes.

Bones grabbed a small stick from the fire and flicked it at Boots casually, turning to look at Cleaver before it even struck home.

"You know, I could really do with some potatoes, Frank," he said as Johnny Boot's face caught fire. Boots screamed and stumbled backwards, losing his balance and falling on his ass near the cook pot, upsetting it. Franklin was already moving, putting out a hand to steady the pot and then thrusting down with the fork. It caught Johnny Boots in the neck and he sputtered and gurgled, trying hard to figure out the trick of breathing blood. He died pretty fast, between the injuries, but not a second of it was anything but hellishly painful.

Edward walked back to his favorite standing spot, looking into the pot and considering the temperature before dumping out his bucket right into it. A sweet sizzle erupted from the pot, smoke puffing upwards tinged with the smell of fresh cooking vegetables.

"We don't have any more potatoes," Franklin said, handing Edward the fresh turning fork, "but that smells good there."

"Thanks, Frank." Edward looked up at the people who stood around. They were gaping, to a body, rooted to the spot in fear. "So who wants a plate?" Edward asked, sticking his hand into the pot to stir.

It only took one moment like that to convince everyone with a lick of sense to steer as clear of Cleaver and Bones as possible. Sadly some of the other folk in town didn't have a lick of sense. They crossed paths with the men and ended up much the same as Johnny Boots, sometimes their deaths were simple and sometimes they were full of complex and strange plans of action, but they always ended up dead. Not once did Cleaver or Bones seem to care about killing a man.

The days continued to pass and the town grew used to Cleaver and Bones, ignoring them where possible and being respectful where they could. Everyone in town was respectful of the pair, except the men themselves. They berated each other and gave one another enough grief that some expected it to erupt into violence, which it never did. Outside of them though, the only other things which didn't learn to respect both men were the Brainers and the weather.

The sun beat down on the town like never before, causing even the weeds to shrivel up and die. Food got scarce and men went hungry. No one knew what to do. There was hardly ever even a wind to help cool off a man's skin and the nights were just as hot as the days, heat radiating back off of the ground in uncomfortable waves.

The Brainers, they made occasional attempts at the wall. None got through, but with the heat and hunger depressing and addling so many hopes dropped and a general feeling rose up in its place: the Brainers would get through and overrun the town.

Hadn't, some asked, the government left the west for dead in the first place? Hadn't they pulled out and then left places like the very town they stood in to defend themselves? Why wouldn't the Brainers over run things, they reasoned. The idea spread and grew and overtook the sense of the town as a whole.

Except, of course, for the minds of two people.

Cleaver and Bones seemed to be having a perfectly fine time of it. Hell, they almost seemed to be expecting and awaiting the mood of the town to shift downward. Franklin smiled more and the both of them conferred in hushed tones, not giving a damn who noticed them whisper to each other.

About a month after they showed up, Cleaver and Bones

walked to the center of town and stood in the middle of the street, looking around and catching as many eyes as possible.

"Listen up, if you wouldn't mind," Edward said with his customary friendliness, "we have something that we think you might all want to hear."

"We," Franklin said with the mean, hard grin of a man thinks he can move boulders with his bare hands, "have a plan."

It was the sentence that was to change everything, and even as it was said, the whole town knew it.

People gathered up inside the church, filtering in as word spread like wildfire. Cleaver and Bones stood near the altar, but not directly on it. They watched the crowd in the room grow and conferred between themselves in quiet tones. Eventually they had to figure the mass of people was as big as it would get and Franklin nodded at Edward and then at the crowd, starting to speak.

"In case you all didn't notice, the current situation won't hold for long," he said matter-of-factly, "and when it gives this town will fall. When it falls, the Brainers will move in, take down the wall and inch further across the land. That needs to stop."

"But it's more than that," Edward cut in.

"Not yet, Eddie," Franklin said with a glance over his shoulder. "One thing at a time."

Barbara Haines stood up and looked around the church. "What can we..." she started to say, before she was cut off by a sweep of Franklin's hand.

"Hold off for now. Let us tell you about where we were."

"We've spent the last few years in the west, and it was..." Edward grinned slowly and tapped his partner on the shoulder. "Hey Frank, it was kinda like that time when we..."

"Don't start, Eddie, just tell them what we discussed."

A murmur spread out along the crowd. I had just gotten to town myself a few days ago and learned all about the two strange men, so when I found out about a gathering you can bet I ran there as fast as I could. Still, at the idea, the simple thought, that these two had spent time out west in with the Brainers made us all wonder. How did they survive, what were they doing, what could they want now?

"Right. Well, settle down some, folks." We fell silent at Edward's words, all attention on the front of the church again. "We were curious, you know how it is. So we traveled west and then came back east. We came back north of here, of course, but we've been going back and forth for a while. At first it was a job, don't worry about that. But the second time we wanted to see what was really up."

People were rooted to their seats. Edward stopped talking for a second to root in his pockets for what turned out to be a smoke and you could've cut the tension with a knife. He took his time lighting the cigarette and then took a long drag off of it, holding the smoke deep.

"The Brainers were a curiosity." Edward exhaled and waved a hand around a bit in thought. "They weren't at all like the old Vodoun ideas of a zombie, but they also didn't seem to fit any other popular mythology concerning the concept. It was confusing. Myth is, I mean, it's an engine and like Joseph Campbell said..."

"Eddie," Franklin broke in, "the facts?"

Edward nodded and shrugged, the cigarette in the corner of his mouth. Something in his eyes though, something deep in there had flicked back on. We could all see it, even Franklin.

"Sorry, Frank. But yeah, we wandered a while. Looking. It was just like that time Frank and I had to deal with Freddie Six-Fingers..."

"Except for the fact that Freddie had otters."

"We dealt with the otters, though didn't we?"

"At the cost of my car. Again."

"Still wasn't my fault. But the Brainers were just like him. They were showing one hand and playing another. We all know they don't kill everyone they meet. Who does, right?" Edward shrugged and then smiled. The both of them seemed to be warming up somehow, breaking out of a shell.

"Bennie."

"Yeah, all right, Frank. Bennie. But the Brainers don't. Some people they take with them. Now from what we heard when we got back the last time they were supposed to be taking them somewhere and using them for labor. What no one knew was how."

They didn't pace and didn't move their arms a whole lot, standing as still as possible while they spoke, but something about the way they started to speak was different. More alive. They seemed younger as they went on, instead of the fifty-odd years of life that had weathered and etched into each man.

"Eddie's right. Everyone had a theory, but no one had seen it in action. So we went and looked. They tie them up and march them out across the desert. The Brainers ride some Brainer horses and corral them, like so many cattle."

"Although traditionally you don't tie cattle when you go on a cattle drive. Then again, I suppose that cattle don't often want to escape. They might, granted, but they seem to be fine just walking."

"Yes. Thank you, Eddie, for that brief, yet fascinating, look into cattle herding," Franklin said with a roll of his eyes. "When we saw that we realized we couldn't ignore it. Humans suffer, they die and they do what they need to in order to survive. We get that, better than a lot of people, probably. This is different."

"Besides, we've seen you all," Edward dropped and stubbed out his cigarette, his eyes scanning all of us slowly as he did.

"We have. You're breaking. There's no fighting back going on. No anything. You are all now sitting here waiting to die. That's it, that's all you have left for yourselves. You'll slowly sink further and further down and the wall over there will get a weak point, but you won't care. Then another. Then it'll fall down."

"Walls fall but they don't have to. If this wall falls, do you think other people north or here, or south, will hold their lines forever, either? What man, my grandfather once asked me…"

"No he didn't, Eddie. Why do you have to attribute bad sayings to this man who, I might add, you never even met?"

"Not the point, Frank. The point is that he was right."

"He couldn't have been right, he never even...why do I bother?"

"I couldn't tell you. But I can tell you that the point is that if you don't hold why should you expect any one else to?"

"But what can we do?" James Higgins, the town butcher, asked.

"We're getting there," Edward told him, "see we would've tried this ourselves but we needed supplies and we needed a few extra hands to help."

"To help with what?" I asked, unable to hold my tongue. The mood of the crowd was shifting slowly. We grew restless.

"Getting there," Edward Bones said with a smile. "We also needed to make sure there would be a town to come back to."

"We intend to bring the fight to the Brainers and disrupt their little herding plan," Franklin said, the glint in his eye unmistakable, "even just one, just to start working out how we can do it again and again and hold the walls and eventually push them back."

"Trust me," Edward put in, "it surprised us to think of this, too. We're not normally your public servant type. Though I did once work collecting garbage."

"You also sold rugs. Let's not push it."

"I wasn't really selling... oh well, no, I mean I really was paid to collect garbage, Frank."

"I couldn't imagine caring any less. Can we get on with this?"

"Sure," Bones said and straightened his shirt a bit. "We need about four guys who can deal with camping out and fucked up conditions and death. Four guys who aren't so afraid of the Brainers that they'll be useless."

"They should also," put in Franklin, "be able to follow orders."

"Are you saying that I can't?" Edward asked, with a hurt look on his face.

"History speaks for itself, Eddie. Still. That ain't all we'll need. We also need supplies."

"Yeah, let's see," Edward thought for a moment, recalling a list the two had obviously spent time thinking over, "we need twenty or forty feet of chain link fence, an equal footage of two-by-four beams, enough so the width of the beams adds up to the length of fence, see? About a hundred feet of solid steel wire, a staple gun, ten or so four by eight wood beams, a few tents, some padlocks and some styrofoam, you can't get rid of the stuff so I'm sure there's a bunch somewhere around here. What else, Frank?"

"Mmm, let's see now, Eddie. As much razor wire as you can find, bolt cutters, rope. Good strong rope, none of that twine shit."

"I hate that stuff, the nylon?"

"Cuts your fingers. About six pounds of raw mint leaves, if possible."

"Don't forget the make-up. We need make-up, women's stuff will do."

"Right. A bunch of wax, enough water for six people to last about a week and dried food to last the same. Heavy duty rubber bands, if any still exist, a few bags of flour, extra boots for everyone involved, heavy gloves, gasoline or the like, and maybe some tennis balls if you can find any."

"See," Edward said with his customary smile growing even bigger. "Simple."

It wasn't nearly as easy as Edward Bones claimed, of course. Some of the stuff they wanted could be managed without too much hassle. Jerry Smitts agreed to give up a section of his chain link fence for the cause without too much bitchin' and moanin', for example.

The wood beams were likewise simply a matter of talking someone into helpin' out. People wanted to help, any way they could, unless it meant personal hardship. That was understandable, to a point, but only to a point. It felt like the town's survival or a few people who had needed goods. In that sorta situation, when the person won't give up what's needed, it gets taken. It gets taken right quick, too, to be honest about it.

Deidre Fontaine had herself a few tents that she never

really used. Still, she saw a potential use for 'em in the future and wanted us to find something else to use. We woulda, except for the fact that hers were the best tents around. They were on the list. One night Deidre put her foot down, firmly, by slamming her door in the faces of some of us other towns-folk.

Well, she mighta' slept well right after, but the very next night she was woken up to the sound of her front door coming down in splinters. The tents were bundled up with the other equipment and when Deidre asked about them, screamed about them, why no one had any clue what tents she was talking about.

While the stuff was being gathered, as best it could be, Cleaver and Bones picked their team of companions. They needed four men and found themselves facing down fourteen volunteers. Both men smiled at that, but they went down the list, asking questions and watching the eyes of the men and women answerin'.

In the end Sally Teekin, a widow who had bigger arms than most men, Otto van Potts, who also supplied all the rope and steel wire needed, Billy McDougal, a damn fine shot, and myself, were chosen. I ain't sure why I was picked above some of the others. I guess they liked the look of my eyes and my steady hands.

It only took a few days to get everything together, the gasoline and tennis balls being the only item we couldn't locate any of. High octane moonshine was used for the gas and Edward Bones gathered up a bunch of avocado saying they'd do as well as tennis balls. The styrofoam packing, which I thought would be a problem, was actually in use as insulation up in the barber's house.

Cleaver and Bones lashed all the equipment into bundles and arranged straps for each bundle, handing them out to us and taking a fair share themselves.

"Ain't we gonna use horses or something? A mule at least to carry this stuff, maybe?" Billy asked, shuffling his pack onto his shoulders and frowning.

"Horses and mules generally are not smart enough to avoid smaller mammals," Franklin said, "and they don't think of them as threats. But everything out there that is not the six of us is a threat to us. Beasts of burden would only cause us problems. We carry the load."

The West Gate was a horrible thing to see, then. It was suddenly all that stood between being brave and being dead. I could read it in the faces of my fellow travelers, all except for Cleaver and Bones. Their faces were neutral, for them this was just another day. But for us, well we hadn't been out west since things started to settle. I knew I was new to town and all, but it wasn't as if I spent the time before that wandering in the wasteland like our two tour guides had.

The west wasn't something you went back to. It was hard enough scratching out a living on the safer side of the gate. The sentries didn't want to open it, looking around for someone to tell them to stop even as they started to pull the thick, heavy barrier wide. Some of their fellow sentries stood on the wall, making sure nothing was in view that could leap out and burst through the gate before they could react.

Once the gate was open wide enough for us to walk, well, we started walking. Ahead of us lay nothing. Sand, the occasional tree and low sitting bush, and the awful power of the sun. It seemed hotter on the other side of the gate, even though that was stupid to think. That was it. Not a Brainer in sight. No animals of any sort. Not even a bird in the sky. We could see nothing worth seeing, but we could see one hell of a lot of it.

The sound of the West Gate closing behind us caused a pit of fear to swell in my belly and I looked around. Otto nodded at me, letting me know that he shared my fear, but wouldn't let it stop him. I nodded back and adjusted my pack. Where we were now we were only gonna come back from one way. If we passed back through the gate into town it meant we were successful. If not, we were dead.

We walked on in silence, the punishing sun doing its level best to stop us. If we kept covered we wouldn't burn but keeping covered enough made most of us feel too hot to move. Damned either way, we would remind each other that the burns weren't going to be worth the temporary relief of removing any protective covering. The guarded friendship that seemed to blossom instantly made the walk a little easier at least. We were watching out for each other the best way we knew how then.

By the time the sun started to dip low in the sky we were well out of sight of town. The wall was behind us, we knew in our minds, but glancing back showed the same featureless expanse as looking forward did. It didn't exactly help our state of mind.

Of course whenever I'm sayin' "we" here, I refer to the four of us that came along with Cleaver and Bones. The two men themselves I wouldn't really wanna guess about. Their minds were their own, and though we traveled with them they weren't in the same space as we were. We were being led, they were leading. They said nothing, so we said not much of anything. They walked so we trudged behind. When Franklin held a hand up and stopped cold, we all froze in our tracks and tried not to look too worried.

"Eddie," Franklin asked, "do you see that?"

"Yeah, Frank," Edward answered, neither men looking at us, "what do you think?"

"I think we keep moving for a while longer, then set up camp." Franklin looked back at us. "That good for you guys, too?"

We nodded and shrugged and made other motions of acceptance and agreement. What could we do, say no? How would that have gone, I wonder? It didn't matter and so we pressed on.

Otto nudged me a few feet later and pointed out to where Franklin and Edward had been staring. I looked off the point of his hand and then slowly turned to look at the man himself.

"I don't see it either, Otto."

"No, I do see it," he told me in a whisper, "and I'll tell the others. It's something moving. You really can't see it?"

I shook my head and tried to look in that general direction

again. If I tried really hard I thought maybe I could see something moving towards us, but it could've been heat waves off the ground or any other damned thing for all I knew.

The sun set and the temperature started to drop. We marched on, regardless, for a while. Our feet hurt from walking all day, our backs shared the pain lugging the packs and our very skin crawled with sweat and grit. When Edward discussed something with Franklin, they were far enough ahead that I couldn't hear 'em. When they turned and gestured to us that we were stopping for the night Sally puffed a gust of relieved air from her cheeks.

"All right, drop the packs and let us get set for the night," Franklin said, "unroll the fence and get out the wood and wire and staples, will you?"

We did as asked, as quickly as we could, which wasn't half as fast as they wanted us to I'm sure. Everything got laid out of the ground in front of us. Edward and Franklin walked around the supplies, nodding. Travel and packing hadn't seemed to have damaged a thing.

"All right," Edward said, grabbing the fence and starting to wrestle it upright, "get this up." Sally and Billy moved to help him and together they strung the fence in a big circle around us. Franklin locked the fence in place and pocketed the keys in silence.

Then he took the two by fours and started to staple wire to them, weaving it in and out of the fence as he did. When he was done, and he asked for no help at all doing it, we were locked into a metal and wood barrier. The four by eights were laid down on the ground inside the circle, causing us to dance a bit as we tried to put boards under our feet.

It was getting cold by then and even with the gloves on I wanted to cram my hands into my pockets for warmth. After the bristling heat of the day the wasteland's night chill burrowed into my bones. In town, at least, there were fires, other people, buildings. Civilization that kept us all warmed, not only in body but spirit. Out here we had ourselves and it was too bad if that wasn't enough insulation.

Otto and Billy got the tents up, cramped though they were, and we huddled into them for a few. Our leaders stayed outside, watching the darkness. Without planning it, Billy, Otto, Sally and I all huddled in the tents facing the still open flaps, watching our watchers.

"Can we maybe light a fire?" Billy asked hopefully.

"What? Light the ground you sit on, now how does that sound good?" Otto asked in response before Franklin could say anything. Instead of speaking, Cleaver just nodded at Otto and went back to watching the land. Both of them slowly turned, taking in everything around us.

It fell silent. The silence of the waste, of death. In that silence I could hear something though, something muffled and out of place.

"What is that?" I asked no one in particular.

"Rabbit," Franklin said over his shoulder, but it didn't sound like no rabbit I had ever heard.

"Brainer rabbit," Edward corrected.

At that we scurried out of the tents at speed. Suddenly we were all standing around looking out into the darkness. Now, even I could see it. See it and hear it.

The Brainer rabbit was trying to hop with back legs that didn't work quite right any more. Moonlight cast irregular shadows on it as it came shuffling on. It would try to hop, back legs coiling and then extending, but the muscles weren't connected right anymore and each hop turned into a horrible shuffling limp that sent the rabbit's ass into the air and then back down a few inches further on.

One of its front paws was totally missing and the other didn't look like it was doing so well, so each hop also shoved its body forward, scraping the front of its body along the ground. Fur and flesh was sloughing off in strips and chunks. Still it came on. Otto let fly with a ragged panicked laugh. Sally cuffed him for it, shutting him up quickly.

"Should we shoot it, maybe?" Billy asked before I could.

"You are a smart one," Franklin said with his back to us, "neither one of us mentioned even having a gun, this whole time."

"Not that we would travel without one. It's like going for a trip without stopping to go to the bathroom first, isn't it? You should always know better than to do that, too," Edward added, turning to us with a shrug and smirk.

"But, to answer your question, no we should not shoot it. It's bad enough we're talking. Let's not make more loud noises than necessary."

We nodded and went back to watching the rabbit shove itself onward, ever closer to us. Yeah, it was just a rabbit. Not a very big one, even. But even a Brainer rabbit could kill us if we were stupid. We all knew that and none of us took its existence lightly.

"Hey, Frank?"

"Yeah, Eddie?"

"I did not think they were out this far, yet," Edward said, stoking his chin and reaching for a cigarette.

"It's just a rabbit," his partner pointed out. Franklin then gave Edward a warning look and Franklin put the match he had taken out back in his pocket, leaving the cigarette dangling from his lips unlit.

"I do realize that, Frank. I just mean where there is smoke there is also fire."

"We would have noticed them by now. Tomorrow." Both men just nodded at that, but blanched. They had to be talking about Brainers. That we would see them was the whole point of the trip, but the idea that there were Brainers not two days march out of town was sobering.

"The rabbit then?" Edward worked the cigarette in his mouth, rolling it from one corner to the other with his lips.

"Would you? Thanks." Franklin moved over and dug the keys out of his pocket, unlocking the padlocks until he could yank open enough of a gap in the fence for Edward to slip between.

Edward slid a knife out from under his poncho and crouched low, running straight for the rabbit. The rabbit saw him coming, or sensed him or something, and perked up, lifting its head sluggishly. It bared teeth and waited for the man to get close enough to kill.

Edward didn't change course of speed, heading right for the rabbit. His knife flashed in the moonlight and the sound of it burying into the rabbit's head was loud enough to feel like it was happening right next to us. He picked up the Brainer hare by the ear and worked his knife free from its skull. Then he flung it far away from us and walked back toward our camp, stopping to clean his knife on a low sitting bush.

"Smaller things are easy," Edward told us, "they can move fast but they also get hurt quicker, which slows them down considerably. Don't think a Brainer will be this easy. Hell, I wish they were. But they aren't, and don't forget it."

We let Edward back into the camp and then locked the fence again.

"They are not much of a threat, when you can stalk them like that," Edward said, "it's when you don't see them that you have to worry." Then he sat down and put his back against one of the tent's support poles and closed his eyes.

We went back into the tents, ourselves, and tried to force ourselves to sleep. It didn't work and when the sun rose we were, all four of us, already watching its first rays brush the land. I poked my head out of the tent and saw that Edward was up, watching the land, and Franklin was asleep where Edward had been.

I didn't say anything to him, I just watched the man in profile. Him and his partner were so different. They were both obviously in their fifties but Franklin looked like he was on the later side of them compared to Edward. Edward was a smaller man, built for speed and sureness, where his partner was made for strength. They fit each other perfectly and I wondered how they had met, originally.

In the spreading daylight I could see a splotch of black tar-like goo where the rabbit had been. I remembered as a little kid hunting rabbits with my father in the woods. They were fast creatures, but more scared of you then you could ever be of them. Hell, you had to rile one to get it to bite, most times. They weren't considered sporting fare, except for their speed. That thing out there last night hadn't been remotely close to what I would have called a rabbit.

If whatever happened to Brainers did that to a rabbit what had it done to men? We'd heard stories but I didn't know many who had seen 'em, and most of those wouldn't talk about it in detail. I wondered, yet again, what we were up against and what our chances were.

Breakfast was a solemn affair of dried meat and bread washed down with a few gulps of water. That shook me out of my revery. Brainer rabbits, Brainer men even, loomed in our near future, but running out of food or water would do us in just as fast. Whose side was the planet on, to give us such miserable hunting grounds. Maybe, just maybe, it was somehow as bad for them as it was for us. Maybe the Earth was an impartial third party to the life and death going on along its surface. Maybe.

We packed up the encampment and put it all back onto our shoulders. Otto nudged me as we started to walk and bent his head close to mine.

"Hey, man, if we have to take all these protections to keep alive out here at night, how the hell did those two do it by themselves without any gear? They didn't have any of this stuff when they came into town, I swear."

"You think it isn't needed, that they're trying to, what, scare us?"

"No, but then, how the fuck did they do it?"

"Ask them."

"No way, you do it."

We bantered like that for a few hours, taunting each other in quiet voices, trying to get the other to ask Franklin and Edward about their own survival skills. Neither of us did though. It'd be real easy, right now, to tell you that we didn't do it because we feared them, or because we felt the answer would make us look soft and incapable of the inhuman feats that Bones and Cleaver seemed to live and breathe.

It wouldn't be true though. No, we didn't ask because any answer had the potential to reduce our guides to being simply human again, and without the reassurance that we walked with people who were somehow far more than we could ever be I don't know if we would have gone on.

Around mid-afternoon we heard a low pitched keening sound. A banshee with laryngitis, maybe. Edward glanced back at us and grinned. Our pace sped up, which felt backwards to me. At the arrival of that sound I wanted to go faster—the other way.

"See, Frank, I told you he'd still be here."

"Well of course he's still here," Franklin said, "where else could he go?"

"Exactly my point."

"No," Franklin corrected his partner, "your point was that I had somehow doubted the idea. Which, for the record, I did not."

"Either way, he's still here, just like I said."

On the ground a twitching lump came into sight. The heat waves off the ground made it difficult to figure out what it was supposed to be that twitched, apparently left here by the men now returning to it.

As we got closer we could all make out what the shuddering heap was. A Brainer. It didn't look like Brainers were supposed to, not by anything I had ever heard. Sure, there was the gray skin and the cold black eyes that shone in the sunlight at a distance. The swollen tongue lolled around like I had heard and the howls and grunts matched up. This Brainer left the garden of the known at that point. He was curled into a fetal position and looked like old leather, cracked and dried. When he tried to move he simply twitched a bit, his skin too stiff and shrunken in to allow for the movement his brain fought for.

Franklin turned to us and nodded. "Yeah, Brainer. The sun doesn't treat them too well. Which is what we figured. We staked this one out last time as a marker, partly to prove a point. He can't grab you unless you get real close. So don't."

With that little speech our march resumed. We gave the Brainer a wide berth, probably wider than necessary, but why take chances with a thing like that? The going was slower after spotting their twisted marker. Off in the distance we could all see a dark shape slowly moving. Cleaver and Bones started to move around it, positioning us directly behind the column ahead.

"There they are," Edward said over his shoulder. "They don't move too fast, and slower still when they have captives, but there are at least three of them for each of us. I am reminded of Custer, except he wasn't on the move and the Brainers don't have arrows. Also, we'll win."

"That is the general idea, Eddie," Franklin said and then turned to face us, stopping our walk. "Here's the thing. The captives won't be much help to us. They'll want to be but they're weak and hungry by now. Which makes them a threat to themselves, really."

"So we should separate them and get them clear," Edward put in, "except that leaves us down a few men, doesn't it?"

"It does. So here's what we were thinking. If we can break their circle and round up the captives then…"

"But they can't run, so we'll be slow getting clear. Which gives the Brainers a good chance to surround us all."

"Which is why we brought the rest of that stuff," Franklin finished and unslung his pack.

The Brainer herding party got themselves a good sight farther from us as we hunkered down and got to work. Work was trying to dissolve the styrofoam in the alcohol and making it a good slush, before we filled some hollowed out avocados with it. Supposedly the rubber bands would hold the avocado together without too much slop.

While Otto, Sally and I made makeshift napalm avocado grenades, Billy helped Franklin and Edward mash some of the mint leaves. The paste of it was then handed around.

"Smear this under your arms and across the back of your necks," Edward told us as Billy passed the glop around, "then apply a handful to your heads."

"They hunt by scent," Franklin said with an evil grin, "their eyes are all right, but nothing special and the mix-up in scent will slow down their reactions."

"As will being on fire," Edward added with a childish smirk.

"One would think," Franklin Cleaver said and nodded.

"Also don't forget, the make-up will make a nice thing to

stripe and prevent glares from hitting your eyes some. Use it, but don't use it up, we may need some to help get away," Edward said as he got back to work.

When we finished up our chores and packed the resulting goodies carefully it was turning towards dusk. Edward and Franklin told us that we'd be on a fast march from then on in and started off. I carried the half avocados with Billy lugging the other half. We lagged a bit behind, trying to hurry without sloshing the stuff around and making the avocados nothing more than useless. The sheer amount of nervousness might have had something to do with it, too.

"We have to get close," Franklin said just loud enough to be heard, "and break their line before we set any fires. We don't want to risk them just tightening their circle while on fire. So first we distract them. Then we get folks clear. After that we douse them as we retreat."

"Then," Edward finished, "we come back for them and finish them off."

"Of course we do," Franklin said with a nod, "I figured that went without saying."

"I said it anyway."

"You always do, Eddie."

"Thanks, Frank."

"That wasn't a com—? You know what? Never mind. You're very welcome."

We drew ever closer, hunched down and moving as quietly as possible. The column ahead didn't seem to notice us, but we could see them clearer all the time. The Brainers seemed to all be riding horses. The horses moved all right, a bit of a lumber, but not slow for horses. That worried me.

"When we get there, Eddie and I will break the rear guard and them move up to start distracting the rest. I want you guys to circle the humans and get them free. We'll retreat as one unit and then go back for more." Franklin looked at us over his shoulder, "Remember, take out the head on the Brainers. And don't get bitten."

We nodded nervously and looked up at how close the

Brainers seemed to be. I realized that we were doin' the hunting here, they were our prey, but it sure felt like we were just a take-out meal waitin' to happen.

Cleaver and Bones didn't give us another sign, or impart anymore advice, they just moved. Suddenly they were ten feet ahead of the rest of us. Really, I guess them breakin' away and startin' towards the goal was a sign for us, so maybe they did give us one after all.

Whichever, we picked up our own pace and stayed as close behind as we could. Moving at that speed we closed with the Brainers in no time at all. We could see them clear as night now, the Brainers in long coats and wide brimmed hats, clearly dressing as they remembered they had when they were alive, or perhaps simply still in the clothes they died in. The sight truly made me wonder if maybe we hadn't picked the wrong group and these were just cowboys on an old style cattle drive.

The sounds they made washed that thought right out of my being, and quick like. It was the same keening and moaning we heard from the staked Brainer back a ways, except there were human moans added in along with an almost barking sound from the Brainers, a dry coughing expulsion of air that felt like someone trying to fake being able to talk. It was all so utterly not human that it sent chills along my spine and I tightened my grip on the straps of my pack until my fingers hurt from the pressure.

Still, we got nearer and nearer until we had fully closed with the herd.

Edward and Franklin were, of course, in front. They came up behind the rear Brainers and even as they were noticed both men drew knives and hamstrung the Brainer horses, sending them toppling. A quick thrust deep into the base of the skull and both horses stopped twitching.

Their riders, on the other hand, were already up and moving. Edward went in close with his knife, slicing and confusing the Brainer until it couldn't keep up. Then he went in for the kill, leaving his knife in the chest of the thing and pulling a gun. Franklin pulled a gun, too, seemingly out of nowhere. They fired a few seconds shy of together and the twin reports sounded like two sharp cracks of thunder pounding across the sky.

It might not have been the best move. All of the Brainers turned to see what was going on, as did the humans in the center of the circle. The gun shots caused too much confusion, on both sides. Not that it stopped Cleaver and Bones. With all the Brainers looking at them, they skirted the inside of the circle, trying to break the line.

We moved in, pushing past the downed Brainers and their horses to start grabbing the humans and tugging, cajoling and forcing them towards freedom. Otto noticed that one of the downed Brainer horses had a sword in a scabbard along the saddle. He grabbed it free and stuck it in his own belt—it was either a prize or hopeful advantage and I didn't know which he was going for.

The humans didn't want to come with us. Their minds seemed destroyed and I wondered if we would have to kill them just to help them. Flames whoomphed to sudden powerful life towards the front of the line and I knew that the mixture worked at the very least decently. Brainers howled and started to leave the humans alone, moving to rid themselves of their biggest distress.

Edward and Franklin shot a few times, and lit a bunch more fires, causing the Brainers to start to hang back. They pulled back and started to go around the fires. Their mounts were ditched as soon as they became a problem to ride.

The humans were panicked and unresponsive, having no idea what was going on. Their hands hadn't even been tied. They weren't being held by anything other than fear and exhaustion. Neither were things we could fix right off, but we hadda push 'em as hard as we could, regardless.

Two Brainers broke free and came at us from the right. Otto stabbed one in the head with that new sword of his and I chopped another in the side with my knife. I meant to aim higher but I was in a rush. Looking back I could see that the

Brainers couldn't locate us easily what with the brightness of the fire hurting their eyes and the mint distracting their sense of smell. Still, we weren't exactly quiet by then.

Time seemed to slow. The fires blazed and moved, Brainer horses and men shambling along the ground, casting hellish light on anything near by. The moaned and howled their pain and frustration to the heights of heaven. It was a sound that would stick with me, clawed into my brain for all time. The sound was animal, sub-animal even, but also oddly human. I hoped like hell there wasn't a live human in the mix, burning alive.

We pushed at the humans, moving around them as we did, screaming at them and growing desperate at their lack of focus. These were broken men and women and I wondered if they could even be brought back to even an approximation of sanity after what they had gone through. I doubted it, but that didn't mean they weren't worth saving.

Eventually, we had the humans moving, somehow I had moved to the back of the mass as we went, next to Billy. Sally and Otto had the front, leading us out. Edward and Franklin were still doing what they did best. Killing things, that is.

But just as suddenly as the sun breaking through a cloud they were right between Billy and I, helping us force the humans out to safety. A few of he Brainers were coming after us, on foot. I felt something sharp tear at my ankle, right through my boot, and cursed. I was sure I had been snake bit until Franklin started barking orders.

"Otto! I saw you grab that sword. Get it here fast," he bellowed. Otto was next to me quickly. I wasn't sure what was going on as time seemed to slide in and out of focus. I looked down, trying to see what kind of snake it was and saw a Brainer with blood on its mouth in a trail that led to my ankle.

I was dead, and I knew it. Franklin didn't seem to agree.

"It's a god damned infection. We have to stop it before it spreads," he said tightly, grabbing the sword Otto offered him.

"Frank, we haven't proven this," Edward started to say.

"Then we will now, Eddie."

I saw the blade rise and then it swam in my vision. The pain didn't swim though. No, it bit down hard and sharp. I blacked out as soon as I started to feel it though, so that was all right.

I woke up a bit later and looked around, confused. I was inside the chain link barrier, but it didn't seem to have been set up right, or at least fully. My leg hurt, the left one where I had been bit. It throbbed with pain, a harsh constant thing that felt almost alive in its intensity.

I looked down and saw that my left leg ended just above the knee.

"He's awake," I heard Sally say.

"Yeah," I managed, "what happened?"

"It looks like they saved you. You haven't turned," she said, mopping my brow with a cloth gently.

"My leg?"

"Small price to pay for living."

She was right. I had to thank Otto for being dumb enough to take the sword in the first place and Franklin for deciding to try his theory. It made me wonder though, if Brainer infections could be stopped that easily.

"Not always," Franklin said, kneeling down next to me and seeming to read my mind. "Sorry, I know what you're thinking, it's obvious. No, I just had to try it. The infection acts like an infection, even if we are not sure if it really is one. You were bitten low enough it was worth a try, but it spreads fast."

"Are we done, then?"

"Not quite. Eddie and I need to discourage anything from following us. There are still ten or so Brainers out there, coming after us. You guys are done. Get back to your town, with the guys we saved."

"See you soon, then?" I asked him. The pain broke down any reluctance I held towards talking to Franklin with my usual deference and respect. He was just another man to me now.

"Sure will," he said and nodded at someone I couldn't see,

"Otto, finish this and move them back towards town, we'll catch up."

Otto came into sight holding an avocado. He broke it open and poured some of the contents onto my stump. Oh lord the pain, the stinging wretched pain. I threw up and realized from the taste of my mouth it wasn't the first time I had vomited from pain.

"Otto?" I managed weakly.

"Sorry, man, we have to cauterize this. It's gonna hurt as bad as the amputation. But it's the only way."

"Sounds good," I interrupted, "just do it before I think about it."

He nodded at me and lit a match.

I woke up to the swaying motion of being carried. I turned my head to try and see what was going on, where we were, but the motion of my head combined with the gentle sway of whatever I was being carried on made me feel sick. I closed my eyes again and lost more time.

I didn't really come to until the West Gate was being opened for us. The cheering woke me up. We had done it, we were heroes. I couldn't figure out, at first, why Otto and Sally, who were both in my line of sight, looked so grim. Yeah it had been a slice of hell but it was done and we all made it. My left leg was a small enough price for that, Sally was right.

When we got into town and settled some I found myself in a small cabin with Sally Billy and Otto. That's when I noticed the problem and why they all looked so down, despite our victory. It wasn't quite a victory after all.

As for exactly what happened, well there were a few different stories on that. They all agreed that Cleaver and Bones went back out to kill the remaining Brainers. That much was certain as anything. Sally thought she heard Franklin scream in pain, but Billy was sure it was Edward. Otto said he didn't hear any screaming at all, just some gun fire. The gunfire was the other thing they agreed on.

Did Franklin die, or did Edward? Neither? Both? We didn't know. Otto and Sally wanted to turn back and help 'em but Billy had pointed out that the hostages were the more critical of the two groups just then. So they had gotten us all back to town. Sally demanded that the three of them go out and look for Franklin and Edward. Billy waffled on the point, sure they would come back of their own accord before too long. Otto just wasn't sure. Me? Well, shit, I wanted to go look for 'em. They had saved my life.

No, more than that they had given us a burst of hope that we all needed to survive. It was the start of things. The first Brainer raid, but not the last. How could we not go find them, or their bodies, and pay them the tribute they deserved?

Well, in the end the three of 'em went off on a recon to see what they could find while I sat watch on the gate for them. Those were the worst three days of my life, possibly. Just waiting, unable to do anything to help.

In the middle of the third day they came back, though. They found a lot of spent shells and dead Brainers and a lot of blood. It didn't tell us anything and they didn't see any sign of Franklin or Edward.

A month or so later when I had learned to use a crutch almost as well as I had used my leg, Sally and I went on another hunt for the two. No Brainer men in the area, just some rabbits and a possum. No live men either. Nothing. The west had reclaimed them as utterly as it did everything else.

Well you know what happened after that. Brainer hunts started to form up and Otto trained a lot of 'em. Sally and Billy became leads with him and they made a bunch of difference between 'em. I took over guarding the West Gate for a bunch of years, keeping my eyes peeled, every dammed day, for two men in dusty clothing sauntering up to the wall.

The desert was still bad enough on its own, but adding the Brainers and their mounts to the mix didn't seem quite as bas as before. We were still losing the fight but now we could see a way to hold it where it was if not turn it, eventually. Civilized areas started to slowly, very slowly, come back. The future

mister binkles and the highly adaptable future

WHEN THEY OPENED the crate, one bright November morning, they expected to find moldy books, some rotting plastic, and maybe some rusting metal. History Revival Team 17 had never expected more than that, and they often got what they expected. Opening boxes and old hidey holes to find treasures of times lost was like that.

It was the future. And in the future the hot thing was the past. The only thing hotter than the past, in the future, was the even more distant future. The now, in the future, was something that no one cared about.

Reynolds picked up the slightly worn plastic evidence bag with skeptical fingers. He turned the lumpy bag this way and that way and every which way he could. Keying his radio, he asked the rest of the team why someone would put a crusty teddy bear, matted fur and rusty spike-like claws jammed into its paws, in an archaic police evidence bag. They all laughed.

Mister Binkles didn't laugh. He was happy to have new friends at long last, and some light to see by. He was happy and content, happier than he had been in a long time. Since Timmy, in fact.

History Revival Team 17 swept up Mister Binkles with the rest of their artifacts and took their entire cache back to the laboratory. They processed and catalogued. They analyzed and prodded. They removed Mister Binkles' claws one by one, a soft furry poof of noise accompanying the extraction of each rusty bit of metal that extruded from his pliant matting. Strange machines cleaned and restored him, inch by inch, synthetic hair by synthetic hair, until he was as bright and soft and cuddly as he had been when first purchased, those many, many years long gone.

Reynolds, as team leader, claimed the bear as his own and took him home, presenting Mister Binkles to his son, Albert, as a birthday gift. Albert hugged and loved Mister Binkles, and Mister Binkles was so happy he thought his seams might burst. Even when Albert renamed him Flibbertyjibber, Mister Binkles forgave him. Wasn't it the right of his boy to rename him as needed? Mister Flibbertyjibber, who still thought of himself as Mister Binkles, purred to himself, as only teddy bears can, and slept each night in the arms of his new boy. Hot drool cooled on Mister Binkles' (he couldn't forget the name) cheek and all was right with the world.

Albert grew up, as boys will do, and loved his bear, as boys should do. He gained access to Glob-i, the Global Internet connection that was wired into every house on the planet and some that weren't even houses, and would sit at his pokeboard for hours and hours with his bear by his side, finding out all sorts of useful information.

Information that he related to Mister Flibbertyjibber, who still thought of himself as Mister Binkles.

One night, while Albert slept peacefully, Mister Binkles made his way slowly given the size of his legs to the Glob-i connection because curiosity had gotten the better of him during the long hours when his boy slept. He looked at the connection and rubbed at his little jaw with one fluffy paw, considering. Then shaking his head he went back to bed, curling up under Albert's chin faithfully.

Every night though, he found himself drawn back to the place where Albert spent so much time. He studied and then wondered and wondered. One night, Mister Binkles started to work on the construction of what he knew, from all he had seen, would be a very important device, a tiny wireless transmitter. It wasn't easy, what with no fingers or thumbs, only blunt furry paws to work with, but Mister Binkles persevered. He was a very diligent bear when he wanted to be, after all.

Before long, Mister Binkles was able to connect himself to Glob-i, which is when he discovered that his essence, his very Binkle-ness was not contained and constrained only by the balled fluff inside his round little head. Within the extremely large confines of Glob-i, Mister Binkles was as real as he knew he was, and realer than anyone else might have thought. Though still far from all-powerful, he had fingers and thumbs and a voice—all powerful enough for his needs.

At first he simply explored. He wandered and made new, secret friends. Mister Binkles never told them who or what he was, but no one asked. It was fun, he realized, to interact with others besides his boy. He made connections and gathered information. The world, he realized, was much, much bigger than he had thought.

Which, in a sense, explains what happened to Joey Ford. Joey Ford made it a habit of being a bully. There was pushing and shoving, lunch credits and sneakers stolen—Joey was something of a young professional. Certainly, Mister Binkles didn't care one whit about Joey and his quickly developing thug attitude, in fact on one level Mister Binkles would have respected Joey's aptitude and ability to learn new concepts.

Joey only became a problem when he knocked Albert down at school. Albert spent that night crying, holding Mister Binkles to his chest and whispering all about how much he hated Joey. Albert's new black eye shone with bruised brilliance in the soft moonlight that filtered into the room and Mister Binkles decided to do something about it.

Late that night, after Albert had faded off into dreams, Binkles activated his Glob-i connection and made some newer connections. He traveled along the darker corners of the Global Internet, the area nicknamed the Glob-I Desert where things that good little boys shouldn't do happened with regular clockwork ticks like the beats of a boy's heart.

It was two days later that Homeland Security took Joey out. They knew him to be a cunning and frighteningly skilled bioterrorist, posing as a schoolboy. Joey cried and protested his innocence, reaching for his Identcard, one grubby hand jamming deep into a pants pocket. Twenty-seven officers opened fire with steel jacketed rounds as he did so. Joey's arm was torn off, followed by his head and leg. His torso was reduced to something resembling the cafeteria's meatloaf and his intestines snaked across the playground, dancing in the hail of bullets like sausage on a skillet.

Reynolds suspected something was wrong later that week. He received an e-mail from MrB@aboysheart.com that asked him to keep closer watch over Albert. That disturbed him on some level. It didn't seem to be spam, or even close, but he knew of no MrB and the domain had no webpage or information for him to discover. That in and of itself would not have done too much to worry him, but the increased Glob-i usage when everyone was asleep set off warning bells in his head.

He didn't have much time to consider it when History Revival Team 17 got called up to investigate a new find in Iceland. He packed his bags and arranged to have Mister Jin, their upstairs neighbor, care for Albert. Albert, for his part, was excited. He loved his daddy's work and was always both pleased that his daddy was going off to do important things and only minorly disappointed that he would have to do without him for a while.

Reynolds was a good man and a good father. He cared for Albert and did good work, sustaining a career easily. He missed Albert's mother, Charise, but she had died in childbirth and Reynolds never found another woman to share his heart with. Mister Binkles wasn't really sure though. Fathers have a tendency to go bad, like milk, reasoned Mister Binkles. They made their boys grow up into hard men, and hard men left Mister Binkles alone and lonely. If only, he thought, he could keep Albert to himself, then Albert could remain his boy forever.

It was a bright and windy Saturday morning when Binkles made his move. Capturing the tools was easy now, for he had learned the darker pathways of the Glob-I Desert like the back of his paw, and he sent the right people the right bribes and as he sat in Albert's lap, watching cartoons. Mister Binkles had learned to multitask.

A command here, an offer of goods there, and soon everything was in place, including Reynolds. The bomb went off quickly and without error. The light blinded anyone unfortunate to have looked at it. The combination electromagnetic pulse and dual shockwaves flattened, rendering useless or otherwise disabling recording devices for miles. To say nothing of the people. Let us, in fact, say almost nothing of the people, whose bodies were reduced to carbon to blow in a soft Icelandic breeze under a beautiful sunset. Iceland, as a country, ceased to exist in the space of thirty-five seconds. Reynolds himself only took .01 seconds to vanish in a puff of smoke, reduced to nothing by an old Russian nuclear warhead.

Albert cried and cried that night. He felt so crushingly alone and grasped Mister Binkles tighter than he ever had before, making the fluffy old bear's heart soar with love. When Albert connected to Glob-i the next day he found e-mail from MrB@aboysheart.com that told him not to worry. Albert was too smart to reply to strangers that seemed to know too much though, so he deleted it.

More e-mail came. Endless streams of it. Albert couldn't ignore it all and eventually he realized who was sending it. Holding the bear up to his face, he smiled warily, and asked, "You're alive, Mister Flibbertyjibber? Why do you call yourself Mister Binkles though?"

New e-mail came through and explained more to Albert, who sucked all the information down thirstily. Slowly he learned and would sit on the floor, asking Mister Binkles, his rightful name restored, questions whose answers would appear in email seconds later.

Albert didn't tell anyone about the communication he carried on with his bear, and Mister Binkles never let on to his friends on Glob-i that he had a boy to love and hold him at night. An easy, happy pact was formed between them. Friends called Albert lucky as he grew up, all of his problems vanishing in all sorts of random ways that seemed almost impossible.

He held down a good job, had a good life and eventually a wife and son.

On his son's third birthday, Albert put Mister Binkles into the crib late at night. Mister Binkles had agreed that though the connection between himself and Albert wouldn't be severed, Mister Binkles also could help raise his son, who he and Mister Binkles had agreed to name Timmy.

And life continued to bloom and grow and spread. Each day was greeted with the warm drool of a boy on his fur, and each night was ended with another deal brokered on Albert's behalf. Mister Binkles had love in his stuffing and everything was right from then on.

Mostly.

flesh wounds

THE FIRST TIME I died I was alone—except for my killer, of course. The sidewalk was slick with recent rain that made pools of reflected light along the gutters. Reflections of houses shone up at me, and I watched them as I trundled back home. It was late, two or so in the morning, and I knew I wasn't allowed out that late, no one was anymore since the problems began. I was seventeen, a stupid kid coming home late from a party. Half drunk, I left Tom's house to the protests of the other friends gathered there to help send him off to the Army. His last night of freedom, my last night of life. Interesting how that worked out.

It wasn't interesting how it worked out. There was no deeper meaning to it, but sometimes it can be comforting to try and assign one. Regardless, my feet landed one in front of the other with almost no side to side deviation and I could feel the buzz of the night's drinking wearing off slowly. Three, maybe four, blocks away my family slept soundly, sure I was safe at Tom's place for the night.

Scraping and rustling snuck up behind me and I spun around, hoping it was Captain Jingles, one of the neighborhood cats that refused to actually live in anyone's home. I spun around and saw that I was face to face with one of them. The undead, a shambler, a zombie just looking at me the way a dog looks at a tasty crunchy bone. It wasn't a look I had ever had turned on me before, a look that simply told me I was lunch. I ran.

I took off as fast as I could manage, shouting all the way. I screamed for the cops, screamed warnings that there was a zombie near by, the whole nine yards. I even tossed in a tenth yard for good measure, but by the time anyone could react, could get themselves out of their homes to see what was going on, I had been taken down.

You have to understand, the things are faster than you might consider. They shamble along slow most of the time, true, but they can sprint when catching prey. It was discussed on the news from time to time, mostly after something like this happened. After they had downed a victim. After they had downed a particularly stupid young punk of a victim who probably deserved it.

Rotting teeth found purchase against my skin, pushing in and trying to scrape my neck clean off. I swung out, my fist hitting its head with a wet thump, this wasn't exactly a fresh specimen, and the flesh eater backed off a bit. He didn't back off enough though, as he latched onto my arm instead. His teeth sank into my forearm as his head tore slaveringly from side to side, worrying off a hunk of my flesh. I screamed at the sight and sensation but managed to stay conscious. I threw up when he ate my thumb, splashing the contents of my stomach across the sidewalk. The thing chewed at the severed bone quickly, sickening crunching and splintering sounds filling the night. My blood swam out of my body, looking for a new home among tar and concrete.

His hands scrambled up my body, dirty fingers digging rents in my skin through my clothing with their ragged nails. He climbed my body like it was a rock face and my consciousness swam in and out of focus. I was helpless, lying there in shock and slipping from the world, as his teeth found my neck again. A blood slick tongue probed at me, finding an artery and his teeth tore at me again. The world went black. I died.

I died. No long tunnel with a blinding white light at the end, no choir of angels, just blackness and nothing. My soul fled my body, escaping the prison of meat and soaring upwards into the endless night. Up and up it flew, streaming towards stars, until it snapped backwards, colliding with my body like a high-speed chase ending in a twenty car pile-up.

Then there was light.

Heaven?

A final reward after all?

I opened my eyes to intense halogen lamps shining down on me. I felt a sheet over my body, but found I couldn't guess the temperature of the room. With a realization like a slap in the face, I realized I had come back. Revived the worst way possible; not some last second save by the police, rushed to a hospital where my wounds were cleaned and treated, restoring me to health slowly while my family chewed their nails to the nub nearby waiting for word that I had pulled through. I had come back as one of them.

I looked around and realized where I was, in the zombie wing of Memorial General, police and doctors spaced around me, waiting for me to come back exactly like this. I knew the procedure, having heard about it on the news before. Once I woke up and proved that I would indeed come back as the undead, I would be put down. It was, they claimed, the only way to be sure. I was nothing more than the latest in a string of zombie infections across the country and, as such, was afforded no special treatment.

The world slid down to a calm level after the first zombie infections of a decade past. At first no one knew what to make of it. The dead rising again? Biblical signs of the end times? There was chaos and mass panic. I remembered it dimly happening all around me, but I was only a kid, ya know? There had been three wars within the first two years of discovery as governments blamed each other for the invention and spread of what turned out to be a very strange disease.

The wars had died down after time, and the world learned to adjust, as it always does. Zombies were hunted, international curfews were in place, and everyone had an agenda of extermination. It made sense, no one wanted the world taken over by zombies. I certainly supported the notion of total extermination, until I became one of them that is. Once I found myself in the communal boat I realized that it was really in need of a good outdoor motor. I needed to live... well... un-live, that is.

The cops waved the doctors back a safe distance.

"Listen kid, we need you to just lie still, ok?" one of them told me. As. Fucking. If.

"Hey, you don't need to kill me, all right?" I told the cop closest to me, "I won't eat anyone, I promise!"

The cop shook his head almost sadly and drew his service revolver. The light glinted off the metal along the barrel of the weapon as it sliced through the air until it pointed directly at my head. I caught another flash of light on metal and saw a second cop had also leveled a gun at me. I did the only thing I could think of, I made a break for it.

I took a bullet in the shoulder as I hopped off the table, the wound stung a bit and messed up my arm some, but otherwise it didn't slow me down. I slammed into a doctor, muttering "Excuse me" as I bolted past him into the hallway.

People in the halls screamed and a few brave folks even tried to tackle me, as the police came screaming up behind me. I hoped they wouldn't try to fire their weapons in a crowded hallway, but even half sure that they wouldn't I could feel an itching in the back of my head, the imagined final bullet. I tried to run faster. I hit the front doors of the hospital hard enough to go through them, glass showering down along me and the street. Shards of plate glass bounced off the sidewalk, but I wasn't so lucky - ribbons of flesh coming off me as I kept running from long slices of glass firmly embedded in my body. I knew what this meant.

Back when zombies had first started to become understood it was realized that while they were technically the un-dead and did feast on the flesh and blood of the living, they couldn't really help themselves. The disease that brought people back from the very brink of death also made them dependant on certain protein chains inside human DNA. Some other animals would do, mostly mammals, but human DNA and bone marrow and the like was the best thing for them. The stuff let zombies regrow some lost tissue and kept their brains going in ways that weren't yet fully understood. The more they... we... I... got hurt the more flesh and bone and blood I would need to keep going. The longer I went without it, the more I would decay, the faster my brain would rot in my skull turning me into a drooling idiot who shambled around with his arms out muttering "braaaaiiiinnnnnssss."

I was feeling hungry.

Well known fact: a lot of zombies still escaped before being "put down," and when they did escape the cops they ran for woods or alleys, somewhere people couldn't find them easily and they tried to pass for the homeless or infirm as much as possible. So I went home. I snuck up on the house, the same way the zombie had snuck up on me. I cased the two-story structure: no cops nearby, neighbors inside, all probably fearful that another zombie was in the neighborhood, as if another of the undead would be lurking—

Oh, right. I *was* lurking.

I fished in my pocket for my keys, having trouble getting them free while missing a thumb. The front door was in front of me, all wood and glass like it always had been growing up. For the first time the situation sank in and I grew afraid. They would reject me, turn me away right then and there. Worse yet, my father would call the cops and have me "dealt with." If blood still fully pumped in my veins it would have run cold. I stopped my hand from shaking and put the key in the lock as quietly as possible. It turned in the lock with a sudden click that I had never noticed as being quite that loud before. Door handle turned, I edged the door open slowly and slid inside into the front hallway.

As I closed the door behind me again, the darkened living room right off the hallway suddenly grew full of light. Mom, dad, my sister Caroline, and even her Chihuahua Sparky all stood there staring at me. Caroline started to move forward but dad grabbed her by the shoulder and held her back.

"Shawn? Is that you?" my mother asked, her voice shaking with fear.

"Yeah, mom, of course it's me."

"That isn't Shawn," my father insisted, face growing red with anger, "it's some undead freak!"

"Dad! I am Shawn!" I held my hands out in front of me, palm forward to show peace and then quickly pulled them back to my sides as Caroline screamed at the sight of my missing thumb, "I just had an accident."

"An accident?" my father's face was something close to beet colored, "You got attacked by a zombie and you're an undead flesh eater now!"

"But I'm also still your son. We can work with this."

"Carl," my mother interjected, putting a hand on my dad's shoulder to try and calm him, "Shawn is our son, we can't just turn him away at the door like a... like a..."

"Undead flesh eating monster, mom?" Caroline offered oh so helpfully. My mother shot her a look designed to wither humans.

"...Like a stranger," she finished, serving Caroline up with another helping of wither-glare.

"Yeah, see Dad, it's still me. I'm your son, okay? I just need to..." I tried to find a good way of phrasing it but found none, "hide out from the law so I don't get killed... again... you know?" My father scowled and stalked out of the room. My mother turned to follow him, casting a long look at me as she did.

"No, Mom, it's okay. I know where my room is." She sighed and left, Caroline in tow. Only Sparky remained behind to guard me, growling loudly now that we were alone. That dog had always hated me. Sparky took a hesitant step forward. I was so hungry.

I woke up to loud banging noises coming from the front of my room. I stretched out in my bed, home and safe felt really good, and rolled over trying to ignore it.

"Shawn! Open this door now!" Caroline yelled out. Sighing

I got out of bed and pulled the door open. Caroline stood there holding Sparky's leash in her hand. Uh-oh.

"Hey, Car, what's up?"

"What's up?" she asked, shaking the leash. "You ate my dog!"

"Well, I didn't really have a choice."

"You did eat Sparky! Oh my God!"

"No, listen to me Car: yes, I ate your dog, but I needed to or I would've died, ok? It was him or me."

"You ate my dog, you undead freak!"

"Hey! Watch the slander. I hear the acceptable term is 'corporeally challenged' now. No need to be rude."

"Rude? *You! Ate! My! Dog!*"

"But I had to, you see…"

"Undead freak!"

"Stop that."

"Brain eater!"

"Bigot!" I yelled at her and slammed the door. I had to think fast, all right, eating the dog was a mistake but I really didn't have a good alternative: Caroline would've fought back harder. Once she told Mom and Dad I knew someone would call the cops. I had to get out fast. I opened the window next to my bed and went back to shove a bunch of clothes in the duffel bag I used to use for gym class. Heading back to the window, I also grabbed a few books and shoved them in next to the clothes. Then I lowered myself out of the window and down the drainpipe to the ground.

I snuck off into the trees by the house and tried to lose myself. I had to get out of town: that much was obvious. The problem was how. I couldn't exactly take a bus or train in my condition, and not many people stopped to pick up undead hitchhikers. We were in upstate New York, I could try and get down to New York City maybe, it was only a three-hour drive. I stopped, leaning against a tree and did some math. A three-hour drive at sixty miles per hour worked out to roughly a hundred and eighty miles. Not too far, unless I had to walk the whole way and it was looking like I would have to.

I walked through the woods towards the highway, unsure

of how I was going to manage to get to the City, or even if it was a good idea. The woods were full of chirping birds and the rustling of squirrels and mice. Leaves coated the ground and I inhaled a big draught of fresh air, letting it fill my nostrils. I wandered through the woods, trying to forget my problems and let my subconscious mind work out a solution by itself.

Luckily, a solution presented itself in the form of a car. I could see the small lake that sat near the edge of the woods, a car parked nearby and some people from my school splashing around in the water. The car was an old Dodge, a big iron machine coated with mint green paint, sitting there unloved. I would love it.

I opened the door to the car as quietly as I could, hoping that the folks down in the lake wouldn't notice me. As I sat in the car, undisturbed, I had second thoughts. Was I really about to steal a car? Not even a week as an undead monster and already I was committing Grand Theft Auto? I felt slightly sick to my stomach at the thought, until I remembered that just last night I had eaten my sister's dog. Things clicked into perspective; at least the car was insured and could be found later, and I turned the keys that had been mindlessly left in the ignition. At the sound of the engine starting up, the kids in the lake looked over and started yelling. I threw the car into reverse and peeled out, tires squealing in my wake. I drove through the woods dangerously, not quite following the normal path out, and hit a road with a hard bump of the shocks. The highway was only a few turns in front of me. I got on an entrance ramp and sped off towards the City.

The drive was uneventful for the most part. Stopping at tollbooths was interesting though, handing money to booth clerks and trying to make the transaction happen as fast as possible before they got more than a passing look at me. I was nervous the entire way downstate.

I reached the city and headed downtown, to Greenwich Village where I had come once before with an old girlfriend. I

left the car on some small side street and just walked off keeping my head low. Sights and sounds assailed my senses,
throngs of people on the streets, all passing me by without so
much as a glance. I had become invisible in a sea of humanity.
Humanity that I was no longer really a part of. When night fell
across the city, the number of people seemed to just increase
by magic. I had been on my feet all day and was feeling a mite
peckish as well as exhausted. Sliding into an alley, I sat down
to wait and consider my new options. A few slow-moving
pigeons became dinner and as I sat and crunched my way past
bone, spitting out feathers unhappily, I saw another body wander down my alley hideout. She was walking almost
drunkenly, head hung low and looking depressed. I was determined to not eat her, no matter how much my mouth watered
at the sight of someone unprotected and virtually alone.

The stranger walked right up to me and said hello. I sat
where I was and fought back instinct. She knelt down until our
eyes were level, which is when I noticed she had no nose.

"New in town, huh?" she asked me, her voice full of friend-
ly welcome.

"Uhm, I, that is…" The words were in my head: Yes I have
just recently gotten to town and if you don't leave, lack of nose
or not, I might have to eat your head but they wouldn't come
out of my mouth.

"Don't worry, sniff deep, I'm undead too." She smiled, and
I could see that dried blood crusted some of her teeth. I
breathed a sigh of relief. "See, you don't want to eat another of
your kind, we aren't very nutritious." I nodded at her and held
out my hand.

"Shawn Jacobs. Pleased to meet you… Miss…" She took my
offered hand and shook it, not caring about the missing thumb
any more than I found I really cared about her lack of nose.

"Irene Cummings. No Miss though, okay?"

"All right. So uhm, aren't we…"

"Hunted? Feared? Abominations in the face of God and
man?"

"Well, yeah."

"Sure, but look around, who notices here?" She had a point, no one had given me a second look all day. "Look, want to come hang out with the others?"

"There are others?"

"New York has the largest undead population of any city outside of L.A."

"Really?"

"Sure, it isn't easy to hide in small towns." I groaned at that, memories of how my sister had looked at me before I had run, of how my father had seen me when I had first come home flooding my mind.

"You got that right. Sure." I stood up with her and she led me off to Washington Square Park.

"We have an old underground system beneath the park," she said as I followed her into the public men's bathroom in the park, "the city doesn't even realize it's there." Inside the bathroom she pulled out a key and opened an old dirt-encrusted janitor's door.

A single dim bulb hung from the ceiling giving us almost no light to see by. Irene didn't seem to need it as she walked purposefully across the room, stopped only to glance back at me as I tripped over a mop bucket, and unlocked a second door. A stairway loomed on the other side, dim lighting set at even intervals downwards. I hesitated as she slid into the dimness.

"What are you afraid of? I'll kill you? It happens to be a little late for that, I should think." She was right and I hurried down the stairs after her, following her billowing black curls that reflected the dank light.

There was a huge room at the bottom of the stairs, filled with zombies just sitting around on old chairs or crates, talking and reading and listening to the radio. The light was brighter down here, and the place looked like a little dinner parlor. Irene turned and smiled at me, the skin around the hole where her nose had been creasing around the old wound almost cutely.

"Home sweet home," she told me, her arms waving with a flourish. Some of the zombies looked up and waved or nodded at us before going back to what they were doing.

"How long have you guys been here?" I asked, incredulous.

"I've only been here two years, but old Bingo, he's the guy in the purple chair over there in the corner," she pointed and sure enough there was an old guy in the corner doing what looked like a crossword puzzle, "has been here since the beginning, about four years ago."

"Wait—four years? And no one has noticed?" I shook my head, it wasn't possible.

"Of course not. We stay away and keep to ourselves and the City forgets we're here mostly. Those that still worry, and yeah there are a lot of those, have no real clue where we are. We're careful."

"What about..."

"Food? Pigeons, stray animals, the occasional almost dead homeless people...we're scavengers." There was no shame in her expression as she said it, which made me embarrassed that I had been ashamed of what I was now myself.

"What do you do for living? Just hide out here?" I didn't look forward to the prospect of spending the rest of my unnatural life in an underground room.

"During the day we can shamble around in the city, if we're careful. Some of us even have jobs," she said proudly, "but that doesn't happen too often." I was shocked, to say the least.

"Jobs doing what?"

"Oh you know, odds and ends. Jerome over there"—she pointed off towards a black zombie reading a magazine—"gets some occasional work as a stunt man. The producers don't care, they can ignore a lot of safety rules using undead stunt-men."

"But doesn't he, you know, lose a lot of flesh that way?"

"So long as he can get it back and eat quick enough he can reattach it mostly. It pays and his money helps fund this place, buying magazines and more furniture and new light bulbs." I nodded, mystified. Irene walked me over to meet some of the other zombies and after a while we sat down and traded life stories. A lot of them were like mine, folks that had been taken by surprise or done something stupid to end up undead and then decided that they didn't want to be put down like animals after all.

"Most of us who try, don't make it," said Tom, a young Asian zombie with only one arm, "but we gotta try, you know?"

I did know.

Hours later, after a fine snack of squirrel, Irene led me to a rectangle of blankets on the floor. She told me how many steps away and in what direction the stairs to get out where, just in case something happened in the middle of the night, and left me to bunk down. The lights were switched off in most of the room, leaving us in darkness. Next to me a slim woman called Katarin muttered in her sleep the rest of the night keeping me half awake.

The next morning I decided I needed to get out for a while and Irene came with me. We wandered upstairs and carefully checked out the public bathroom before coming out of the janitor closet. Finding it empty, as it usually was she told me, we exited and wandered around the park. Over near some old fountain that no longer spat water fitfully a woman was performing some kind of show, people gathered in a large circle around her.

"Come see Miss Mysteriosity perform her daring feats of blinding brilliance!" she proclaimed to the crowd that was already gathered to see her. Hopping off the milk crate she stood on, Miss Mysteriosity lit a bowling pin on fire and lit some paper with it. Once she had proven it was real fire coming off the club she proceeded to pass it under her arm, wincing a little as she did. Club passed by her flesh, she raised both arms to the sky and let out a loud "Taa-Daa!" The crowd responded with a smattering of clapping and a few people wandered away. Next she did some card tricks and a rope trick.

The card tricks went ok and garnered her more applause but the rope trick fell apart and more people left. She ran through some more tricks, working at about a sixty percent success rate and then passed a hat around what was left of the crowd. A few people put coins in the hat and then everyone slowly wandered away back to their lives. Miss Mysteriosity sat on her milk crate, sifting through the change, her head hung in defeat.

I pulled away from Irene and went up to Miss Mysteriosity myself, her head snapping up as I drew close.

"Nice act," I told her lamely.

"No, I fucked up a lot, as always."

"No, no...it wasn't that bad," I insisted, staring at her dull blue eyes. "Really."

"You're sweet to say that." Her eyes caught my hand, stupidly left out of a pocket and she gasped, "You—you're—"

"Undead," finished Irene as she came up behind me. Miss Mysteriosity blanched, gathering her things quickly.

"Just stay away from me, okay?!" she yelped, "I know my show sucked but that isn't cause to just eat someone!"

"Hey, now," I told her, taking a step back, "no one is eating anyone, all right?"

"Well, probably," Irene said and I thumped her on the shoulder to shut her up.

"No really, don't listen to her," I said, extending my hand, "I'm Shawn."

"Miss Mysteriosity, but you knew that," she told me, ignoring my offered hand and still packing up her things with due haste.

"Look, you just need some more work and your show," I said with a smile that was only partly false, "could be a hit."

"Maybe," she grudgingly admitted, packing away her clubs and cards.

"What you need," I told her, an idea springing to my mind, "is a willing assistant."

"Someone who can work for nickels and get burned a lot," she said shaking her head at me, "yeah, that'll happen."

"I'll be your assistant," I told her happily, "I don't care if you burn me or cut me a bit, you know?" Her eyes found mine and the look of fear they held was slowly replaced by one of curiosity.

"You're serious?"

"Why not? I don't have anything else to do, and it could be fun."

"Shawn, it's a little too" Irene butted in, jabbing me in the back with her fist, "public. Don't you think?"

"People will be so busy watching the act, they'll assume I'm made up to look like a zombie to fool them even more. It would be great!" Miss Mysteriosity had caught on to the idea too, smiling now and reaching out for my hand. I shook it and to her credit she only turned a bit paler when the lump of my ruined thumb joint brushed her palm.

We spent the next few weeks meeting at her apartment in Queens late at night and practicing tricks. She set my arm on fire, which stung like hell, and then had me douse it in a bucket of water that steamed dramatically when I put myself out. Later we tried cutting me in half, and I was patient until she learned to do it without actually cutting me in half. The first few times she tried it we had to go grab a bird from the cage I made her keep so I could piece myself back together again.

Irene wasn't too happy with the situation, grousing whenever I came back to the park and spending days not talking to me, but she started to come around to the idea too, after a while. Miss Mysteriosity (whose real name was Sasha I found but she hated it so I just started calling her Myst in private) picked up her tricks a lot faster once she didn't have to worry about hurting anyone. I felt like I had found a way to cope with my new un-life after all and all too soon came the day of our big first show.

It was a clear sunny day and the crowds were pretty good. Myst went into her opening spiel and lit her club. I held my arm out, I was known as the Great Deadgimi to the crowd, and she lit me on fire. There were gasps and cries of shock as I stood there lighting things with my arm, pieces of wood and paper mostly. I dunked it in the prepared bucket and let out a sigh of relief as the stream hissed upwards. The cheers were loud and prolonged.

The box of swords trick went off mostly without a hitch too, and I kept quiet when one went through my side cleanly, so that the crowd had no idea anything had slipped up. I wore gloves, the thumb of my right glove stuffed with cotton so it looked like I still owned that digit; if anyone noticed it never moved, they didn't comment on it.

While Myst did her card tricks, a bit of a pacing problem that we had to change having them come after the bigger numbers, I circled the crowd with the hat collecting money. I shambled around stiffly and whispered "Bbbbrrrrraaaaaaiii- nnnnnsss" to the crowd as I passed, getting little cries of laughter and surprise, along with bills shoved into the hat. We made a hundred bucks that first show, a pure hit.

By the second week we performed, the crowds were big- ger, word had spread. Our tricks had gotten more extravagant too with a new finale tacked on before I passed the hat where Myst would run me through with a sword right before the crowd's eyes. We warned them the effect was not for the faint and intoned great deep magic was involved. The sword passed clean through my liver and hurt every time, but doing it almost guaranteed us another fifty bucks of take for the show, so I put up with it.

I'm still there, doing the show Mondays, Wednesdays, Thursdays and Saturdays, like clockwork. I moved out of the park and me and Irene got a small place in Brooklyn where no one knew us or bothered us, paid for by my work and Irene's new job in construction.

We eat out on the town every night, but really—what other option do we have?

dead side story

"ROMERO! ROMERO! WHERE the hell are you, Romero?"

Julia ran as fast as she could. Her boots slapped against the pavement, and she willed herself to move even faster. She wore the all-black outfit that had become her normal hunting clothes: combat boots, black jeans with matte, spray-painted shin and knee guards strapped on and a black turtle neck over a light Kevlar vest. Every inch of protection, she knew, wasn't protection enough. Somewhere along the line you had to trade speed and maneuverability for strength and she made her choices carefully.

Unlike, she reflected, her choice to shout just seconds before. Her panic, her fear, and her frustration had led her to make a move that could draw everything to a close much, much, sooner than anyone was ready for. Still, she hoped she was wrong and kept running.

On either side of her she could hear moans and shuffling feet as she passed by buildings and alleyways. Julia fought down all the doubts that threatened to rise up against her and made herself believe, truly and firmly believe, that Romero would be where they had agreed to meet. Of course he would be. Why wouldn't he be. No one else knew where he was, except his... friends, and they wouldn't blab to anyone. Certainly the Clean Sweep team had no idea about it and Julia was, she thought with a grin, their scout.

The building loomed before her suddenly, windows broken

and brick starting to crumble. Julia came to a stop at the front door, her heart thudding in her chest. She peeked into the lobby of the once-posh Upper West Side, New York apartment and found it clear. She pushed the door open, its lock long since busted off and leaving a dismal empty hole where it once proudly kept people at bay. Julia ran for the stairs at the back of the lobby, taking them two at a time. She hated that she still felt the need to run, but gave into it regardless.

She opened the door to the third floor slowly, and then made herself walk at something approaching a normal stroll down the hallway to apartment 3F. Her hand touched the knob gently, the knob she had reinstalled herself so that the door would latch properly again, and turned it. The door opened and her hand pushed, forcing it to swing wide. One foot over the threshold, then the other. Julia started to close the door slowly, breathing a sigh of relief. She was there. She was in. She was, at last, safe.

A hand, made of slowly rotting flesh and broken nails, closed tightly on her shoulder from behind the door as it closed. The hand threatened to root her to the spot, paralyzed in abrupt fear. She fought it and kicked the door fully closed behind her with a bang and rattle. Turning, she faced the undead thing that held her: prepared to die, to fight, to live.

Instead she fell against the corpse of a man that still walked and, muffled against his chest, released the urgency that had almost made her attack.

"Romero! Oh, gods above I was so worried, so... stupidly... I'm sorry. I know you wouldn't have hurt... it's just all the training, really. Oh, love, I'm sorry!"

Romero grunted, trying to shrug but managing only a slight jitter and shake. The two moved over to the couch and sat. Romero looked at Julia and held her hand and stared into her eyes.

"You have to run, honey," Julia told Romero, matching his gaze with her own, "I can't lose you. Not after... I just can't."

Romero moaned deeply and patted Julia's hand. He was hungry, damned hungry, and the scent of her filled him to bursting. Her eyes held him captive, though, and he was content to sit and be near her. He wouldn't eat her, he knew that. As deeply as he knew the hunger he also knew that he couldn't bring himself to give into it around her. She meant too much to him.

He nodded at her and did his best to shrug again.

"How long?" she replied, deciphering meaning from his crude actions, "I'm not sure, just not very. You have to get out of here. Take Merc and Monty with you, I don't want them getting hurt, either. Anymore than I want my family... oh Romero, what can we do?"

Romero gave Julia's hand a firm squeeze and stamped one foot gently on the ground.

"Yes, we will be brave, love. We will. Something will work itself out. I..." Julia stood and glanced at the door, "I should get going before they miss me."

Romero nodded and let go of her hand, his own landing limply on his leg. He stood, without too much struggle, as she opened the door. Julia left, running down the stairs faster than she had ascended them, fleeing her lover, her safety and her fears.

She turned down different blocks as she ran back the way she came, so that if you mapped out her path it would look like less like a circle and more like random jagged lines that happen to describe something like a circular path by some accident of artistic interpretation. Julia Capritzi had been well trained by her father. She was the best scout that the higher New York City Clean Sweep teams had, and she knew it. It was her ability to get in and out of places, at speed, that had allowed them to pinpoint the raids of '67, '68 and '71 before they happened. Julia was often considered too young for her job, but her record spoke volumes to any doubters.

She knew just where her father and the rest of the team would be. Like always, when she went scouting along the Upper West Side of Manhattan in daylight, the team would hang out near Columbus Circle. Tyrone would probably be leading the others in a snipe hunt—standing near Central Park and taking aim at anything that moved, teasing the undead to come out and swarm. The ones that lived in the park never seemed to leave during the day. No one knew exactly why, but the CST used it as sniper training to take advantage of the situation.

She approached from the East, turning around the old Lincoln Center buildings and cut down to Broadway. As she got close she could hear the sharp, solid cracks of sniper rifle fire. A few seconds later she could see them, her father standing watch in case something came at them from another direction while Tyrone led the others in sniper practice, just as she had thought.

"Julia!" her father bellowed, raising a hand. He assumed, as he always did, that if she came back without a gun raised then it was safe enough to talk and shout and not slink about. Julia's father hated slinking about.

"Father," she said curtly as she stopped by his side. She wasn't even winded from her run, but her face was flushed and she ran a cool glove along each cheek slowly, trying to will her body to settle.

"Is it clear then?" Her father asked.

"Yeah," Julia said, willing her body to relax, "if we... uh if we go a bit west, skirt the Park, I think we'll have better luck today. They must be all hidden and scared of us, huh?"

Her father sighed. "Julia," he said, "I held out hope, you know."

"Hope for what?"

"Hope for you!" Tyrone spat, suddenly beside them. "Hope that you weren't a damned traitor!"

"What? But I'm not! I mean how," Julia thought fast, her mental footing lost, "could you even think such a thing? Father?"

"We march," he told the rest of the CST. He started to walk and then glanced at his daughter who had fallen by his side as they walked, "Julia, I had you followed. Skiff did it. He radioed in. We know, all right? We know. And we're going to kill it."

"What? No, Father, listen to me! They aren't all mindless husks!"

"No? That'd be a first!" Tyrone said.

Julia's father held a hand up to Tyrone and flicked it, gesturing him away to have privacy for this discussion.

"Julia, darling, they are mindless husks. That's exactly what they are. Soulless flesh eaters. Look around you," he gestured while he spoke, pointing at buildings with the muzzle of his gun, "at this pathetic waste of a place that used to be filled with life and action and everything you could want. Now, now if it's anything it's a graveyard and they live here. Our job, our reason is to rid our race of theirs so that maybe we can rebuild. Have you forgotten that somehow?"

"Of course not, father, but be reasonable! Things change, people change, why can you not accept that the undead can change as well?"

"There is nothing in them to change, Julia! You say you wish that I was reasonable, try it yourself. Mindless brutes, empty husks of men, they can not be more than that. They are soulless and mindless, what in them could possibly change?"

"They have minds, oh, father, they really do. Please, just slow down and let me prove it to you!"

"I think decidedly not, Julia."

They marched on, Julia's mind and heart torn. Skiff met up with them a few blocks further uptown and wouldn't meet Julia's eyes at all. He was the backup scout and even though he had long wanted Julia's key position he hated the way he was forced to take his first steps toward replacing her.

Tyrone handled the rest of the team. Brian, his short cropped blond hair mussed by pilot's goggles that he always kept sitting on his head, took the right point. Lucas took the left point, swinging his snub nosed pistol back and forth like a scanning extension of his consciousness.

Tyrone's report from Skiff must have been perfectly detailed, thought Julia as the team turned off of Broadway and slid over a block to Amsterdam. He was acting like a missile, a missile pointed directly at Romero.

"All right," Julia said through clenched teeth, "will you please listen to me for just a second here?"

Her father gave her a tired glance. Then he waved the rest

of the team forward slightly, giving his daughter an edge of privacy. "I am listening," he told her softly.

"You know what you're about to do. And yet you won't let me prove that you are making a mistake. That's all I ask for, the chance to show you. The merest chance."

"Julia, do you understand that there is nothing I can do? I won't risk all of us by stopping to... to what? To try and have tea with the undead? No. It is silly."

"So don't talk to them. Stop long enough for me to show you, at a distance, I swear at a distance, that they are not just dumb brutes. Then, if I can prove that to you, you can not kill them and we can... we can discuss it and not just shoot them, all right?"

"We will see," her father said after a thoughtful pause, "what happens. If Tyrone is startled, if they shoot first, well then I can not stop that. But if luck is on your side then perhaps I will allow your foolish plan to be tried."

Tyrone, of course, heard every word. He planned, fully, to ensure that he shot before any counter-offer could be given. There was no way, simply no way at all, that Tyrone intended an undead.... thing.... to prove that it was a thinking and feeling person. Besides the sheer stupidity of such an idea, it would mean that he had been killing actual people for a few years now and not just destroying walking dolls who didn't have the sense to fall down without his expert aid.

Lucas, to Tyrone's left, had also heard everything. He thought about it, digested it in his own way and came to two conclusions, back to back. The first that he wanted to see this proof for himself. The second, that Tyrone would try to make sure no one saw it and so Lucas would have to spoil his shot somehow.

The two men walked together, exchanging hand signs and small words of advice, but they also moved against each other.

Brian, to the right of all of this, had no idea what was going on. He had Billy Joel's "Uptown girl" stuck in his head, and was trying to not hum it loud enough for anyone else to hear and get annoyed by.

They came to the same building Julia had visited. Tyrone

kept moving past it and Julia looked at Skiff. Skiff, for his part, blushed, as much as admitting that he had followed Romero, explaining why he had met the team further on. Julia cursed under her breath.

Tyrone found his prey a few blocks further north. Romero shambled forward with Merc and Monty in tow, the three of them wearing tattered rags of clothing that might as well have served as a uniform, all of the cloth so dirty and aged as to be devoid of color or distinction.

Tyrone fired four shots in quick succession, as did Lucas. The difference was that while Tyrone's shots were aimed directly at the undead in front of them, Lucas' shots were aimed high, and as he swung his gun barrel over to aim he managed to knock into Tyrone. It was enough to throw Tyrone's aim off and Lucas smiled to himself.

"What the…"

"Sorry, Ty," Lucas said. "I got excited."

"Tyrone. Lucas. Stay your hands. Julia deserves a chance to prove herself truthful to us," Julia's father rumbled.

Julia stepped forward, nudging past an angry Tyrone and a satisfied Lucas.

"Romero!" she shouted, "it is safe to approach! I swear by this! Come and show them what you once showed me, so that they too might learn!"

Romero's head swung from side to side, scanning. At the sound of gunfire he had started to flee, but hearing Julia gave him pause. He saw her, recognizing her shape, her sound. He knew the danger, but he found he could not turn away from her or deny her anything. And so Romero urged, with wordless grunts and groans, his companions to follow him.

The CST stood its ground, guns aimed tightly along the undead, but Julia's father stayed their hands. He also stopped Julia from running out towards the shambling beasts. She strained against the demands of not rushing to her love's side, but did as her father asked. There would only be one chance at this and she knew that if she blew it she could never forgive herself.

Romero stopped roughly twenty feet away and nodded.

"You see, father," Julia said, "they aren't mindless. He stops at a respectful distance."

"Oh, come on," Tyrone said, "we should listen to this? So she has taught one of them tricks and treats it like a pet. So?"

"Shut up, Tyrone," Julia snapped, "Romero isn't a pet, he's a person. Just because you won't admit it doesn't make it bull-shit."

"Have them show me," her father said, considering.

Before Julia could say or do anything, Romero bowed, awk-wardly to be sure, but it was still a bow. His two companions followed suit and the members of the CST looked at each other.

"This is bullshit!" Tyrone raged and fired a single shot.

Merc fell in a heap, appearing to be surprised as he did. Romero and Monty both looked over at their friend and then locked their gazes with Tyrone.

"Tyrone!" Julia and her father screamed as one.

"Doing the world a favor," Tyrone said to them, turning to look at them, "come on, you can't be buying into this."

Romero moved faster than he had known he was still capa-ble of. He was on Tyrone while Tyrone's back was still turned. He wanted blood for blood and in his rage he didn't consider what he was throwing away.

Tyrone screamed, the back of his neck being gnawed on, and fell twitching to the ground under Romero. Romero didn't stop to feed, simply killed Tyrone, stood and seemed to realize what he had done. He turned and moved as fast as he could, urging Monty with waves and grunts to do the same.

The CST was too shocked to react. It was the time Romero needed to get away. They had gathered around Tyrone and tried everything they knew to stop the bleeding and infection. They knew it was too late, but they tried anyway, and, in their attempts, let Romero and Monty escape.

"This is what I get for listening to you, Julia," her father said after Tyrone had been put down so that he would not rise again, "this is what we all get."

"Father, no. Tyrone started it. He had no call to shoot, you know it as well as I do. No call in the least. They weren't attacking, hell they weren't even moving except to pay respect to us. And he killed one of them for it. Wouldn't you seek revenge for that as well?"

"You go too far, Julia," her father warned.

"No! I love Romero and you can't change that, or change the fact that he's intelligent."

"We're going back to base."

"No!"

"Yes! We are going back to base to bury Tyrone and discuss our next course of action."

"Then you go without me," Julia said, her face flushed. She sprinted off then, choosing a street at random.

Her father started to order Skiff after her and then shook his head.

"Let her go," he said to no one so much as himself. "She'll come back to us when she realizes what she has been a party to. Come, we need to bury our dead."

Julia ran until her legs burned. She had no clear destination in mind, simply escape. She loved Romero, but she also loved her father. She was torn between two lives, two destinies, and didn't know where she would land. Her heart thudded in her chest, cracking it seemed to her, as she went. Still she wouldn't let herself stop. Stopping would mean choice, and choice, she felt, would mean losing. No matter the answer, she could not win, there was no way to have it all.

That much she knew as well as she knew the icy cold lump in her stomach. She ran her mind through the options she had: she could go back to her father and to her team and face their judgment or she could go to Romero and try to seek comfort in his love.

If she went home, she knew what was ahead of her. Trials, discussions, replacement. She wouldn't be allowed back in the field for a long time, if ever. She'd have to give them all of

Romero's hiding places in a show of faith and send him and Monty to their second deaths.

Going to Romero she would lose her entire life, leave it all behind, for a chance at what? Happiness? Love? Could she, Julia thought as her feet skidded around corners and down long empty streets, hold those things in her hand? Could she trust that he was truly in love with her as she was with him? Then again, could she afford not to trust him?

Her feet, she realized, were a step or two ahead of her. She found herself outside of Romero's building, and was suddenly sure that he had returned there to wait for her, knowing the risks.

She took the stairs as fast as possible, though her legs protested the movement. Her hand on the door didn't wait for caution or reason, it grabbed the knob, turned it and flung the door wide.

Romero and Monty were in the middle of the room, standing close together, their heads bent towards each other as if whispering. At Julia's entrance the pair broke apart and started to move towards her, expecting trouble.

Romero realized who was at the door, and put a hand against Monty's chest. Monty groaned, unhappy with her. Romero shook his head and patted Monty's chest a few times before lumbering towards the door, the speed he had shown earlier seeming to have left his limbs. If anything he seemed slower, tired.

"Oh, Romero, I'm so sorry," Julia said.

Romero nodded and held his hand out to her. She took it and gave it a squeeze.

"They'll never listen, will they? They'll never let us be together, or agree to give your kind a fighting chance, the whole world is just..."

Romero reached his other hand up and his papery, dried skin crushed her cheek gently. She leaned into his caress and sighed.

"What can we do?"

Romero had no answer to give, even had he been able to

speak. He longed to tell her how beautiful he thought she was, how radiant she seemed to him. He wanted to tell her all about how he had regained consciousness, though undead, and how it seemed to grow sharper every day. Still, words escaped him, his voice box long since destroyed.

Monty, who had felt that possibly, on the outside glimmer of a chance, Julia would be able to sway her people, now felt only the coldness of anger when he looked at her. Merc was dead, because of her. There was no good hope left, because of her. He would die alone, again, because of her. It was all her failure, in his eyes. How he wanted to give in and rip her flesh from her bones with his teeth. He longed to feel the hot spurt of her blood dribble down his throat.

Romero felt the change in Monty, the rise of the bloodlust and tugged Julia's hand towards the door. A look, a glance, at Monty and Julia saw the problem, followed Romero.

"We can just run," Julia said, as Romero led her down the hallway and to the stairs, "and we can go, I don't know, somewhere safe. Where's safe? Canada? Could we make Canada do you think?"

Romero didn't reply, knowing that there was no way they could make that sort of trip. Not together. He knew he would hold her back no matter what he did and it pained him like nothing except the hunger ever had.

The whole way down they could hear Monty shuffling after them, the pant and groan of his breath coming out tortured from his chest. Monty wasn't very fast, and his wheeze of a moan echoed along the stairwell.

Romero and Julia hit the street and wandered down the block, hand in hand, keeping to the side of buildings as much as possible. Romero could sense there were not other undead, except Monty, close by. Julia was sure her team had gone back to base.

Only one of them was right.

The CST turned a corner, facing Julia and her undead love. There was no love in their eyes, only wariness tinged with the harsh lights of disapproval and sadness.

"Julia, you need to come back with us," her father said.

Julia realized what had happened. The team must have started for their camp and then turned back, sending Skiff out to track Julia and report back. Then, following some alternate route of his own devising, they had followed Skiff to where she was. She was, in a sense, impressed.

"Hey, Skiff," Julia called out, "good work. You totally deserve my spot."

Skiff's face went beet red and he found somewhere else to look. Anywhere but Julia's face was a good place to be staring just then.

"Julia, you need to come back with us," her father repeated, "and we can deal with this. Just move away from that... thing and it'll be all right. I promise."

"No, don't you see? It won't be all right until you can accept him for who he is!"

"Jules," Lucas said stiffly, "get out of the way. That bastard killed Ty."

Julia, in response, pulled her own pistol out of its holster and leveled it towards Lucas. There were tears in her eyes and she blinked, trying to clear her vision. The world seemed to float away from her.

"Lucas, don't. Father, tell him to stand down!"

"Julia, just walk over here and put the gun down and we can resolve this," her father said, his voice betraying that he was nearing the edge of his patience.

Julia thought about it and her hand shook. Lucas knew she wouldn't shoot, he was sure of it. Brian watched all of this unfold and decided that, for a change, he was going to be the hero. That would surprise all of them, he felt, and maybe they'd stop treating him like the extra man on a sinking ship. Or maybe he simply lost his mind. Either way, for a change, he took action.

Brian knocked Lucas out of the way and ran full out towards Julia. He raised his rifle as he ran, not intending to shoot her but intimidate her into submission. Julia reacted, swinging her weapon to aim at Brian as his legs carried him ever closer.

"Brian," she barked, "stop!"

Brian didn't reply, he saw her weapon come around towards him he reacted as he was trained and shot her. His reflexes took over and the head shot was a clean one, spraying blood and brains and bits of skull all over Romero's face and chest.

Romero howled in rage and pain and leapt forward, grabbed Brian and his gun, and wrestled the man to the ground. Brian's head hit the ground hard and bounced once, knocking him out cold.

Romero stood, Brian's rifle in his hand. The remaining members of the CST were too confused to simply open fire. Romero and Julia's father locked eyes across the seemingly impossible distance that separated them.

"H-hold your fire," Julia's father said through his mounting grief.

Romero nodded and set down the rifle. One hand came up and touched his chest, over his heart. He bowed, stiffly, and simply stood there.

"Sir, we can take him, it's an easy shot," Lucas said as softly as possible. He ached to pull the trigger, but somehow it felt like firing quickly had lead to all of the mess over the last day. The fear that he would only contribute to wrongful deaths held his hand dead still.

Monty came up behind Romero then, and slowed as he approached. He saw Julia dead on the ground and fumed. Though he hadn't liked her and was ready to give into his hunger for her flesh, he knew what she had meant to Romero.

The two groups stood like that, facing each other in the empty street as winds whistled past and birds flew overhead. A cloud passed over them and the sudden shade, sweeping past to grant sunlight across their bodies again made Lucas shiver.

"I think he is as sick of the killing as we are," Julia's father said, wonderment in his crisp voice.

Romero nodded in reply and spread his open hands in supplication.

"We should have listened to her…"

"No, Sir, it's an undead killer, we…"

"Shut up, Lucas. My daughter is dead because of this. No more need to die, if she was right. And by God it seems as if she *was* right."

Romero looked down at the body of his slain love and deep in his brain he wondered if her death was worth the progress made. He liked to think, in later days, that she would think that it was.

He liked to think, in later days, that someday he would become truly convinced of it as well.

crazy little thing

Chapter 1

I DROPPED THE still-smoldering filter onto the ground and crushed it out with the toe of my sneaker. Back and forth, back and forth, the toe of my shoe went, grinding the filter and its dreg of tobacco into dust that was taken by the breeze. I watched it go. I loved to watch the dust swirl and move into the daylight. Life was calm and good, and they said things were looking up some.

That is when I first saw her: the most beautiful woman I had ever seen. Instant *bang!* love at first sight. No doubt in my mind, no room in my heart for anything else; just like that I knew and knew well what my destiny was going to be. We would fall in love and it would be amazing and pure and romantic as pigs in shit.

Her hair streamed downwards and was caught by the same breeze that my dust had wandered off in, so that it flowed like the gentlest of rivers. Each tendon and ligament and other bits of her neck under her wonderfully smooth skin all strained hard, chording like piano wire. It pulsed and rippled as she fought against the leather band that crossed her forehead. Her fingers, the nails bright day-glo pink, made claw shapes that were still beautiful as they struggled against the bonds that restrained her wrists. The wide leather strap across her chest crossed her body just under her breasts, accentuating them enticingly under her white floral cotton gown.

I turned to her and waved, a happy wave, a hello wave, the kind of wave you give the love of your life right before you ask them to marry you. I had, secretly, practiced that wave in the mirror a lifetime ago. She turned and, glimpsing the motion of my hand out of the corner of her eye, spoke to me.

"You stupid motherfucker! Release me! Help me! Fuuuuck! Get me—*ugh!*—out," she strained and tensed, trying to rip the leather straps free, "what good are you, you piece of shit?" The orderlies shook their heads and Jim waved at me. It was a sad wave but it was also a hello wave. "Shitbag! Kill them, release me!" They pushed her through the doors, while discussing medication under the volume of her cries. The doors swung shut behind them, and I stood, giving a last glance in the direction my dust had traveled. I walked to the doors myself and put a hand on the bar. "Simon B. McGee" the glass door read. It wasn't real glass. It looked like glass, but it was much, much stronger. They told us so once. The other door, the one I never used because it made me feel bad—didn't like that door—read "Mental Health Facility" and completed the name. No one called it the Simon B. McGee Mental Health Facility, though, unless people in very nice suits were around. Otherwise we all, even the staff, called it "McGee's" and left it at that.

I walked in and waved at Sally, who was working reception that day, and nodded briefly in Clyde's direction. I didn't like Clyde much. He worked security and he had helped a lot of us at one time or another, but something about him made me feel wet inside, like a sack of something not quite solid. Loose. I hurried on and went in my room to figure out how I would meet up with my dream girl again. Maybe she'd be in my group. Or maybe she enjoyed a rousing game of ping pong. I liked ping pong, because the ball was small; and yet also very white and it bounced. I also liked golf, but there was nowhere to play golf.

I paced and thought about it for a while. Ping pong balls and my mystery woman with no name, and bouncing and Clyde. They didn't quite add up to anything useful, but I felt sure that they would some day.

I sat on my bed and lay down to think better. I think better lying down. I needed to request a change in medications, my current ones made my thoughts too hard for me to follow; I used to be so sharp witted. Of course I also used to believe that John Quincy Adams was out to kill me, so things can change for the better. These days I knew it was Abraham Lincoln who was going to kill me one day. Not today, he was waiting for the time to be right. That was how he worked. "Honest Abe" indeed. They couldn't fool me with all the ping pong balls in the world.

Clock number three buzzed and that meant it was time for dinner. Clock number one told me to wake up; clock number two was for breakfast, three for dinner and four for bedtime. I took lunch when I got hungry.

Chapter 2

MY EYES SKITTERED across surfaces and the walls seemed to move in on me. They loomed, moving too fast for me to track, until I realized that the only thing moving was my eyes and my head as I tried to find a space to belong, somewhere in the space I already occupied. The off-white color of the painted brick was streaked with blacks and reds and grays. What looked like scorch marks and blood met up with grime and soot, the mixtures working to coat the walls as completely as they could. I felt sick just looking at it, my stomach starting to churn as fast as my eyes had moved. Suddenly a single thought came to me out of the depth of sickness and lurching: I wasn't sure how I had gotten here. I thought I knew where I sat, my back against another wall just gazing across the hallway to study the mosaic of wrongness. The corridor felt familiar, but that was wrong too. The lights didn't flicker so much as they had gone out and occasionally forgot, coming back on for a harsh fluorescent burst of stark relief driving me into fits of blinking and head turning.

I curled my legs up, tucking my knees under my chin, and

just stared blankly at the wall, trying to piece it together, trying to come together. Things had, obviously, gotten worse. Had
I caused it? Was this all my fault after everything? I didn't
know, I didn't have the tools to process and I ached for them,
I really wanted to rent them or lease them perhaps from some
higher being, just for long enough to understand what was
going on. I shook my head and tried to fit everything together
like a puzzle of a kitten hanging onto a tree: thousands of little cardboard shapes, each one a mystery by itself. I couldn't
find an edge piece at all.

I had been taken back to the room. I had that piece right
in my grasp when I reached for it. I had it and lost it again. I
dug until I located myself, remembering what felt like a key
day, a while back. The sun shone brightly then, brighter than
it did now, but maybe it had always been dimmer in reality
and simply more stunning in memory. A lot of things seemed
to sparkle in retrospect.

I stood, shakily, and put a hand against the wall behind
me, palm down. I wrenched it away quickly, almost too quickly, causing myself to stumble. A sticky wet sensation slid
against my flesh. Biting my lip, I turned around to confirm
what my skin made me think: the wall I stood against was as
bad as the one I looked at. What must the rest of the place look
like?

Was she okay?

The thought burned through my mind, charring its way up
to my consciousness like a comet falling in reverse, making
my stomach lurch again.

Was she alive, injured, lost, trapped, worse?

The possibilities pounded at me, reminding me of how I
felt, back at the beginning. If it could be called a beginning. If
it had happened. If this was—no! It was too easy to get lost in
the thought train, too quick a trap to spring on my mind.
Thinking along those paths would squelch me down and
reduce me to uselessness. I didn't have to be useless anymore.

I walked down the hallway, wincing and squinting as the
lights gave another show of luminescent force. Realizing that

I was walking down the hallway towards the dining room I let instinct take over, gratefully only half noticing the signs that were a combination of pried and burnt off the walls. My bare feet scraped against grit and small sharp debris from the walls and, I confirmed by looking up, ceiling. When had my feet become bare? Footwear should rank near the least of my worries, I knew. I repeated it to myself until I could, if not believe it, accept the concept. Then I stepped on something that gave a bit as my foot came down on it, something that felt like flesh. I went still, debating the sense of bothering to look, for a few seconds. I found I could hear a crackle and hiss from the dining room in front of me in the silence created by my lack of movement, and closed my eyes in a weak attempt to block everything out, not just sound. It didn't work. I hadn't thought it would.

I moved my foot and looked down, seeing a severed finger on the ruined linoleum floor, half on a black tile and half on a white one. Strange the details that chaos imparts. The crystal clear excerpts of order that leak into your brain, or at least into mine.

I felt dizzy and sat down, just outside of the closed dining room. I couldn't face it yet. It felt too big for me. Everything started there, after all, if it had happened and if it had ever truly begun. I closed my eyes again and lost myself, willingly this time, in the past.

Chapter 3

AFTER QUESTIONING BENNY during dinner, I found out my love's name was Abigail. She was still too new to join us, being sedated and all, but Benny had seen a guy who knew a guard who had helped find her a room, which is how we knew her name was Abigail, or just Gail. It might have been just Gail, but Abigail was a prettier name so I decided to stick with it until I knew better.

After dinner, Benny and I hung out in the rec room, watching other people play ping pong. There was a line, so we couldn't play for a while. I got us some cups of juice, orange, and wandered around waiting for some chairs to open up. Two did and we wandered near them, except Benny spilled his juice, and while looking for the spill managed to slip in it and fall on his ass, missing the chair by a few inches. I tried not to laugh and gave him a hand. He muttered angrily and wiped at his pants while I got him more juice and some napkins. After that we sat and talked about what Benny had learned today.

"John, you gotta know, they're gonna come any day now." Benny nodded as he spoke, constantly. A big white bobble head doll, Benny was.

"From the radio still?" I thought Benny was a bit crazy, but I didn't want to tell him that. He was my friend. If Benny thought that the radio sent sentient waves out disguised as sound, then I had to accept that as part of who Benny was.

"Of course from the radio! John, don't you listen to anything I say? They're biding their time…"

"Like Lincoln," I said, trying to be helpful and show Benny that I really did understand.

"Lincoln is dead, man. Dead. He isn't going to kill you, because he's dead."

I sighed and shook my head, stopping to sip my juice. I knew Benny was my friend; he just had trouble being as accepting and open-minded as I was.

"Benny. Benny. Lincoln is as real as the radio thing. I mean, maybe the radio waves are just radio waves? That's what Doctor Pinser said isn't it? But if you really think it's true, then I'm willing to extend you that friendship, right?"

"Of course you are, because the radio waves are out to get us…"

"No see, but then I need you… I mean Lincoln scares me Benny, he scares me bad." Benny was about to say something to me when Doctors Lensher and Vandrell stopped their rounds to look at me. They talked to each other in hushed tones, the tones that we all knew meant they didn't want us to hear them at all, and came over, all smiles.

"John," Doctor Lensher began, consulting a chart in his hand, "do you have time to meet with us?" His voice was polite and eased, and Doctor Vandrell winked at me. I shrugged and stood up, giving Benny a neutral, goodbye wave.

They took me to one of the big white labs and asked me to sit down. I sat and Doctor Vandrell handed me a fresh cup of juice, apple this time. I thanked him and he smiled and nodded at me, taking a step back as Doctor Lensher took a step forward.

"How have you been feeling, John," asked Doctor Lensher. I considered the question while I took a big sip of my juice and rested the cup on my knee.

"All right. I mean, sometimes I still can't find words, or I need to know the time. I just talked to Doctor West this morning. You can ask her, she takes good notes I think. I always see her writing, and she has a really nice pen, too."

"Yes, Doctor West does take good notes," Doctor Vandrell agreed with a smile, "and we read them over before we met up with you. I think Doctor Lensher was asking if there was anything," his eyes flicked over to Doctor Lensher for agreement, which Lensher gave with him with a small smile, "you didn't think to mention to Doctor West. Have you been depressed recently?" I shook my head and thought about the question at the same time, something that Doctor West always asked me to not do. Then I shrugged and smiled at them. "Okay, well, John, we wanted to try a new treatment on you, so it's important that we know." I nodded again at Vandrell.

"Not that I know of. I was sad today, but it wasn't depression, I was just sad. That new woman who came in. She didn't seem happy, and that made me sad. The day was so clear and bright before that, but she didn't enjoy it at all." The doctors exchanged a look and both started to talk at once. Vandrell stopped and gave Lensher a small turn of his hand.

"Well, our new friend just moved here. You remember how you felt when you first got here, don't you?" I did, and they were right. I hadn't put it in the right context, like Doctor West encouraged me to do more often.

"Yeah, so what's the new procedure?" From past, not always unpleasant, experience I knew that if they were asking me they had already asked my sister and she had already agreed. I didn't mind, it worked that way here at McGee's, and more often than not it worked out pretty okay for me too.

"We want to recharge your clock," Lensher said with a quick look at Vandrell. I liked clocks. They really helped me keep track of things, time for example. More than time, though, clocks helped me know where I was supposed to be and when and what time it was. Clocks were good, and helping my clock would be good, I decided. I smiled and nodded, giving Lensher a thumbs up.

They both worked to find a good time and gave me a slip of paper to remember it by. I knew they would come get me if I did forget, but I wouldn't. I didn't like to let them down if I could help it. There was no reason to.

I left, giving both doctors a happy goodbye wave and wandered the hallways for a while, just seeing who was around. I went out for a smoke, and sat by myself on one of the benches. There was still a small breeze but it had cooled down, and I smoked quicker than I would have liked, staring at the sky and thinking. I ground my cigarette carefully into the ground and tried to watch the breeze carry it away, but it was too dark and the remains too small to see really well. I watched anyway, as best I could, and went back inside, straight to my room and to bed.

Chapter 4

I SQUINTED, MY eyes trying to adjust to the difference in brightness levels between inside and outside, as the door swung shut slowly behind me. I waved at Sally, a happy hello wave, and padded my way down to the rec room. It was early yet, a lot of people didn't like to be around and awake yet, but my clock insisted so I took its advice. I knew, like every morning, that I had time before breakfast. Even without being close to my clocks I could still hear them, just in my head. They really helped keep track of things.

The rec room was empty, at first sight. I wandered to the ping pong table and twirled a paddle on my hands, just letting the aloneness settle over me. It was funny, I knew I wasn't really alone, I was never alone here. Not really, not for real. There was always someone, usually within shouting distance, wandering by. That was part of why I liked it here. It was safe, even if you didn't want it to be safe, it was. That safety wrapped around us like a blanket. They gave us decent blankets for our rooms here, too.

The emptiness of the room felt both big and small to me as I stood there, putting the paddle back down.

"Schmuck."

The word rang out, large in the suddenly small room. It echoed, more in my head than in the space, and caused me to startle. Dropping the paddle, I spun around and around, and finally spotted the shape of a person on one of the chairs by the TV.

I walked closer and I admit I was kinda nervous. That safe feeling had vanished with surprise and I thought of what time it should be, looking for the clock on the wall. Not much time had passed, thankfully. "Come on over here already. I won't hurt you." The voice cooed at me with an undertone of dislike. I recognized it then. I moved closer and saw that I was right, it was her. Abigail, or just Gail, but really Abigail.

"Abigail?" I tried, intending to settle it for myself.

"Schmuck," she repeated, using it as my name. I sighed and sat down near her, gazing lovingly at her: her soft skin, large green eyes, long hair slightly straggly and unkempt, her legs crossed with one foot jangling quickly to a tempo I couldn't hear.

"John, my name is John. We met, I mean I saw you, you know when you came in?"

"I remember. Want to help me get out of here?"

"You mean you want to go for a smoke? I have a few more, we could go for..."

"I mean out of here, fucker. Vamoose, leave, get of out Dodge."

"What, why?" I asked.

She sighed at me, shaking her head slowly, a look of utter disappointment creasing her face. "I shouldn't be in this mad-house. Jesus, fuck. Come on, man."

I wanted to reassure her that the place wasn't so bad. They took good care of us here. I wanted to settle her down and strike up a friendship, but I knew it would take just the right words to do it. Something simple but calming. I could tell her about Doctor Vandrell, or how nice Sally could be. The brownies were really good too, when we had any. She needed to see things from the right

perspective, like Doctor West told me. It could, she said a lot, make everything come into the right focus. The right focus was very important to Doctor West. I tried to remember the things Doctor West had told me, thinking I could pass them on to Abigail and help her adjust.

"I love you," came out of my mouth and I blinked as I heard the sound of my own voice. It wasn't really what I had in mind at all.

"That's rich. You're crazy. *You?* You stay here. I'll get out. Sounds right."

I looked at my feet, my hands twisting together. Crazy was a word we weren't allowed to use. She could get in trouble for it. It was also mean, really. I wasn't crazy. They told me that. I just needed some help sometimes. I tried to look back up at her but found I couldn't. She was so perfect but she just didn't see things right, yet.

"We aren't allowed to use that word," I whispered. A whisper wasn't the tone of voice I had reached for but it was all I had in the face of the word. She laughed, her head going back to expose a perfect throat. I loved that throat then.

"What word? Crazy? Can't call a spade a digging tool around here? Fine… John, right? John," she remembered my name and used it, a sign that she was seeing things the way they should be, "listen close, okay? You are crazy. That's why you're here. It's fine, lots of nutters around, and you're one of them. I, on the other hand, was put here by my evil step sisters. Totally different thing, got it?" Or, then again, maybe not. She got up, shaking her head at me and heading past me, out of the room. I sat there, shocked and confused as she walked away from me. "They're just jealous, but I'll get out and get revenge. I just need to find the mice," she muttered to herself as she left.

I didn't exist to her, and when I did it wasn't in a good way. I really wanted to stop her, to explain things to her, but I wasn't any good at that. I waited until she left and got up myself, looking for Doctor West, hoping she was in already.

Chapter 5

THERE WAS NO use in putting it off any longer. I opened my eyes with a shake of my head and forced myself to stare at the door to the dining room. The doors were almost never closed, and they looked unnatural to me that way. Sure, they were pock marked with long scrapes and one of the glass windows set about head high in the door was busted, leaving bloody shards like teeth, but even without all of that it would have looked odd to me. Now it just confirmed my feelings about this place. Except it hadn't been like this. I knew it hadn't. I was pretty sure it hadn't.

There was nothing to be gained from staring at the doors, nothing worth gaining at least, so I carefully opened one. The door swung cleanly on its hinge, revealing in full what I could only see a hint of through the tiny square of broken glass: the room was worse than the halls. It was, thankfully, mostly empty; but what people were in there though weren't a pretty sight. What was left of them. I didn't let myself recognize anyone in the room, I just refused. That might've been Sally's head, that half a skull there, but I wouldn't let it be. I couldn't let it be.

I rejected it. It wasn't real, none of this was real. I had problems, I did. Turning, I started to leave the room but stopped cold. I had to know if she was in there, which meant

I had to recognize the bodies, as best I could. I wanted to cry. My stomach churned at the thought but I turned back into the room.

Checking the bodies, and body parts, to see who they were did me in. I added vomit and bile to the mess of blood and rubble on the floor at least twice. Dry heaves crippled me, leaving me leaning heavily on a table, slick with grease and rotten spilled milk. It was while I hunched there, bent over the table with my stomach trying to claw its way out of my body that I noticed the bullet holes in the floor and chairs.

Those puzzles they used to sell at malls, the fields of dots that you would stare at endlessly until a picture formed out of them, swirled into focus from hidden view, it hit me like one of those. I looked around the room again, the missing piece in place, and saw it all over again for the first time. There had been a gun fight in here, fight was the wrong word; there had been a slaughter in here using lead slugs as a medium for its dark art. Carnage. Massacre. Terms swarmed to my forebrain in a useless attempt to make sense of it, to label it and lock it in a nice box. Each severed limb, splotch of bone and strange shaped bit of meat and gristle had been part of a person. I couldn't secure it away all safe and warm. It had to be dealt with.

She didn't seem to be there. Dealing with it became easier suddenly, like a breath of slightly less rancid air. Maybe I would taste fresh air again sometime, but until then I'd take what I could get. I fumbled in my pants and found nothing, cursing slightly. On one of the tables near the door was a pack of cigarettes, only a small splash of blood on it. I stole a smoke from the dead and lit my ill-gotten gain, drawing hot smoke deeply into my lungs. A bark of laughter escaped me, turning into a cough and then another series of dry heaves as I noticed the no smoking sign by the door.

I left the room and kept searching.

———

Chapter 6

THE EXAMINATION ROOM was chilly, but it was all right, I had my slippers on. They asked me to not wear sneakers or anything, since this was a medical thing. Clock number two had gone off that morning, but instead of breakfast it told me to go see Doctors Vandrell and Lensher for my appointment. Vandrell smiled at me when I arrived on time, pleased I suppose that I remembered and was punctual. That made me smile. Thinking that he was pleased made everything a bit easier. They were just looking out for me, and like they said, they wanted to recharge my clock. That sounded good to me.

"Hi John," Lensher said, gesturing me towards an exam table, "do you want me to explain what we're going to do?" I nodded, sitting on the table and giving Doctor Vandrell a small hello wave.

"That would be great, I like to know what's going on. It makes everything so much easier, don't you think?" Vandrell nodded and Lensher just smiled at me, reaching out to pat my shoulder.

"Yes, yes exactly. Why don't you lie down here," he asked, his hand still on my shoulder, friendly and calm, "and Doctor Vandrell will start preparing you while I explain." I lay back on the table, my arms at my sides and shrugged a bit. I always felt a bit funny lying like that, but most times doctors don't like it when you lay on the exam table with your arms dangling. I guess it gives everything the feeling of play, and lots of doctors take themselves very seriously.

"John, can you take off your shirt for me?" I nodded at Vandrell and half sat up again to take my shirt off, handing it to him. I was happy to see that he took it and folded it for me, placing it on a chair behind him. That was really nice of him. Some doctors, before I came to McGee's, would just toss your clothes on the chair. I always felt it told me a lot about how they would treat me. The doctors here, though, were really good about that sort of thing. They liked to, like Doctor West always told me, put you at ease.

"Now, Doctor Vandrell is going to put something on your chest to monitor your heart rate. We don't want you getting hurt during this, do we?" I shook my head and watched the little contact sticky get pressed down. "To make sure you aren't scared either, we don't want you scared or hurt, we're also going to give you an I.V., just something to make you sleep. You can sleep this whole thing away."

As Lensher talked, Vandrell acted out his words. It made me want to laugh and distracted me so that I didn't even feel the I.V. go in my arm. Then Vandrell asked me to count backwards from twenty. I grinned at him and started to count.

"Twenty. Nineteen. Eighteen. Seventeen. Sixteen." As I counted I started to feel like I was drifting away. Like a rocking boat on the water, maybe. It reminded me of a time I went fishing with my dad when I was a kid, and the sun was bright and happy and we didn't catch anything but the boat swayed constantly and made me all sleepy, made me feel like I could coast forever. It felt just like that time. My eyelids grew heavy and I stopped really hearing or noticing either doctor.

A flash of light. A sharp sudden crack, deep in my brain. Something came loose and ran away from me. I was being chased. The sky was floating away. The ground drifted by, except there was no ground. I was giving chase.

Teeth. Eyes. Fear. Panic. Pain.

Even as I felt and thought and struggled, the memory of it slid away like a snake. The well was deep, the water warm. I sank.

Down.

Down.

Up.

I woke up and felt like I had been beaten. My jaw ached and my temples felt hot. My arms and legs and back all burned, the muscles sore, and I winced. The crinkling of my face made me notice the plastic mask over my mouth and nose. I opened my eyes, confused and frightened and saw Doctor Vandrell standing near me, moving to help me sit up slowly even as I came awake.

"What... did I make the appointment?" I couldn't remember it clearly. I had gone out for my smoke and then gone back to my room. My second clock had buzzed at me to remind me to go to the examination room and then things went blurry, like static on a television set. Vandrell nodded at me and gave me a soft smile. He didn't look concerned for me, he looked relaxed and fine, helping me to feel a little better.

"You did fine, John. That was what we call electroconvulsive therapy, and sometimes it can hurt your memory for a little while. I'm sorry for that, but it should help your clock recharge. Hopefully you'll be able to think clearer now, hmm?" It seemed like the kind of question that wanted an answer.

"I... maybe? Ow, I dunno, I feel... really bad right now. Are you sure this helps?"

"It will, John. Here," he handed me a cup of orange juice from a table by his elbow, "drink this and relax. You'll be fine. When you feel up to it, I'll walk you back to your room." Electroconvulsive therapy contained two things I knew, electro and convulsive, and I didn't like either. If Vandrell was really sure that it would help though, I decided to trust him.

"I think I can stand now," I said quietly and swung my legs slowly over the side of the exam table. Doctor Vandrell helped me, keeping a hand on my shoulder.

"Where's Doctor Lensher?" I asked, looking around the room. The movement of my head made me a bit dizzy but I didn't realize that until after my head moved.

"Doctor Lensher wasn't in today, but he asked me to go ahead without him." That was wrong, I was sure of it. I remembered... well it was fuzzy, but I thought I remembered Lensher there too, talking. A bewildered look crossed my face and Doctor Vandrell studied me carefully. "Are you okay, John? Do you need to sit back down?"

"No," I shook my head, again suddenly remembering that moving my head made me dizzy, "I just thought I remembered him here." He helped me put my shirt back on, and we walked slowly out into the hall together.

"Well like I told you, ECT can hurt your memory a little sometimes. I wouldn't worry about it." I nodded and we wandered back to my room, his arm on my shoulder still and the cup of orange juice still in my hand.

We passed the front desk and Sally got a small hello wave from me, but instead of smiling she glanced away from me and ignored it. She must've been having a bad day. I let it go. We all have bad days and you can't hold them against a person. I'd make sure to come back later and say hello to her for longer, maybe ask if everything was all right.

Doctor Vandrell opened the door to my room for me and nodded at me, letting go of my shoulder. I set the cup of orange juice down and looked around slowly, not turning my head.

"You rest, John. I'll have someone check in on you later, okay?"

"Sure, thanks, Doctor Vandrell. Hey if you see Benny maybe you could send him by? That'd make me feel better." Vandrell looked away and shook his head, gradually coming to rest looking at me again.

"Benny Rico?"

"Yeah, Benny. You know him?"

"Benny died a day or so ago. John, you were there. Maybe we should do a few tests..."

"No, that's... he died? How?" I sat down heavily on my bed, leaning forward to rest my elbows on my knees. I had seen Benny not too long ago, and I knew I would've remembered if he had died.

"He slipped and fell on a chair, it broke and a piece of it stabbed... We shouldn't discuss this, John. I really think I should set up some tests." Benny slipped, when I was there? Sure, I remembered that but he just fell on his ass; he didn't hit a chair or get stabbed or die.

I was sure of it.

Sure.

Mostly.

"No, I remember now," I lied to Doctor Vandrell, not really sure why I was lying other than something in me telling me it was a good idea, "I must still just be a bit confused. I think I'll take a nap." Vandrell nodded at me, telling me again that he would make sure someone checked in on me in a while and left, shutting the door gently. Benny was dead? That didn't make any sense at all, not really. I checked my clocks and curled up in bed, laying on my side and pulling my knees up to my chest, tugging the blanket up under my chin. Why would I remember it differently?

I fell asleep, turning the question over in my mind.

Chapter 7

I WOKE UP in the middle of the night and stretched slowly, squeezing my eyes shut. Things still felt off, but they felt off outside, not on the inside where I normally would feel off about the universe. An external tilt had taken me.

I staggered out of my own space and headed down to the rec room, just hoping for a larger space to be alone in. Pushing the door open I spotted her. My instincts ran in two directions at once: I wanted to go to her and I wanted to leave. I still loved her. I knew that, but I also didn't look forward to more of her cutting tongue.

"Uhhh," I started bravely, "hey there." My feet took me to the couch she was curled up on all by themselves. They never even asked me, just happily walked me right up to her. Her knees were held tightly to her chest by her arms and she seemed to be looking at the floor through a cloud of her own hair. At my words she glanced over at me.

"Hey, John, hey. What are you doing up this late?" She looked back at the floor and held out a foot. "What size does this seem to be to you?" I decided she must be distracted, to be speaking calmer. Then I remembered the time, she had to be tired. That was it.

"I... I don't know. A seven or eight maybe? I never really sized shoes real good, you know, and uh, yeah. So why are you up so late?"

"Couldn't sleep, I need a better reason? Nightmares, that's the normal one around here right? Did you have nightmares then?" Her arms unwrapped from her legs and she held her hands up in front of her face, wiggling her fingers, "Big scary nightmares maybe, chased by some guy who had your mice captive and wouldn't give you the right shoe?" I sat slowly on the edge of the couch, not too near her and shook my head.

"No, I've never had a nightmare like that. I mean, there was time I had a dream that I was a hamburger but that was a long time ago and I..."

"Yeah, okay John, thanks. So why are you up so late, huh?" My fingers plucked at the couch cushion and I looked directly at her, quickly changing my mind and looking away from her eyes.

"I just got up, the clocks didn't tell me to," I said fast, "it just happened, okay? Have you seen Benny?"

"You mean that guy who died?" My stomach lurched. "Oh, you were there when it happened weren't you? I'm so sorry." She leaned over and hugged me. Just... she hugged me, right then and there, clutching me to her awkwardly but firmly, bent far over with one leg coming up to rest on the couch while the other balanced her against the floor.

"See, I don't remember it that way. I thought he just... it's not important," I fell silent and hugged her back. After a minute or so she let go and sat up straight. I stood and looked around the room, trying to place everything. "I should get back to bed, clock number one is going to go off way too soon, right, and I don't want to... I should go." She raised an eyebrow at me but shrugged, dismissing me.

I went back to bed, totally unsure of why I remembered things wrong and adding her behavior to the list of things that made no sense to me. Abigail had seemed far too nice to me, but Doctor West said that I should embrace new friends and I did love her and embracing her was pretty high on my list of ideas. She hugged me. It wasn't the warmest hug in the world, but she had hugged me.

Chapter 8

DOWN THE HALL again to the stairs. Upstairs to the sunroom. I walked by rote, memory guiding me while my mind tried to refuse looking at anything. I almost slipped on some blood that splashed along the stairs but caught the handrail and kept moving. The sunroom door was open, propped that way by Horatio Fersetter, my old next door neighbor, his body inert on the ground. His eyes had rolled back in his head and his hands clutched at air dangerously, as if it had knives and teeth. I stepped over him, not wanted to, muttering an apology to him while I did, and took in the room.

The sunroom itself was largely untouched. Fairly clean and, except for Horatio, devoid of bodies, the only issue was a few broken window panes. The sky was dark, bruise colored and heavy with clouds sprinkled throughout. It didn't look like rain; it didn't look like much of anything except bad. I stared into the dim sunlight a while, closing my eyes and just breathing but I couldn't relax. I knew I had to keep moving, to try and work out what had happened and make some sort of sense out of things.

More importantly, I had to find her. Alive or dead, I had to know. Everything was so dangerous now, even if the danger felt like it had passed. I wasn't sure what happened, no, I had no idea what had happened, but it was obvious that fights broke out. Deadly fights, the kind that no one walks away from.

So how had I missed it and why didn't I remember it? I didn't remember anything leading up to it, the concept simply wasn't there before... before what?

Before the changes, the shifts and the swirls.

My tongue felt large in my mouth and I worried it along

the side of a tooth, the structure of the problem feeling like a sliver of vegetable caught in my mouth. So I worked at it, rubbing my tongue. It wasn't really caught there of course, I knew that, but it felt like it and if pretending was going to help me solve this then I would go for it.

I wondered what time it was as I left the sunroom and headed for the stairs again, down to the basement. We weren't allowed in the basement, but we all knew it was down there, heavy and solid like a fist of emotion. We weren't allowed down there but I was sure that didn't matter any more. I really wanted to know what time it was.

Chapter 9

DOCTOR VANDRELL CAME and got me for a second treatment.

I didn't want to go. I really wanted to tell him no, and started to, but I got nervous. The doctors had always been nice to me, for the most part. When did I start thinking that addition to it? When did the "for the most part" creep in? Doctor West was watching my case, even if I kept trying to see her and couldn't seem to make a time with her. That was strange to me, too, since before this she would make time for me.

I followed Doctor Vandrell down the hall to the examination room. The table he had me sit on was in the same place as the table from before—it was the same room, I was sure it was—but it was dented around the edges now. The straps looked more worn and the room itself seemed to have seen a few bad days, but there hadn't even been a few days between sessions. I shook my head and shut my mouth and sat down, giving Vandrell a hint of a smile. He didn't even bother to talk to me as he was putting me under and I closed my eyes.

I woke up in my room. No, that was wrong, I regained conscious control of my mind in my room, but I had obviously been awake before then since I woke up standing up in the room, looking out the window. The time between didn't exist for me, lost again, but a bigger slice of time than had been lost previously. It scared me and made me hide my smiles, even from myself. Clock number three went off and I hit the button to silence it.

I had to eat dinner. Still, my nerves were jangly and a smoke might calm them some. I wasn't sure I could get anything down if I didn't stop and have a cigarette before I tried to eat. The hallway was mostly empty and the lobby was even more bare, having only Sally, Clyde and a new guard I didn't recognize. I smiled at Sally, giving her a small hello wave but she glared at me in return, so quickly my hand fell down by my side and my smile hid itself again.

"Mister Dillon," Clyde said from behind me as I walked past him and put a hand on the door, "you know occupants aren't allowed outside." I froze and moved my hand off the door, turning to Clyde and the new guard.

"What? But I always go outside to smoke." I held up my pack of smokes and my lighter to show him, shaking them slightly. "Always, every morning before breakfast and after dinner and sometimes, if I really want one at other times but I don't know when those will be, like now." I tried to catch the other guard's eyes but his were hard and challenging so I looked somewhere else.

"That simply isn't true Mister Dillon, the Facility has never allowed smoking inside and does not allow occupants to go outside without escort." For the life of me, I could not work out why Clyde was being this mean and telling lies. Clyde looked at the other guard who nodded.

"Mister Dillon," the other guard said softly. His voice was a lot nicer than Clyde's even if he looked somewhat colder, "you know that is how it has always been here. I don't know how or where you got those cigarettes but you aren't allowed to use them here. We've had this discussion before."

"We have? We've never even met before…"

"Now, Mister Dillon… John," he gave me a patronizing look, the kind of look they weren't supposed to give you at all, "why don't you go get some dinner. Clock number three must've gone off, right?" For a new guy he did seem to know a lot.

I nodded dumbly and left, heading to go get dinner and figure out what was wrong, outside or inside, something was wrong.

Chapter 10

"ABIGAIL?" THE SUNROOM was fairly warm and inviting, after the strange coldness of the dining room during dinner the next night. The coldness down there was no more temperature than the warmness in the sunroom was. She was curled up on a couch with her head thrown back to catch some of the sun on her face. At the sound of her name her head lowered and her eyes opened to search the room and find me, fixing on me quickly.

"Call me Abby." She smiled at me and patted the couch next to her. I blinked, but refused the urge to frown, allowing my smile to return one to her and giving her a small hello wave. "Are you feeling better? I'm feeling better." She stretched like a kitten, suddenly all limbs and angles. I walked to her and sat down near her, folding my hands in my lap. I wondered about the change in her, change that felt too fast.

"I'm... so the doctors are helping you? Did they give you any good medications yet? I always talk to Doctor West about my medications..." She frowned at that and turned, slugging my shoulder gently.

"I'm not on anything yet, John. Can't a girl just be happy?"

I supposed yes, but somehow I wanted to answer no. She muttered something about her step-sisters and leaned against me like I was a comfortable piece of furniture. How I loved her. Even as everything... the thought stopped me cold, making me go stiff. She felt the change too and pulled away from me. I turned and looked at her face, taking it all in. It was like the world got worse but somehow even as it did she liked me more. There was a word for that. I didn't know what it was, but I knew it existed.

"Are you okay?" she asked, carefully trying to lean against me again.

"Hmmm? Huh, yeah. Yeah I'm, thanks, yeah I'm fine, Abby." The name tasted strange in my mouth, but not a bad sort of strange, the sort of strange of a new flavor of gum that could become your favorite flavor and easily beat out strawberry with some time.

"Good, I was thinking, John, that we should do something tonight."

"Like what? Ping-pong? I like ping-pong." I shrugged and turned to her as she kissed me. So many thoughts swam around my head then at incredible speed, but all of them were chased by or chasing the singular thought that she kissed me. I gave in to it and enjoyed it, not wanting it to end by the time it did.

"Not," she said softly, "ping pong."

I nodded dumbly but happily and wasn't really sure what she did mean. Maybe she liked a good game of foosball. "So, John Dillon, what do you think?" I didn't remember telling her my last name, but it wasn't hard to find out really. I shrugged and nodded at her again, looking into her eyes.

"Well Abby... I don't know your last name... I think that would be fun."

"Lincoln."

My jaw fell open an inch. Now I was hearing things.

"My parents thought it was funny, okay? Abby Lincoln, like the president, but less male."

I stood up quickly. Everything made a sudden, sick sense.

"You won't, you know."

"I won't what?"

"I know!" I knew. She was trying to lure me into calmness to kill me. Abe Lincoln, Abby. It fit. It did.

I headed for the door at speed.

"John, you knew what?" she asked, getting off the couch and coming after me. Oh lord she was coming after me. I hit the door with the palm of my hand and ran down the stairs. I could hear her feet slapping the floor behind me.

"John! Wait!"

I wouldn't wait. I knew, and everything made suddenly sense.

"No, I know, okay? Stop trying to... just... stop!" I didn't want her to be my destruction made flesh. Such sweet, wonderful flesh. She had kissed me; I could still taste her on my lips. I turned back from the door out of the stairway and caught a glimpse of her face, screwed up with passion and anger and resentment and fear. A huge melting pot of emotional breakfast cereal that condemned me and begged me to stop at the same time. I shook my head at her and walked out of the stairwell.

"Damn you, fine. Bastard," she shouted at me as I left. I felt a tightness in my chest. I loved her, I did, even once I knew she was going to eventually kill me, but I couldn't let her kill me even if it broke my heart. It felt like she already had killed me.

The new guard, who seemed to not be new, stopped me outside the stairs with a cold smile.

"John," he used my name instead of trying to be bossy like Clyde, "Doctor Vandrell sent me to collect you. Follow me?" I closed my eyes for a second while I nodded and fell into step behind him. Suddenly Doctor Vandrell felt I couldn't be trusted to get somewhere on my own and I didn't care anymore.

"What's your name," I asked him as we walked. I didn't really care but I wanted to know at the same time.

"Warren." And that was that apparently. Warren ignored me and kept walking me down to the examination room. The table had been removed and in its place was a large metal chair. The thing had a lot of padding and didn't look uncomfortable but it loomed there. The table had fit the room; the chair fit some other room that thankfully wasn't the one I was in. Except I was still expected to sit in the chair. I sat in the chair.

"Thank you, Warren," Doctor Vandrell said as he slid metal cuffs over my wrists and ankles to secure me. "Now, John, I need you to just relax." He slid the black rubber mouthpiece into my mouth and smiled at me, but it wasn't the smile I was used to. Unfriendly and fake, his smile loomed in front of my eyes while he flicked his fingers against a needle and reached down to inject it into my arm.

Somehow fragments stayed with me.

Another flash of light, dazzling in intensity but not sunlight. Light from inside me. Interior lighting, self-lighting, that chased away shadows haunting my brain and replaced them with things all its own. A snapping sound, a displacement and I knew, as certainly as I knew that I was still breathing, that something chased me.

Lincoln.

Not Lincoln—*time.*

Time was chasing me, I was out of time, I was full of time. The clocks knew my name and had my address and they didn't want to give me a check, they wanted me to check out.

Tick.

Tock.

Tick-tock.

Tock-tick.

And the alarms went off.

Bells and gongs and a troupe of truth marched by, leaving me alone with my nothingness. Everything I remembered moved away from me as I tried to hold on to it. I knew I could. I realized I couldn't.

I came back to my senses in my room. I was sick of coming to my senses; no, I was sick of losing them and having to find them all over again. Each time felt longer and harder, a struggle back. I was in my bed and I laid there, eyes closed, slowly letting feeling come back to me. My toes all wiggled, my ears followed suit and my muscles all ached in the right places as I stretched. Whatever else the ECT did, it beat me up. Then again I also found that I felt broader, not physically but mentally. I was sharper, like the brightness on a television turned up after years of being dim, the greys resolving into images you knew were there but could never quite make out.

As I stretched I realized I was also naked under the sheets. That was new and I had to wonder why they had undressed me, or why I had gone to bed nude. I never slept that way, my pajamas made me happy so there was no reason to. Every time I went through this I came back and things were different. Different in so many ways that I couldn't even second guess myself and now the blackouts that followed were getting longer and the things I did while my short term memory wouldn't save seemed to get odder.

I started to get out of bed and heard a noise next to me. Freezing, I thought about it and realized that while I stretched I had felt skin against my own, skin that wasn't attached to me at all. My confusion level ran up the flagpole right off the scale as I debated turning my head and seeing what I had done.

"Mmm, John?" I didn't have to turn. I knew that voice, even if I hadn't heard it filled with sleep before. She was in bed with me. I was naked. I felt her skin against... she was probably naked. She was plotting to kill me! I jumped out of bed, realized I was, as I thought, really naked, and grabbed a piece of clothing off the floor to cover myself. Glancing down at myself, even as she raised her head and propped it up on a hand, I realized I had grabbed her bra and was holding it in front of my crotch. I dropped it and reached down again to grab my own underwear and slip it on.

"Uhhh, Abby." The name was hard to say, a struggle to get out when all I wanted to do was run. "Hi?"

"Hi, baby," she smiled at me. "What's wrong?"

I started to say something, anything, an excuse to leave when she shifted and the sheet slid to reveal her right breast.

"John, what are you doing?"

I tore my eyes away from her breast and tried to not think about what the two of us in bed, together and naked, implied.

"I should... I should go. I mean, you know, I, we, well, you're going to kill me." I nodded and gave her a small shrug.

"Okay, first of all? You aren't going to leave your room because of me. Second of all we talked about the whole 'me killing you' thing and it's settled. Wasn't it settled? I could've sworn," Abby sat up and crossed her legs in my bed, the sheets pooling in her lap, "it was all settled before we fucked. You didn't lie to me just to get me in bed did you?" I sighed, loudly, and pulled my chair out from the desk, sitting in it and facing her.

"No, it's settled. I mean if we settled it, we settled it—but the procedure..."

"That thing they take you for?"

"Yeah. It messes with my short term memory. It... it does things like that. So I'm not going back on anything I said or anything we did, okay, I just don't remember it."

Her head shook, her hair shifting with the motion like hay in the wind.

"You don't remember talking to me about all of this already?"

I shook my head sadly, I wished I did remember it—I really did. "You don't remember... us... fucking? I mean it wasn't exactly porn star sex, but forgettable?"

"Abby, I didn't forget it because it was bad or forgettable; I forgot it because I was under the influence of electroconvulsive treatments. I really don't think it's fair to blame me for memory lapses, considering."

She gave a little laugh and patted the bed.

"We can go over it all again then. Are you sure you'll remember it this time?" I left the chair and moved to sit on the edge of the bed both happily and hesitatingly.

"No," I said softly, "I can't promise that. I think I will, but I'm sure that I thought I would before too. I wish I did know for sure, but I don't." I looked at her hopefully, trying to hide the underlying fear I had of her, and of what I was sure was her destiny. She shook her head again and put a hand on my knee gently enough that I was able to squelch the flinch I felt building inside of me.

"Okay, John, okay. My parents named me Abigail as a joke,

a sick little joke. That's all it was. Abraham Lincoln isn't out to kill you and neither am I. I know it's hard to swallow, but you told me that you loved me more than you thought Abe wanted to kill you, and that you trusted in that." I wasn't sure if I had said that. How could I be sure? It felt like something I would say, though, and as she said the words I could feel almost an echo of them in my head. The memories tried to swim back from unknown shores.

"Just for the sake, okay the sake of, you know, argument, okay? You could be making this up. It's not that I think you are, but you need to see the problem here." I frowned and considered everything.

"I see that, John, I really do see it. I just don't know what else to do, what else I can do." I nodded at her and patted her hand. A small happy smile crept out onto my face by itself and shone towards her. She returned it, adding a sly grin. I liked that grin, the way it played with the corners of her mouth. A mouth I could still taste, and that I was slowly getting hints of memories about.

"So, if I do trust you and you turn out to really be Abe Lincoln out to kill me, then what?"

"I... John," her laughter was loud but warm, not directed at me but only my words, that much was thankfully obvious, "I don't even know how to begin to respond to that, dumbass. I guess if this is all a ploy to catch you unaware and kill you, then you'll die. But you said you loved me, and that has to count too, right?"

"I do love you," I insisted, "and I guess so. Everything is just so confusing recently and I don't know why. It's on the tip of my tongue maybe, but I can't quite find it." Something occurred to me then that made me squeeze her hand tightly, "Did you say it back, I mean do you...?"

"Love you? I like you a lot, John. I do. Ever since I came into this place and you waved at me in the lobby. When I told you I liked you then, I meant it." That certainly didn't match my memory, but a lot of things, more and more, weren't. "But love? John, I don't think so, and don't take it personally." She exhaled loud and long through the corner of her mouth, "This was hard enough to say the first time. I like you a lot, obviously, okay? I don't just sleep with people I hate. You can blame it on a bias after you saved me from that Clyde guy when we were in the rec room, but that really only reinforced what I was already feeling." I saved her from Clyde? If I added up everything that didn't match my memory of events I would shut down completely and just start drooling on the floor.

"Okay," I told her softly leaning over to hug her, to take that first move myself; even if it wasn't a first move to her anymore, it was to me, "okay, thanks for going over it all again. I didn't mean to sound... crazy, I guess." She leaned into the hug and buried her face in my neck.

"We're all supposed to be crazy in here, John. Crazy little things, moving like unexpected clockwork until they beat us up, drug us out, or lock us deeper away, right?" she asked, muttering the words into my flesh. I held her and we lay back down, curling tightly around each other and falling back to sleep slowly.

Chapter 11

THE NEXT NIGHT Clyde and Warren came for me. During the day I noticed the guards all carried guns, Abby told me they always had but I knew different. At least I thought I knew different. I had no proof, except what my memories told me.

"Guys, I'd rather not go... I don't feel too good." I gave them both a fake smile, a nervous one that I tried to put an element of queasy into. A weak gambit, a simple ploy but it had a chance, I thought. I thought a lot of things that were proven wrong it seemed.

"John, don't make this hard for us," Warren said as one of his hands drifted toward his belt and the thick wooden stick that hung there. Clyde's hand drifted towards his gun. He was gonna shoot me? Was that even possible?

"I don't want to make it hard on you, but really I just don't feel..." A soft snap cut me off. Clyde's thumb unsnapped his holster and his eyes drilled into mine.

I shrugged. "Let's go," I said glumly.

When there was no choice, there was no choice.

As we walked through the building I saw other guards, more than we ever had around, wandering and giving the residents grim looks. I saw one of the residents go down in a quick flurry of sticks, beaten to the floor for some transgression or another, I couldn't tell what they had done to deserve it where I was. The only sounds from the altercation that reached me were a few screams and some wet, meaty thuds. We kept walking.

The examination room was dim, only every other light functioned, and chilly. Vandrell stood near the doorway and nodded at the guards as they brought me in. They both turned to go and I considered Vandrell carefully.

"Look, Doctor Vandrell, I think these treatments are bad for me." The facility hadn't done me wrong, but then again, in the facility I remembered none of this would have happened. It was time to stop taking things for granted. It was time. What time was it, exactly? I spun around looking for a clock but there was none. I did, however, notice the chair. It looked like an old electric chair and not like any good examination device I had ever seen. The skull cap was there, the wooden frame slightly charred from use. I felt sick just looking at it.

"John, get in the chair. We must continue, don't you see?"

I didn't see. Not one bit did I see. In the realm of seeing why, I was the blind.

"No." I tried to put some force into the word, to hide my fear. Vandrell, for his part, stabbed me in the arm with something, taking advantage of my glances at the chair.

"'No' isn't a word we like here at McGee's, John. You know that," he said as I grabbed at my arm, blackness swirling up to drag me under.

Damn it. What time was it?

———

I woke up, I came to, whatever term is right for it, in a hallway. Then I got up and started looking for her. The gore disturbed me, it made me feel cold and harder than I wanted to admit to myself.

I worked my way down the stairs to the basement and my sense of self seemed to expand with every step. It wasn't a sense of answers being below, it was just time, time was my answer for this. Snatches of memory flooded my brain when I would let them, I just had to stop trying and let them. The problem, I found, was that I couldn't let them. I had to keep moving and keep trying to find her.

The basement door was pristine. There was no blood, no bodies and the door was firmly locked. I shook the doorknob a few times anyway, just to be sure, and then put my ear to it to listen. The metal surface was surprisingly cool against my skin, making me shiver. I blamed the shiver on the metal, wanting it to be that and not fear. It was a dead end, but I tried banging on the door anyway. The metal was too thick to be heard through and I was only hurting my hand so I climbed back up the stairs reluctantly.

Turning down the hall I watched the smears tell a story. It was a story I didn't know and one I had trouble piecing together. It looked like war had hit the facility, but it was all too quiet now. I headed towards the lobby.

The reception desk was battered and cracked but thankfully Sally wasn't behind it. There was blood on her chair, but I had no way of knowing if it was hers or not, so I assumed not and glanced out the front doors. About thirty feet beyond the doors there was a wall. Thick solid looking metal glinted in the low sunlight. There had never been a wall beyond the grounds. I knew it, I was sure of it. Running to the doors, I grabbed one and shook it hard, trying to get it to open but it was firmly locked. I could see a gate, a closed gate, in the wall and started to outright panic.

Nothing was right and nothing was true. I pounded on the doors with my fists until they started to bleed, wet smears running along the glass that wasn't just glass. I sank to my knees and smashed my forehead against the doors next, it wasn't worth anything. My head was worthless, the lump of meat in it confused and bad and wrong. Hope had run out and when it had it left only despair behind for company. I cried, I wept and railed and got up. Backing up a few feet I started to throw myself against the doors as hard as possible. I needed to get out, I had to get out. It was all wrong, so perfectly and horribly wrong. Everything was wrong and I lived in a world of shit and evil. I had problems, that's why I was sent here in the first place. Big problems, they said, but they only showed as little ones most of the time. Indicators, they called it, and put me away.

I felt clear now though, come full circle past madness to clarity and in clarity I was madder than before. The doors shook from the force of my body flying into them and my cries of powerlessness echoed around the lobby.

"John?" A dimly heard voice said, washed out by the thuds and rattles of my relentless attack on the doors. "John," it repeated louder and with a strong sense of panic behind it. I stopped moving, bracing to be hurt. "John, hey, will you... will you stop?"

I spun and faced her, her voice breaking through where reason wouldn't.

"Abby?" It was more than a word, it was a question full of every shred of hope I had left, the shreds that weren't currently spreading slowly across the surface of the doors. She was bruised and bloodied, wearing a loose yellow sundress. She had a plastic bag in her hand, clutched tightly like it was her anchor in a rough sea. Just from her eyes I could tell she was as close to losing it as I was. "Oh fuck all, Abby, where were you? What happened, where is... what..." the words wouldn't come out right, my brain and mouth both fighting for dominance.

"You don't... you don't remember do you?" she asked as we embraced. "I thought you were one of the ones who didn't make it, but I," she pulled away from me and offered me the bag, "I stole these for you from the exercise room, in case." The bag had three small plastic stopwatches in it, the kind you hang around your neck while you jog. Each one was a different color and they all told the same time. "I thought maybe they would help you some, you know how you like clocks and I thought maybe..." she trailed off and just watched me as I put each one around my neck in turn.

"This is just the greatest, the best thing anyone has ever done for me." The words spilled out of my mouth, their truth pure and simple.

"Well, I love you, what else was I supposed to do, schmuck," her eyes settled and a bit of her old fire crept back in, "leave you lost and hopeless?" She loved me, she didn't even have to say it, the act alone told me volumes, but she loved me and suddenly nothing else was wrong. I kissed her and held her gently and thought.

"Okay, this is going to sound crazy," I began and stopped, both of us laughing and then started to cry, "but when I was, before I came here, I got electrocuted." Her head tilted and I started to walk around the lobby looking for something, anything, that could help us. Clyde's body was hidden behind a large floor pot and I walked up to it as I continued.

"I'm telling you, Abby, this place wasn't anything like it is now when I first got here. No one but me seems to remember that though. And it only started changing when," I bent down and picked up Clyde's gun, "I got those treatments."

"So you think that, what, each treatment changed everyone but you?" She followed me and grabbed Clyde's metal-shod nightstick.

I walked to the doors, standing a few feet behind them and held the gun.

"No, yes but no. I think maybe I changed where I was. Not, like, what room I was in, but what world I was in. It kept getting worse each time I went through it. They said I would lose some memory."

I pulled the trigger and shot the door twelve times in generally the same area. The not-glass grew spider webs.

"But this wasn't memory loss, I mean there was that too,

but it's like each time I got shocked I ended up in a different world entirely." Abby walked up and started smashing at the door with the stick, the spider webs pushing outward as they fractured worse. "When we first met, that I remember, you screamed and hated me. This place was sunny and bright and happy, I liked it here. Now this. What happened?"

The door shattered and the pane of not-glass fell out with an unsatisfying noise. We stepped out into the daylight and fresh air.

"I think you're crazy," she said nervously, "but I suppose, for you, it makes as much sense as anything else. It's what do you call it, subjective reality?"

I shrugged and nodded as we walked around the grounds.

"As far as I remember though, this place has always been what it is. They brought me in, drugged, and my first night here when they dragged me into the dining room you came and snuck me some extra food. Anyway, your clocks went off and Fernsetter, what was..."

"Horatio," I supplied as we started to walk around the building, looking for a way through or over the wall.

"Horatio. He lost it and started screaming about the noise from the alarm and attacked that guard, Simon, when they wouldn't break down your door to shut the alarm off. Simon panicked a bit and fired a shot. He missed Horatio, who ran off, but he hit poor Ms. Klienstock. The other inmates"— inmates they called us now, it used to be residents—"got scared and a few of them tried to get the gun away from Simon. Doctor Lensher came out and started screaming and soon everyone was screaming and running and the guards tried to shut us all up. They started killing people and getting killed and everything just went wrong at once." I nodded at her as we walked.

"So we're all that's left?"

"I think so? I don't know, I hid in a supply closet until the noise died down and then went looking for you. I didn't see anyone else moving though, so I guess..." A noise startled me and I raised the gun, not sure if I had any bullets left. I let go of Abby's hand and lifted one of the stopwatches, the red one. It was early afternoon and I felt like lunch or possibly a smoke or both.

"Get back in the building, John, Abigail." Warren shook his head and raised his own gun at me, his eyes growing wide as he talked once he saw I had a gun myself. "Put the fucking gun down now, John."

I fired, I don't know if I meant to or if I just freaked a bit but a bullet took him in the leg and made him drop his gun in surprise and pain. I pulled the trigger again but it just clicked at me. I started to turn towards Abby but she was already rushing towards him, screaming.

"Don't you ever try to shoot him," she bellowed, bringing the nightstick down on his head and shoulders rapidly.

A sharp crack as the metal shod stick connected with his head. "You don't try to kill him, or me," a crunch underlined her point, "or the mice, or anyone ever again!" Wet things slid against hard things as her arm pistoned up and down in the direction of his skull. "You don't raise guns at the President!" His head deflated as she caved it in, wet gray meat and blood running across the grass and seeping into the ground. Did she say President? I shook my head and moved to her side, hugging her from behind.

"Abby, Abby, it's okay, he's not going to hurt anyone." Her body shook for a second in my grasp and then she calmed, turning her head to look at me over her shoulder.

"He was going to kill us, John. We have to, can we even get out of here?" I turned her in my arms to face me, running a hand down her arm. It was coated from the elbow down in blood and gore but I didn't care. I wasn't exactly pristine myself.

"We can get out of here. Look, Abby, I feel sharper, bigger inside, than I have in a long time. Moving around worlds, losing my mind, whatever else the process did to me it seems to have opened my head some. I don't know if it'll last but it's here now, okay?" She nodded at me and we started to go on when she stopped.

"Wait," she said and left me, running back towards Warren's body. She came back to me quickly holding two small lumps in her hands, the bloody nightstick tucked under an arm. "He had grenades. Why would he have grenades? I don't know either but he did. He did and now we have them." I laughed then.

"Of course he had grenades." He was looking for a way out, too, I think. And I think then I knew why he had them. I dropped the useless gun and took the grenades from her, walking up to the wall. I pulled the pins of both and ran, giving her a hurried follow-me wave. She followed and we were only thrown to the ground by the force of the dual explosions, but not hurt. I spat some grass out of my mouth and sat up, looking at the small jagged hole in the wall. I gave it a big hello smile, that I turned on the sky and then finally on Abby.

We stood up and ducked out of the hole, a piece of hot ragged metal tearing at my shoulder.

"Hey Abby," I asked as we clasped hands and started walking down the road together, "what did you mean by 'you don't raise guns at the President' anyway?" I looked at the red stopwatch. It was certainly a fine time for lunch and a smoke, and maybe a change of clothes. In the distance I could see fires and smoke, the craziness of the planet didn't end at McGee's, the whole world seemed aflame.

"Huh, oh that. Just a... it was *uhh* just a childhood thing, you know, when people would make fun of my name, huh?" She beamed a smile at me that faded fast as she pointed towards the horizon. "How are we gonna..."

"We'll get by," I told her, shrugging. I had some freedom, three new portable clocks and the love of my life with me. What was the end of the world compared to that?

"Just a childhood thing, huh?" I asked, glancing at her with a small grin.

"Yeah, stupid name." I decided to trust her, for now. If she really was out to kill me, I would deal with that too, in time.

"Do you like golf?" I asked her as we walked.

"I always lose the little balls. Fucking things drive me insane."

ode to brains

Gnnahhh. Unnghh grannnh, huurrrr, ughn nnnnr. Graanh uhh ghuun nuuuhg grannhhh.

Ghuun grannnh huurrrr. Ughn nuuuuhg, gnnahhh uhhn fuuhg, ghah. Huurrrr ghunn grannnh naahg gnnah uhh.

"Fnuuh," hunng gruunhh. Gnnahhh: fuh hunnguh hurrr uhhnfg. Gruun. Ruuhhhggg, uuhn funaaaa. Aaahhrrgg.

Huunnaag frug gunhf. Uhhn aag ruhhfug, aannuuh. Gnnahhh nuuuhg naahg haanuh funaah.

"Huggfunaaaa," gunnfa hanaaaa, "grraaahhh, uhnng, grrrunnnaa."

Gnnahhh ruhhfuhh fuuhg grannnh funaa. Nuuuhg, ghah, huurrr grunn.

Grannnh fuh huggfunaaaa, aag nuuuhg naahg gnnah. Uhhna grnnah uhhn uhhnfg. Hunng gruunhh naahg.

Bang!

Thud.

afterword

EVERYTHING IN MY life is a story. Everything. What I had for breakfast becomes, in my head, a possible sprawling epic of life and death, ageless and deep. Walking to the corner to get a newspaper can become a life lesson, learned through the eyes of a child whose mother is dragging him along behind her, his fist clenched in hers with a vise-like grip.

People I know, relationships I have, my family, my job—all fodder for the mill. Nothing is safe and nothing sacred in the temple of my brain. Each tick of the clock is a thunderous moment towards another story, another tale yet to be written.

You don't escape it. At least, I don't escape it. Once you start telling stories you don't really ever stop. When I was six or so (every age when I was a child is 'six', my father used nine instead, but we both drop back to the same issue: the smaller you are the more time was utterly fluid and who-knows-fuck-all-what so you need a plucked year to pin down an event - this time though I actually mean *six*, unless it was *five* or *seven*) I asked my father to tell me a story.

Now my father was a writer by trade and I already knew that by that tender age. At least I understood that my dad got paid by some mysterious 'they' to tell stories on paper. I figured, in my six-year-old way, that he could give me a story too and I wouldn't have to pay him, being related and asking for no paper and all.

He looked at me, arching an eyebrow and running a finger

down the bridge of his nose as he always did and smirked. Then he shook his head and told me to tell my own story. I wanted to cry, then. I remember being upset and annoyed at this man from whom the stories were supposed to come. I was only a kid, who was I to tell a story? I didn't know any good stories. I must've sulked for a good ten or twelve minutes.

Then I told myself a story.

I don't remember it now—thankfully—but I am fairly sure, based on things my mother has told me, that it must have involved the death of every main character by the end of the tale. I had a fascination for people dying in stories. No, that's bullshit, it was just easier than finding a good ending. Nowadays I have the fascination. Back then I was just lazy.

Wait, I'm *still* lazy. *Fuck.*

Anyway. My childhood is littered with stories like that, ones I told and ones I was told. Things I saw and lived, and events that were told to me by my father (after I started to tell myself stories he went back to telling me some of his own as well, he apparently needed to be convinced that I could do it on my own first, is all) and passed down from other members of my family.

My life is a house of stories, each room a living thing that cycles endlessly and waits for me to pluck it back to life like a tensed string. New stories flow around me and into me every day, every hour. Some of them get written down, many of them end up chopped to bits and tossed into my fiction. They all get used and reused eventually.

It informs my writing, enhances it, and lets me remember my days a little stranger. Because that egg and cheese I had for breakfast the other day isn't just an egg and cheese on whole wheat anymore. It's tied to the guy that made it, the jaunt of his hat and the flick of his wrist as he stirred the eggs. It's tied down to the fumble as he separated a slice of cheese from its family. My very breakfast is only a small part of the mix. How did the eggs taste? Hot. No real taste besides that, overwhelmed by the melted cheese and the warm bread. The breakfast itself isn't the story. The story though, that makes the breakfast taste better. They two stop separating in my mind.

That's the sound in my head, at all times. I can't turn it off, but I doubt I would if I could. Plus, I'm lucky enough that people seem to occasionally want to read the noise from my head. But all stories do have a start point, somewhere, and below are a few of the stories in this volume (in no particular order) and as close as I can come to where they started for me.

"High Noon of the Living Dead"

I have an irrational fondness for *Lonesome Dove* (the novel, not the TV thing) and for the Sergio Leone westerns. Hell, I just love a good western. I realized one day that westerns and zombie stories are often the same thing. A good western uses the landscape to help tell the story. It informs and isolates. The story becomes, at a core level, the fight of man against nature. Zombie stories are much the same. A good zombie tale is never about the *zombies*, it's about the *people*.

So I wanted to throw both those elements into one pot and stir. How do people react when everything is against them? Every single thing is on the other side, what do you do, then? You stand and fight or you cower, hide and eventually die.

"Futuristic Cybernetic Assassin Fairy Hasballah"

I was asked to join in on a fairy anthology. I wasn't going to, actually. Then I decided that if I went completely off the rails with it I might have some fun. So I decided to take a Mickey Spillane character and turn it up to Spinal Tap and then, when in doubt ask myself "What Would Adam Warren Do?" to solve any issues.

Bunny, however, was originally going to be the name of Hasballah's gun. Then I decided that a talking gun would just be silly. Which means, I'm sure, I'll use a talking gun in something soon.

"Flesh Wounds"

Really this story only gets a mention here because it was the first fiction sale I made. I had stopped writing fiction for a handful of years and was just dipping my toes back in, here and there, when I got word of an anthology about zombies.

I thought "what the hell?" and tossed my hat into the ring. Sold the story, met Vince Sneed and the rest is history. Or, if not history, then it's at least the first brick in a road that leads us right here with you giving me money to read this sentence.

"Mister Binkles and the Curious Case of Changed Perspective" and "Mister Binkles and the Highly Adaptable Future"

The Binkles tales really started years earlier on a site called writethis.com, run by a guy named J. Tyler Blue. J. Tyler asked me to toss him a story for the site, if I could, and I said yes. I'm a cheap whore, understand, so asking me to write something is often a fairly easy win/win situation.

I was just sure that I couldn't sell the story in print anywhere. Which is not busting the chops of the intardwebs at all, I still do a lot of work for intertube places, but still - print is a different animal. So the first Binkles story sat for years. Until one fateful day, at a convention, C.J. Henderson (this is his fault, get it?) introduced me to folks at *Cthulhu Sex* Magazine.

They loved Binkles. They bought it and ran it and asked me for a sequel. A... *a what?* Well fuck. So I wrote a second. They had me broken down to try a third when they decided to close the mag down, thus sparing me.

I make fun of Binkles all the time, mind you. But I love the little bear. Something in him just makes me smile. Still.

"Dead Side Story"

Have I mentioned that I love musicals? I do. So really, in my head this story has always been set to a Leonard Bernstein score. There's also a dance sequence, but I decided to leave that out. And some of you think I'm kidding. The rest of you know exactly where it was.

Fans of either the original Shakespeare or *West Side Story* will hopefully notice that I completely abused the story, beat it with a bat and fucked it in front of the family dog. And then I slapped my name on it and laughed.

People who are not fans of either of those works may have also noticed this. But I don't care about them.

"After These Messages..." and "Pretty Little Dead Girls"

A lot of me says I shouldn't lump these two together, because they have vastly different histories but I think they both boil down to the same point: I don't trust parents or the media with children. Furthermore, I don't trust children. I don't trust much of anyone, huh? I mean I trust the guy who makes my lunch at the deli across the street. He's a good guy. Lives in the apartment above me, in fact.

But I wouldn't trust his children, or what he lets his children watch, or anything silly like that. No, children are being brought up by horrible media things that skew the whole universe into an evil conundrum of the sort that *Star Trek* would use to scare you into thinking that in the future we would all wear skintight velvet-spandex blends and yet not live in malls.

"Crazy Little Thing"

"Crazy Little Thing," the title story (sort of title story? Title story but for an added 's'? What the fuck *ever*) of this volume, started as something completely different. In fact, when it was first proposed (with no title) the story had a framing sequence involving a nun. The story itself didn't really take place in an asylum, except the frame, and that involved a possessed guy and madness and... well, I wrote the opening for it. So, for the first time anywhere, here it is:

SISTER NANCY SULLIVAN sighed and undid her bra, folding it and placing it on the table next to the rest of her clothes. She hated this part of the trip, hated it more than anything, but she knew it was also part of her duty. The floor was cold under her feet, and she grimaced, enduring the cavity search yet again. She knew some of the older sisters refused this duty on the grounds that the enforced cavity search was degrading. Sister Nancy also knew that a few of the younger members of her order tried to request the duty, their vows of celibacy still fresh and that sometimes even the cold impersonal touch of a latex glove could give them a cheap, immoral thrill. Sister Nancy forgave them in her heart, remembering herself at their age, her own early doubts and second thoughts.

Her exam finished, Sister Nancy hurriedly dressed, going so far as to nod and offer a smile to the guard but not so far as to actually thank her for being professional. Did you thank someone for a slightly demeaning cavity search, so long as it was all above board and quick, or was that in poor taste. Sister Nancy hoped she didn't draw this duty enough to have to ponder the problem too deeply.

Moving down the bare, painted, brick hallway behind a second guard she considered what laid in store for her. She was hardly a first timer, but each time walking down the hallway to the elevator felt like the first. The cold dread that rolled in the pit of her stomach, no matter how much she told herself to just trust in God. The sullen desire to return the sad stares of the guards as she passed them, stationed every twenty feet or so. Their eyes spoke of a sense of pity held for her, gazing at her as if to wonder what she had done to end up here, walking among them.

At the end of the dull gray painted plain brick hallway was a door marked in large black letters with the simple words 'No Admittance'. To the right of the door was an elevator, a single car whose doors were painted the same flat gray as the walls around it. Sister Nancy Sullivan said a small prayer to Mary and pressed the down button lightly. One of the guards, seeing the button light, turned away from her. The elevator came and Sister Nancy got on, taking the car swiftly down to the basement. The 'Trouble Ward,' as it was labeled.

She stopped at a final check point and signed her name, showing a letter from the Cardinal quickly, agreeing to the rules of visiting Patient 17: No physical contact, nothing taken from the cell, nothing left behind that was not strictly laid out in her letter of entrance, nothing incendiary. Sister Nancy was cleared to see Patient 17.

She hated to think of him, to refer to him at all, as Patient 17. She still remembered him as Bishop Albert Thompson, a pious man who had a gift for the obscure and the unorthodox. Now, here, he had been reduced to a nameless shell of a creature in the back of a small cell. It was, she reflected, at least a comfortable cell; not the sort of place you would find a prisoner but rather a ward of some higher power. God's power, Sister Nancy supposed, God's, the Pope's and the Cardinal's. A trinity of sorts, deciding that Bishop Albert, Al as she once knew him, was no longer fit to see the light of day or to know the comforts of fresh air.

Pushing the thoughts that edged towards blasphemy out of her head she found his cell quickly, found it right where she left it, she thought wryly. It had been eleven months since his internment, and each had weighed heavily on someone who had been proud to call him friend and confidant.

Patient 17, Bishop Albert, Al, stretched across his bed and looked peaceful for a change. Sister Nancy's left foot half turned as she considered leaving, swiftly drumming up a half-baked story as to why her visit was aborted. The options ran through her head like a grocery list, but each item was crossed off as they came around leaving her with only her duty before all else.

So I sent this off and it got approved. Except then I realized the story was all wrong. It didn't fit the size requirement, and I just wasn't into it. So I switched gears. Eventually I came to *Crazy Little Thing* and wrote it instead, as it came to be finished. However, by then, Vincent Sneed, the guy in charge at Die Monster Die! Books, expected the first story shown to him.

I tried to explain what had happened, but I have to admit now that it was a dick move on my part. If you happen to be reading this and you want to be a writer let me explain: Never swap out shit on your publisher with no warning. It backs them into a corner. He had already slotted a space on his publishing schedule, and expected story *A*. Then I come along and say I shot story *A* in the face, but here's story *B* to make up for it.

It's like... did you ever see *My Blue Heaven*? When she has to get the new turtle because the old turtle got sucked into the trash compactor? This is like that except instead of getting Vince a new turtle I got him a camel and then when he noticed I pointed out that he never truly loved the turtle anyway.

Thankfully for me, Vince liked the story. So he ran with the punches and we put out "Crazy Little Thing." That would be the end of the story.

Except.

Except except except...

Every now and then Vince will ask me when I am going to write him that "nun story." He really did like the idea of an opening with a nun getting a body-cavity search. It appealed to his sensibilities (take that how you will). Except there is no "nun story", see, that was only ever supposed to be a framing sequence anyway, the nun would have been in very little of the story *and*... I am resigned to being asked to write him the "nun story" for the rest of my life. I won't, mind you. Because there is no such story. I suppose this is my punishment for swapping out stories.

"The Nun Story"

This story does not exist. I promise. No, *really*. It doesn't.

"The End"

No, not a story, I mean this is *the end*. That's it. There's nothing else. This line, in fact, is being intentionally not left blank. Because I've always hated that. "This line intentionally left blank", well it isn't is it? It isn't blank, it's a fucking lie! So this, this is me striking back at the world for spreading lies and general dishonesty through out the land to...

Oh. *Right*.

The end.

Printed in the United States
104304LV00003B/19-66/P